THE SEARCH FOR NEWTON'S MOON

SAINT ADRIAN
PRESS

THE SEARCH FOR NEWTON'S MOON

BY BEN SCHAFER

Published by Saint Adrian Press
PO Box 36 Windemere, FL 34786

ISBN-13: 978-0999231814
ISBN-10: 0999231814

First Edition

This book is dedicated to my mother, Debra Schafer, for her undying support and for first introducing me to the amazing world of science fiction through her love of Star Wars.

CHAPTER ONE

THE CNS *Antonia Estrada* was the perfect face of the new navy. Massive battleships that bristled with weapons may have won the war, but they were not effective for winning the peace. The new navy would need to be sleeker, faster, and more capable of tracking down asymmetric threats wherever they hid.

The past century had been a time of war both between and within the three star systems that mankind claimed as their own, and the peace forged from those conflicts was still tenuous at best. The *Antonia Estrada* was one of the few *Scorpion*-class destroyers to see action in the closing battles of the last war, and she had the scars to prove it. But her crew didn't mind. They saw each gouge in the hull as a badge of honor, and they would never forget what victory had cost.

Those few who remained, anyway.

"Commander," a young man shouted from his station at the front of the ship's bridge. Eight years ago, the bridge would have been abuzz with constant activity. Now, however, with its skeleton crew the whole ship seemed to echo with every footfall on its metal plating.

Commander Marcus Caron looked across his bridge and sighed. He was less than two meters from the man, but he still remembered the days when it required a miracle to hear someone that clearly without a headset. Of course, that was back when Caron had been a mere lieutenant. Back when he had been the one manning the Navigation station.

He had been so eager to show his prowess in battle against the petty tyrants that had corrupted the vision of mankind's birthright among the stars. So eager to show that, despite his aristocratic heritage, he was a committed New Center man. A man of vision.

As he regarded his reflection in the computer screen built into the console in front of him, he mused that he had purchased his promotion at the cost of his hair and waistline. His scarlet jacket sat too tight across his abdomen, but he refused to have it retailored. He had already been forced to transition to an embarrassing size for his black trousers, but he drew the line at so visible a symbol as his officer's jacket.

Unlike the rest of his crew, who wore the basic working uniforms of the Centrality Navy, Commander Caron wore his service dress uniform while on his bridge. Regulations didn't require it, but he felt that the commanding officer of any respectable ship should project the pride of his navy at all times. He'd be damned if he allowed himself the indignity of admitting that he'd let himself go.

The commander shook his head. He needed to stay focused on the present, not relive the glory days. He nodded to the blond young man who had his arm held aloft. The junior officer grimaced. "Sir, are you sure this is the correct course?"

Commander Caron's eyebrows lowered in anger. He had set this course himself, designed to cut across normal traffic patterns to reduce the time in transit. Traffic through the Tedros Cloud was not forbidden, exactly, but neither was it encouraged. The only thing that mattered to Commander Caron was whether his chosen path would get them to Chelsea Station ahead of schedule.

He would show those vultures in the Ministry of the Navy that he was still as disciplined and driven as he had ever been. His bloodline may have been too cozy with the Old Centaurs, and he didn't have the legendary wartime career of some of his fellow officers, but he was determined to make flag officer before old age forced him from the service.

If only these pesky new commissions would learn to do their damned jobs.

"Are you doubting the calculations?" Commander Caron asked, leaning back in his chair as he studied the young officer. His tone carried a weight of disapproval.

"N-no, sir," the young man said. "It's just," he indicated his display console which shone with an orange light, "we entered the Tedros Cloud twenty minutes ago without receiving anything from the nav buoys. If we're getting close to Chelsea Station, sir, we should have heard something by now."

"Commander, if I may," said a pale woman who looked to be closer to Caron's own fifty-two years than the youthful Navigation officer. Caron nodded for her to continue. "Sir, the cloud is exhibiting a high degree of ionization. That could be disrupting our ability to detect the nav buoys."

Another young man, this one with dark hair and a grim expression, said, "That could explain these sensor readings. Sir, I think you should take a look at this."

Commander Caron nodded. "Put it on my screen."

The display on Caron's console shifted from a block of text to the simplified image of the ship and all surrounding sensor contacts. Most of the screen was that orange glow, indicating the plasma cloud that they were passing through on their way out of the Tau Ceti system. On the very edge of the screen, a small blue pulse flickered once, then vanished. "What am I looking at, Lieutenant?"

The young man turned back to his computer terminal and said, "I don't know. Gravitational anomaly, from the look of it. Reads like a battleship with a faulty gravity drive."

Commander Caron scoffed. "Impossible. The only battleship in the system is parked in orbit around Yu-Kiang."

The lieutenant's head bobbed in agreement. "Yes, sir. That's why I thought it was odd. But the ionizing effect could just be causing an echo from our own ship's drive."

"Very well. Flag it and then drop it. If something is out there, it's someone else's problem." Three sharp tones sounded from the ship's speaker system. Impact warning. "Lieutenant? What's going on?"

The dark-haired man furrowed his brow in concentration as he studied a rush of incoming data. "Lidar picked up an unknown object moving toward us. Must have been masked by debris within the plasma cloud. Projected contact in four minutes."

Commander Caron looked at his own data terminal. When there was an alert, the information from the Sensor officer's station was relayed to the commander's terminal in real-time. The simplified map became a tactical display highlighting the incoming object and projected time to impact. "Torpedo?"

"Negative, sir. There have been no velocity adjustments of any kind. Whatever this thing is, it isn't running on its own power."

Commander Caron frowned. If the young officer had disrupted his bridge over a mere piece of space trash, he would see the man disciplined. Order still meant something in his navy.

As if picking up on the commander's frustration, the officer stammered, "Uh, sir, I only bring it up because we've been able to identify it. I think you want to see this." The young man placed his haptic gloves onto his screen and wiped it up, transferring what he saw to the main display.

The commander stood and leaned on the railing that separated him from the crew pit below him. The image was hazy, a composition based on several sensor scans. But what it showed was clear.

"ARTI, is that what I think it is?" the commander asked.

A ghostly male voice answered through his implanted earpiece. "Yes, Commander Caron. Lieutenant Galloway's analysis is correct. I have run the numbers and can say with ninety-five percent certainty the object in question is a ArgoTech 9141 Model EVA suit."

Commander Caron grunted. If there had been any real danger, the ship's artificial intelligence would have crunched the numbers and deployed countermeasures before any of his officers could have reacted. "Any signs of life?"

"Negative. Though there seem to be limited power readings emanating from the suit. The 9141 Model has a noted history of fouling scans for life signs, which is the reason the model was discontinued two years ago in favor of the 9141-A."

"Thank you, ARTI. Please plot a course for intercept."

"Of course, sir."

"And thank you, Lieutenant Galloway, for bringing it to my attention. Helm, ARTI is plotting an intercept course. Follow it in and let's see if there's someone out there who needs our help."

The young lieutenant gave the commander an uneasy smile and returned his attention to his station. The blond Navigation officer who challenged Caron's route was also hard at work, though his eyes continued to flick over to the commander's chair every so often as if asking for silent forgiveness. Unfortunately for him, Commander Caron was not the forgiving type.

It wasn't that Commander Caron distrusted the men and women under his command. It was just that, since the Automated Reconnaissance and Tactical Intelligence program had been introduced in the final years of the war, Commander Caron had learned to depend on it above any flesh-and-blood crew member. ARTI essentially *was* the ship, the first ever computer intelligence system powerful enough to run all the systems of the ship simultaneously. Caron had learned over the years just how capable these living computers were, and even his own gut instinct took a back seat to the computer's analysis.

Of course, a system of such potential power also carried tremendous risk. That was why only Commander Caron had the implants that allowed him to directly interact with the ship's computer. Only he could issue the commands that would allow ARTI to override the programmed limitations that prevented any artificial intelligence from causing harm to a human being.

A ship's ARTI could bring up firing solutions and prepare the weapons to fire, but it could not engage those weapons without the express command of a ship's officer. Certain limitations were built into the system that prevented the system from intentionally harming any humans without the approval of a human overseer. This kept the AI system under human control despite its fearsome capabilities.

It wasn't fears of a robotic revolution that kept such tight limits on the artificial intelligence program. Rather, a powerful lobby in the Citizen's Assembly on behalf of lifelong naval servicemen protested the idea of allowing machines to make the decisions previously left to officers with decades of experience. Beyond that, a fully automated navy would put thousands of spacers and tens of thousands of support personnel out of work.

On larger ships, or even small ships that boasted a full crew compliment, the entire senior command staff had the implants enabled in case the commander was incapacitated. But it was just Commander Caron and twenty-one crew members on this rocket. He didn't even have an executive officer at the moment, though it was rumored that the Ministry had picked someone to fill the slot when the *Antonia Estrada* made its scheduled stop at Chelsea. For now, Commander Caron wielded unlimited authority, which was just the way he liked it.

With the new trajectory, the ship intercepted the piece of floating debris within two minutes. Commander Caron watched on his terminal as the ship's cargo arm extended and snatched the space suit out of the vacuum. Once it was inside the cargo bay and the bay had repressurized, Commander Caron said, "ARTI, contact Sergeant Wyatt. Have him meet me at the cargo bay."

"At once, Commander."

Ken Wyatt was the understaffed ship's lone Marine, responsible for ensuring the protection of sensitive information and the command staff. He carried the responsibility of a whole twelve-man squad on his shoulders, at least until they were restored to full strength at Chelsea. But he was good at his job. Commander Caron only wished he could say the same about the rest of his crew.

Commander Caron addressed the officers in front of him. "Sensors, try to clean up our feed. I don't want any more surprises." The dark-haired man bobbed his head once in acknowledgement.

Commander Caron turned his attention to the center of his bridge. "Helm, I want to make sure this little detour doesn't delay our arrival at Chelsea Station. See to it that we make up the lost time."

The blond man nodded and began inputting information into his computer. "Aye, sir."

Commander Caron turned on his heel and stepped through the blast door that led to the rest of the ship. The *Antonia Estrada* was not a large vessel, and he reached the cargo bay in short order. How he longed for the days when these corridors were filled with frantic activity. How he missed the days of combat.

The only other man who had served on this vessel as long as Marcus Caron was Sergeant Kenneth Wyatt. The middle-aged man wore dark grey fatigues with subdued rank patches on the sleeves. His dark hair remained full and colorful, a fact which Commander Caron envied. The Marine threw Caron a sharp salute, then grinned at his old friend. One of his teeth was a gleaming synthetic, a replacement for a tooth lost in a training accident when he was still a recruit.

"We picking up passengers now, Marcus?"

Caron considered chiding the man for not using his title, then reconsidered it. There were no subordinate officers around who could get the wrong idea. He would let it slide. Once. "You know the law as well as I do, Ken. If we find someone in distress, we are obligated to investigate."

"How do you know they're in distress?" Wyatt asked.

"There are no other ships for hundreds of kilometers. Hell, there aren't even any charted asteroids out here. The Tedros Cloud is basically the edge of the map."

"What you're saying is there's no reason an EVA suit should just be floating through space giving off power readings." Commander Caron nodded. "Peachy." Wyatt tapped the sidearm at his hip. "Well, if it decides to give us any trouble I can punch some nice holes in it."

Caron put his hand on the door control for the cargo bay. The ship's computer scanned his handprint, then opened. The lights were off in the bay, and the entire room was shrouded in darkness. The only faint light came from the readout display on the EVA suit in the middle of the deck.

"ARTI, can I get some lights on in here?" Commander Caron asked.

There was no response.

"ARTI, activate lights in cargo bay," Commander Caron repeated, phrasing it as a command. Still nothing.

A beam of white light suddenly snapped into focus on the helmeted space suit. Caron turned his head to see Sergeant Wyatt with his sidearm drawn, underslung light attachment providing the illumination that ARTI had failed to produce.

The visor on the helmet was lowered, completely obscuring the interior of the suit from outside eyes. But something about the way it lay on the deck made Commander Caron realize that there was someone inside the suit. It made occasional tapping sounds on the metal deck as the motorized joints spasmed, a typical sign of low power on a mostly automated suit like this. More than one spacer had gotten an arm twisted out of socket by a malfunctioning EVA suit.

Commander Caron knelt and examined the suit more closely. It had a commonly used white-and-yellow paint scheme to help make visual identification easier in the darkness of space. The suit itself was unremarkable, a metallic exoskeleton intended to provide its user with more survivability in deep space than the standard emergency vac suit. It had a backpack rig of some kind attached by clamps to its waist and the base of the helmet. It was marked with numerous abrasions, which was not unusual for a suit that saw regular use.

"You think they're still alive?" Wyatt asked.

"I don't know," the commander replied honestly. He held up a small hand scanner that interfaced with the suit's internal monitoring systems. "But I doubt it. Based on these power readings, the suit's been floating out here for a long time. Months at least. More likely a few years. Though it's possible some cheap bastard was just using the same suit for multiple EVAs without recharging to squeeze every bit of money out of it."

The light from Wyatt's gun shifted from the helmet to the rest of the suit. "Look at this," the Marine said. He aimed his light at a thin tube that ran from a spool attached to the backpack rig. It was roughly a centimeter in diameter. Commander Caron started to follow it, gathering it in his hands. He reached the end and held it up for Wyatt's inspection. The red tube ended with an abrupt slice at the end.

"Detached from a safety line, then?" Caron guessed. "Maybe he was doing a spacewalk to perform repairs to his ship and some debris severed the line."

"Two problems with that," Wyatt replied. "You said there were no other ships in sensor range. If this guy left his ship abandoned, you would have at least picked up a debris trail from whatever cut the line. Not to mention the ship itself."

"Maybe," Commander Caron said. "Sensor readings are anything but reliable out here. But what if someone else was on the ship?"

"Well, that brings me to my second problem. Look at the edge of that line again. That wasn't clipped by debris. See these markings here? Someone sawed through the line with something sharp. A switchblade, maybe, or a machete. Though it's anyone's guess why someone'd bring a machete on a spaceship."

"Maybe they picked up a souvenir on Bakuwana," Caron said.

"Ugh." Wyatt groaned. "Only things I ever picked up on that forsaken planet were leaches the size of Admiral Chernavin's pet schnauzer and a bad case of croaking fever."

"Way I heard it, that wasn't the only disease you picked up on Bakuwana."

Wyatt's grin was wicked. "Maybe. But I can't really blame the planet for what happens with pretty girls during shore leave."

Caron chuckled and shook his head. "ARTI, bring up Communications and tell them to issue an alert to Command." Once again, the ship's artificial intelligence system didn't respond.

He stood up and rubbed a spot under his ear. "Damned implants are failing."

Wyatt didn't look at him, instead focused on the details of the suit. "Maybe the suit is giving off some kind of interference."

Commander Caron hadn't considered that. It had been years since he'd had to bypass jamming technology. It was possible this suit had been floating around since the days of the war. Maybe this, too, was a relic of those days long past.

"Okay, Marcus," Wyatt said. "I'll stay and see if I can pop this guy out of here. Head back to the bridge and try contacting ARTI again. I'll let you know if I find anything." As Commander Caron stepped back toward the now-blinding light of the corridor, he could hear Wyatt talking to himself. "There are some kind of vambraces on here. Looks like mining or salvage gear, useful for cutting into—"

Commander Caron stopped at the edge of the doorway. "Wyatt?"

He turned around and saw that the handgun had fallen out of his friend's grip. It rested on the deck at an angle. Sergeant Wyatt was nowhere to be seen. The suit had vanished, as well. The light streaming from the handgun's attachment shone on the robotic payload delivery arm that had snagged the suit out of space. It cast a bizarre shadow against the far bulkhead.

"Ken, what was that you were saying? Something about salvage gear?" Commander Caron's voice echoed in the cargo bay, and suddenly he felt very much alone.

He stepped back into the bay and retrieved the handgun. He hadn't carried one of these things in years, but his training kicked in and it felt like second nature. He didn't put his finger on the trigger, though, because he didn't want to shoot Wyatt by mistake.

He swept the light across the spot on the deck where the suit had been and froze. The suit was gone, and so was Wyatt. "Sergeant, I swear, if this is some kind of joke I'll see you court-martialed."

"I'm not joking," said a man's voice, though it was modulated and lifeless, like it was being transmitted through a speaker. But Commander Caron was certain of one thing: it wasn't Ken Wyatt.

"Who are you? What do you want?"

"This is mine. I won't let you take it from me."

The commander kept moving the light, but even on a small vessel like the *Antonia Estrada* the cargo bay was a dozen meters across and filled with plenty of places to hide.

Sudden movement caught the commander's eye. He swiveled to orient the gun on his target, then gasped in horror at what he saw.

Sergeant Kenneth Wyatt, veteran of countless combat missions, was dead. His body slumped at an unnatural angle, impaled on a wicked blade. That blade was attached to the armored forearm of the space suit Caron and Wyatt had been examining only moments earlier. It seemed that the man was not dead, after all.

Commander Caron would fix that.

He fired at the suit, each round finding its target and punching holes through fabric and glass. The gun in Caron's hand finally went *click* as its ammunition was expended, a dozen rounds designed to shred human flesh without punching holes through the armored hull of a spaceship.

The man in the suit stood undaunted.

"I won't let you take it from me!" The man in the suit surged forward, a small circular saw popping out of his other forearm.

The man in the suit screamed.

Commander Caron screamed.

Then the only sound was the whirring saw and a *thump* as Commander Caron's body hit the deck.

CHAPTER TWO

"YOU'RE a dead man," the man with the plastic teeth scowled. This close, the scent made Val Tanner gag. Val wasn't sure if the smell of the man's stained denim overalls or his breath was worse. It ultimately didn't matter. The fact that Val could smell the man clearly over the press of unwashed bodies in this backwater saloon on the sleepy moon of Parson told him all he needed to know.

Stench or no, Val wasn't the kind of man who was intimidated by simpletons. Though, he did admit, things looked grim at the moment. Fortunately, luck always had a way of turning around.

Val ran a finger along the line of his slim mustache. "Is that so?" he asked. There was a chorus of chuckles around the table at that. "Look, I've got places to be and I'm sure you've got a date with your right hand that you can't reschedule. Let's not make this any more complicated than it has to be."

The small crowd gasped as Val pushed a sizable stack of colorful coins into the center of the table. The coins were low-tech stand-ins for the encrypted plastic chits, known as Imperial scales, that were the standard currency of the Tau Ceti system.

"I'm all in."

The man to Val's left, a skinny man whose hair was flattened out into a disk in defiance of gravity, let out a snarl. "Damn it. That's too rich for me. I'm out." He tossed his cards onto the table. The man with the eyepatch on Val's right hand also tossed his cards down with a curse.

That was two down, one to go. But the man across the table wasn't so easily intimidated. He was a barrel-chested man who looked like he had gorilla DNA spliced into his family tree. There were extensive scars on the knuckles of the man's vast hands. If Val were to guess, and reading people was what he did for a living, then he would say that it wasn't an industrial accident that had cost his opponent his front teeth. The man's sunken eyes glared at Val and he scratched at the stubble on his chin. Then he pushed his own stack of coins into the center of the table.

Up until that point, the saloon had been a lively place, full of music and laughter and all the sounds associated with loosened inhibitions. But when those coins entered the pot the entire place went silent. Even the live performers on the stage beside the bar stopped playing their instruments, though Val knew the screeching sounds they emitted could only generously be labeled "music."

Val looked at the cards on the table in front of him. The Five of Hearts, the Five of Clubs, the Queen of Hearts, and the King of Clubs. He didn't have a great hand. In fact, odds were good that he was about to lose. And, to make matters worse, he was working on credit with the bar owner. If he lost this hand, he wouldn't have the cash to pay out. He absently pulled a small totem out of his vest and ran it through his left hand under the table.

"Hey, what you got there?" the eyepatch man said. Val was surprised that he could see him at all. Maybe he was hiding a cybernetic implant under that thin fabric. But that was unlikely so far out from real civilization. It was more likely he was simply paranoid.

Val lifted his totem onto the table. It was a small bit of fur on the end of a thin chain. "It's a rabbit's foot," Val explained. "It's my good luck charm."

"Been damn lucky so far," the man with the flat hair remarked.

Val's opponent across the table let out a wicked chuckle. "Little bit o' rabbit ain't gonna save you now." He looked to his right. "Do it."

The man with the flat hair drew the final card.

It was the Ten of Diamonds.

The man across the table broke out into a plastic grin. "Well, well. Looks like I win." He showed his cards: the Nine of Hearts and the Jack of Spades. "Straight, nine through king."

The big man began reaching for the money when Val held up a hand. "Hold on." He tossed his cards onto the table. It was the Jack of Diamonds and the Ace of Diamonds. "Seems I also have a straight, though I take it with the ace."

Val started to scoop the coins over to his side of the table. "With that, gentlemen, I believe it is time to call it a good night."

The man on his right grabbed his arm. "Not so fast." He flipped over his own cards, revealing a Three of Clubs...

And the Ace of Diamonds.

Val recoiled. "You dirty cheater!"

The man seemed surprised by that response. So did the other men at the table. They glanced back and forth at Val and the one-eyed man. "No, it's not—" the man protested.

And with that moment of uncertainty, Val yanked his arm out of the one-eyed man's grasp. As he tumbled back, he kicked the table onto the big man across from him. The heavy wood slammed into the man's chest and knocked him to the ground. The impact sent most of the coins clattering all over the room.

The moment of crystalline calm was shattered as dozens of patrons began shoving and punching and clawing at one another in an attempt to scoop up as much cash as possible. Even the owner of the tavern, a broad-shouldered man with a yellow walrus mustache, got in on the action, kicking one patron's hand away from what the owner was loudly proclaiming to be his money.

Val cursed. He hadn't intended to waste that much money on the diversion, but the chaos would hopefully give him a chance to sneak away with at least some of his winnings. He twisted around a pair of middle-aged women whose skin and outfits had both seen better days. They ignored him as they clawed at each other to get to the money scattered across the ground.

The door was in reach. Before he could cross the threshold, however, a heavy weight slammed into Val from behind and shoved him against the nearest wall. The impact made the whole tavern shake.

Val twisted and tried to dodge away. The man with the disk hair stabbed at him with a big Bowie knife. It didn't pierce his skin, but it left his maroon-colored vest pinned to the wall. "You think it's funny, taking money from working men like me, huh?" asked the man with the disk hair.

Val shrugged. "Yeah."

The man flew into a rage and slammed his fist into Val's stomach. "Okay," Val coughed. "I can see you're upset. But I don't even have your money. It's over—Whoa!" The man threw another punch, this one aimed at Val's head. Val ducked and the punch went wild, breaking the man's fingers against the wall. The man recoiled in pain, clutching his injured hand as he stumbled toward the melee around the fallen table.

While one threat was down, another re-emerged. The barrel-chested man picked up the poker table and tossed it across the room. It collided with the bar with a heavy crash and knocked several bottles of alcohol to the floor.

"You!" the man screamed, pointing his finger at Val. "I'll kill you!"

He pulled a thick chain from around his waist, which had apparently been serving as the man's belt. He gave it an experimental swing, then let it dangle from his fist.

Val tried to pull the knife out of the wall, but it was stuck and he couldn't get decent leverage. He tried ripping his vest free, but the material wouldn't tear. "That's what I get for investing in quality fabric," he muttered.

The big man roared in fury and charged at Val. The gambler put his arms above his head in a futile protective gesture.

There was the sound of glass breaking and then something heavy hit the floor at Val's feet. He opened his eyes to see the brute on the floor, bloody welt forming on the back of his head.

A woman with straight black hair stood on a wayward wooden chair, using the bit of furniture to boost her otherwise unimpressive height. She held the remains of a whiskey bottle in her hand, and the stain on her blue coveralls told Val that it hadn't been empty. She hopped off the chair and took a menacing step toward Val, brandishing the broken bottle like a knife. "Oh, come on," Val said.

Then she slashed through Val's vest just below the spot where the Bowie knife had him pinned to the wall. Val fell to his knees, the remains of his vest drooping on his shoulders. "You all right?" she asked.

"Of course not." Val looked up at the woman and gave her a look of anguish. "Did you really have to destroy the vest?"

She rolled her eyes. "Thank me later," the woman said. She helped Val to his feet and they began pushing their way out of the tavern.

They cleared the doorway and made their way out into the snow. A flurry must have come through at some point in the evening, because there was fresh powder up to his knees. The small, single-story dwellings that made up the bulk of the settlement nearby had a uniform square design with a domed roof to make the interior space a little more livable. With snow this thick, they began to look like igloos Val had seen in old vids of Earth. It was beautiful and peaceful to see the town at night covered in snow.

It was also hell to run through.

Val staggered in the cold wind, trying to follow the path without losing his footing. He kicked some snow off of his dark corduroys. Cold slush found its way around his ankles, and Val wished that he had thought to wear better shoes.

"We need to get to the ship." The slight woman followed Val, relying on him to break a path through the heavy snow.

"Charity, I thought you *were* in the ship," Val said.

"And I thought you were going for a 'quiet drink,'" Charity said.

Val shrugged, conceding the point. He pulled his lucky totem out of his pocket again. He pressed down on one side, depressing the concealed button beneath the fur exterior. "Tell me you at least left the ship running hot."

"Of course."

The wind whipped around them furiously as it was channeled through the mouth of the valley two hundred meters north of the town. They marched directly into the wind, trying to get out of the shallow valley to the wider plains beyond. The ship's simulated intelligence would need a landing site large enough to set down, and it couldn't do that in the middle of the street. Fortunately, the bar was at the northernmost edge of town, a rest stop for travelers who had other business in this sleepy settlement.

"What are you doing here?" Val asked.

"You mean besides saving your life?"

"Yeah, other than that."

The woman grinned. "Looking for a hot date."

"Huh. Anyone I know?"

Before she could answer, a shotgun blast echoed through the still night air. Small birds that had been brought to the planet as part of the terraforming process fluttered out of a nearby tree, disappearing into the night sky.

Val and Charity turned to see the bar owner pointing a sawed-off shotgun at them. Like all civilian weapons, it was one of the classic models that used chemical propellants instead of magnetic rails. It was no less fatal for its centuries-old design. "Running out on your tab, Val? Bad way to do business."

"What are you talking about?" Val asked. "I left plenty of money in there to cover my debt. You should be in there picking it up."

"This ain't funny, boy," the portly man in the apron said. "I'm gonna give you to the count of three to come back here and pay me what you owe me." He racked the slide. "Or I'll take it in your hide."

"Sir, put the gun down and we can talk," Charity said.

The hills shook as something large flew overhead. "That's our ride," Val said.

"Oh, no, you don't," the bar owner said. "Count of three. Get back here or die. One. Two." He raised the shotgun and aimed it at Val's head.

A blinding hurricane of snow and dust whipped up around them. The bar owner had to raise his hands to keep from losing his vision entirely. The faint outline of something moving in the twisting fog solidified into the solid shape of a spaceship.

The huge object above them pierced the gale and revealed itself as a light transport ship about thirty meters long. It was a sleek craft, shaped like a tube that tapered on both ends. It featured stubby wings at the rear of the ship complimented by stabilizing fins just behind and below the cockpit. Four powerful engines, one built into each wing, swiveled down to allow the ship to hover a dozen meters above their heads. Two more engines on top slid together to act as a tail while the ship was in atmosphere. The ship was painted a light grey with white highlights and had the name *Lucky Rabbit's Foot* stenciled on the nose.

A turret mounted to the chin of the craft swiveled toward the human figures on the ground. The turret featured twin 35mm auto-cannons that were designed to fire a range of ammunition but most commonly used armor-piercing high-explosives. The rounds were useful for obliterating small chunks of space debris and belligerent shopkeepers alike.

It was a threat, nothing more. Val knew the limited programming on the ship's second-hand simulated intelligence would prevent it from firing. No one, not even the Centrality of United Planets with their vaunted "true" artificial intelligence, trusted computers enough to let them do the killing for them.

The bar owner was recovering from his shock, but he didn't dare move with those big guns pointed at his face. Val moved quickly. If the bar owner decided to call Val's bluff, there'd be little the gambler could do to stop him.

"Come on, come on!" Charity yelled. The ship settled onto the snow-covered ground, thick struts sinking into the mud. A narrow boarding ramp opened just behind the turret, leading up into the shelter of the ship.

He clambered up the ramp after the woman in the blue coveralls. The entrance hatch to the freighter swung open and he followed her inside. "Yeah, it's a boring town after dark, anyway."

They cycled through the airlock, which wasn't a problem in the thin atmosphere of this backwater moon, and made their way deeper into the ship. Just past the interior hatch were metal rungs cut into the bulkhead that led to the cockpit and a short corridor that led to the passenger areas of the ship. Val reached for the ladder, but Charity put a hand on his and pulled him in for a kiss.

They broke off after a moment and he looked into her eyes. "I've got to get up there. The barkeep is going to realize we aren't going to shoot him and I don't want him putting holes in my ship."

Charity pouted. "You mean *our* ship. Mom always told me you flyboys loved your ships more than your women."

Val smiled. "Didn't stop her from marrying one. Or you, either."

Charity's expression shifted to a sultry grin. "Maybe I just enjoy feeling like the other woman."

Val laughed and gave her a kiss. "You know I only cheat at cards."

Charity smacked him on the backside. "Get up there, flyboy. I've got a coolant leak I need to work on, anyway."

She released his hand and stepped away, pulling a set of tools from a locked compartment in the bulkhead. She wrapped it around her waist and moved down the corridor, then reached for a hidden switch that revealed a trapdoor that led to the lower deck.

"You also know you love me," Val called out after her.

"Do I?" She tilted her head, but her smile never faded. "Well, it certainly is an adventure," she replied. She shut the trapdoor over her. Val stared at that spot of deck grating for another moment, amazed at just how lucky he really was.

CHAPTER THREE

THE universe exploded into a million stars. Of course, Ulysses Walden knew, that wasn't what *really* happened. The coldly rational part of his brain understood that it was simply an optical illusion caused by the Doppler Effect during the transition out of a warp bubble. While moving apparently faster than the light emitted from those stars, their light shifted out of the visible spectrum. It was replaced by a more general bright glow, the background radiation of the universe edging into visibility.

All of this was academic, given that the massive ship had no genuine viewports, instead relying on external cameras that fed into screens located along the so-called "Observation Deck." Ulysses spent a good deal of time there for the first two days of travel, but as days turned to weeks he found his attention drifting elsewhere.

Now that they were finally arriving, however, he was among the crowds gathered to see a new sun emerge from the blurry glow of radiation. The more seasoned interstellar travelers shook their heads at the "tourists" who watched, awestruck, as the huge rings around the ship's core activated, warping the very fabric of space-time to cheat the laws of physics.

Calling these new travelers "tourists," however, undercut the true difficulty of arranging passage on one of the government-run warp ferries that traveled between the three settled star systems under mankind's control. Getting a berth on one of these vessels was incredibly expensive and heavily restricted. As Ulysses shifted in his seat, he ran his hands into the interior pocket of his jacket and pulled out his identification card.

He barely recognized the face on the picture, a face that he saw when he glanced at the faint reflection in the view screen. His natural wavy black hair and brown eyes were long gone, replaced by stringy blond hair buzzed short on the sides. His green eyes were genuine replacements and not simple lenses. It still gave new meaning to seeing the universe through new eyes, since these particular organs had been produced in a laboratory less than a year ago.

Some parts were hard to conceal even with advanced medical technology. The cocky smile with just a hint of teeth, the set of his shoulders, the way that he could never seem to grow anything longer than peach fuzz despite hailing from a proud line of bearded Martian men. He had trained for weeks to adjust his habits and had gone so far as to implant pins in his legs to adjust his gait. It had worked so far. But out here there really was no going back.

Ulysses Walden, Martian war criminal, was dead. Chico Wallach, entrepreneur and second-cousin to a cattle baron on the pastoral moon of Dulcinea, would walk out of this warp terminal into a new system and a new life.

As long as he didn't screw this up.

The ship rumbled as the warp field fizzled completely. Ulysses heard a shriek and twisted his head to look behind him. A woman in an elegant blue dress was cartwheeling toward the far bulkhead in a decidedly inelegant flail of limbs. She, like a few others Ulysses could now see bobbing above the crowd, had declined to listen to the captain's warning and failed to strap into the crash couches that littered the Observation Deck. Most of them reacted quickly and held fast to the straps or recovered with the help of fellow passengers, but the woman with the fancy dress drifting around her head had been in motion when the gravity field shifted and found herself flung into the air.

When the ferry shifted out of its warp bubble, it would take about a minute for the gravity drive to come back online. Until that point, the ship was little more than the old rockets that had launched the first colonists into space hundreds of years ago. That meant no artificial gravity and no inertial compensation. Simply put, a woman in motion would stay in motion right until the point when she collided with a bulkhead or gravity reactivated and she plummeted five meters to the deck.

Fortunately for her, the ship's crew had prepared for an event like this. With precision that bordered on rote procedure, two of the ship's attendants, both small men with the classic Asiatic features that were common in this system, unbuckled their own restraints and kicked off from the bulkhead toward the woman.

It was a delicate ballet. The first man to reach her arrested her momentum toward the ceiling with his own. The second man, who had climbed up the bulkhead to adjust his angle of approach, impacted a moment later, driving all three back toward the woman's original position on the deck.

They landed awkwardly, but the attendants rolled and caught themselves on their heels. The woman tumbled until she hit a crash couch, at which point her fellow passengers reached across and pulled a restraint belt across her waist. The attendants, meanwhile, simply held onto handholds built into the deck plating to remain in place.

Ulysses was surprised that they weren't wearing the magnetic boots commonly used to allow spacers to walk around in microgravity. It was likely due to the fact such footwear would have clashed with their otherwise formal attire.

A gentle round of applause went up from the crowd and the two attendants bowed their heads graciously. The woman was red with fury and whispered something to one of the other passengers. The man, a mature gentleman with dark skin and a thick black mustache that drooped over his upper lip, laughed and shook his head. He whispered something in reply. It was not the reaction the woman had been hoping for, and she balled her hands into fists and struck at the couch in frustration. The impact sent her flying again, but this time the belt caught her as she let out a strangled gasp.

Ulysses shook his head. These were the kinds of people who were issued a coveted license for warp travel: vain, self-important elites who had never worked a day in their lives. Or, worse, the kinds of bureaucrats who kept the massive machine of the Centrality of United Planets moving, crushing the life out of the men and women who wanted nothing more than to be left alone.

He forced himself to take a breath. He couldn't afford to lose his cool. He had come too far. There was too much at stake to get sloppy now. He plastered a vacuous grin on his face as he seethed inwardly. The lights dimmed twice in quick succession, the sign that the artificial gravity would be reactivating within moments.

While he waited, Ulysses brought up the computer pad that he carried with him and studied the information one more time. The Tau Ceti system was mankind's farthest reach from their homeworld and centered around a single star slightly smaller than the sun that had seen humanity take their first steps into space. Depending on who you asked, it was a lawless frontier or a center of civilization amid the stars. Ulysses chose to see it as a land of opportunity, a place where a man could make a fresh start.

As he examined the travel brochure, an alert streamed across the bottom of the screen. It was a green banner with gold text that read: "The Eternal Dragon welcomes you to Tau Ceti. Please remember to respect local customs during your visit. If you have any questions, visit the Imperial Informational Resources kiosk when you arrive at Chelsea Station. Thank you for visiting." The message then repeated in the dozen or so languages most common for new arrivals.

With the gravity restored, passengers were free to walk around the Observation Deck or return to their staterooms to collect their belongings. Ulysses had everything he needed in an old military surplus vac bag, a loose canvas hold-all similar to the old kit bags from Earth. He had cleared his room this morning, ship time, of any traces of his presence. Even the most detailed forensics sweep wouldn't pick up any genetic traces that could lead back to him. Now all he had to do was wait in silence until the ship docked with Chelsea Station.

"Seems like a good seat." The dark-skinned man stood above him. "Do you mind if I join you?"

Ulysses shrugged. "It's a free system."

The man chuckled and slid onto the couch beside Ulysses. The safety restraints had withdrawn into the red cushions of the couch, allowing total freedom of movement. The mustachioed man extended his hand. "Akash Kulkarni."

"Chico Wallach."

"A pleasure."

"If you don't mind me asking, what did that woman say to you after her abrupt landing?" Ulysses asked.

Kulkarni sighed. "She was rather insistent that we should be able to simply ride the warp bubble all the way to the station instead of using the more conventional methods of travel for the last leg of the trip."

"She said all that?"

Kulkarni shrugged. "More or less. There was a considerable degree of profanity involved. She didn't like it when I told her that we could warp all the way to the station, but only if we wanted to cook everyone inside with a lethal dose of radiation and probably destroy both this ship and the station in the process."

"Yeah, she didn't look very happy about that."

"The ignorance of some people amazes me." Kulkarni looked at the travel brochure on the pad in Ulysses's hand. "First time in Tau Ceti, I take it?"

"What makes you say that?"

"Well, you say things like, 'It's a free system.' Anyone who's been here knows that isn't true."

Ulysses frowned. "What do you mean?"

"This system isn't like Centauri or even the Solar system. Those places at least have their populations under control. Here in Tau Ceti, the outer planets are rife with pirates, warlords, and terrorists. The worst kinds of scum. Take my advice, son. Stick to Yu-Kiang and its moons. You'll be better off."

"I take it that you've lived here before," Ulysses said.

Kulkarni nodded. "I've lived just about everywhere, at one time or another. Most recently, I was in the Solar system on business."

Ulysses slid the handheld computer into his pocket and straightened his jacket. "And exactly what business are you in, Mr. Kulkarni?"

"Oh, it's nothing interesting. I'm what they call an 'executive asset specialist.'"

"You mean you're a security contractor. A private spy."

Kulkarni gave him a fierce smile that showed his teeth. "I see you speak bureaucracy, Mr. Wallach. Are you a veteran?"

Ulysses shook his head. "Small business owner. I see plenty of bureaucracy without having to sign up for the Navy."

Before Kulkarni could reply, a short tone carried over the ship's speakers. It was followed by a woman's voice, smooth and professional. "Ladies and gentlemen, if you'll direct your attention to the view screens, we will be shifting from an exterior view to a live feed from Chelsea Station. Our estimated time of arrival is one hour and eighteen minutes. If you have not already done so, please collect your belongings and prepare to disembark. On behalf of myself and the crew, we hope you have enjoyed your journey across the stars."

Kulkarni slapped his palms onto his knees. "Well, Mr. Wallach, it's been nice chatting with you." He reached into his pocket and pulled out a small plastic card. It had his name and the logo of an unnamed security company with a simple contact address. "If you find yourself ignoring my advice and heading to the outer planets, please look me up before throwing your life away."

"I might just do that." Ulysses accepted the card, then shook his hand again.

Kulkarni stood and stretched. "Ah, well. Vacation's over for me, I guess. Until we meet again, Mr. Wallach."

Ulysses waved as he departed, then sagged back onto the couch. That had been a test, he knew. A man like Akash Kulkarni didn't make random small talk with strangers. It was possible that he was internal security for the ferry who was keeping an eye on suspicious passengers. But he could work for someone far more dangerous, and he had just singled Ulysses out for his little test. Whether Ulysses passed or failed was difficult to say. He hadn't been arrested, but Kulkarni might be playing a long game to see if he would lead him to bigger fish.

Ulysses shook his head. This paranoia was going to kill him. No matter what else Kulkarni had said, one thing was true. The vacation was over. It was time to get to work.

Chelsea Station was actually a series of three space stations whose carefully maintained orbit around the system's single star kept them in close proximity. The first facility was where passengers disembarked from their warp ferry and were processed by Customs and Immigration. It was only a few hundred meters across, just enough space for all the appropriate security checkpoints as well as a collection of shops where travelers could pick up last-minute items for their journey starward.

The passenger station also played host to a gaggle of shuttle companies that provided transportation to the various planets and moons of the Tau Ceti system. Despite three settled worlds and eight settled moons in the system, not to mention numerous settled asteroids and artificial space stations, ninety percent of traffic was bound for the planet of Yu-Kiang. It made sense that the system's capital would be a common business and tourist destination alike, and the fact that it was the second most populated world outside of the Solar system meant that there was no shortage of traffic headed the other way.

The second station struck Ulysses as a massive butterfly net whose invisible strings contained all the commercial freight that passed through the warp junction. A wide ring represented the edge of a restricted zone, and this zone housed tens of thousands of cargo containers of every conceivable shape and size. Swarms of drones flowed among the containers, preventing collisions and ensuring that every piece of cargo was in the optimal position. These drones also served as tugs, guiding the cargo containers into the cargo hold of the warp ferry, a hold that was large enough to fit a whole *Crusader*-class cruiser without scratching the paint.

This was the beating heart of interstellar commerce, the only way for corporations to transport goods from one star to another. Before the advent of warp technology, each star system had been virtually cut off from the others and forced to develop independently. Now that interstellar travel had been reduced to a matter of months instead of decades, corporations from every system were making up for lost time and the volume of trade was staggering.

In truth, that trade was the real reason for the warp ferries to begin with. A few such ships existed prior to the war, but nothing on this scale. Construction of such complicated vehicles required an investment of capital and resources that made it impossible for anyone except for the centralized government bureaucracy to organize such a task. Only the richest, most advanced corporations could even hope to construct a single warp-capable vessel, let alone a fleet. The warp ferry allowed the government to subsidize interstellar trade in a way that would allow it to flow freely.

At least, that was the official line. To Ulysses, it just seemed like the best way to make sure that everyone had to follow the government's rules or else lose out on trillions in profit. Control the purse-strings and you control everything.

The third and final sub-station at Chelsea was by far the largest, although you wouldn't know it by looking at the view screens. In fact, the third station didn't even appear on the digitally-altered feed for security reasons. But Ulysses knew what it looked like. A lifetime ago, he had been assigned to a task force to determine the best way that a team of saboteurs could go about crippling such a station. The results had been disappointing. Nothing less than engagement by a full naval fleet would threaten a station like that.

It was the lifeline for all Centrality forces stationed in the system. If they lost their base at Chelsea Station, they would be stranded light-years from reinforcements or effective resupply. It was comprised of two parts: the station itself and the Ring Field. The station was a fortress, bristling with guns and patrolled by a flotilla of support ships. In wartime, they would have stationed at least three cruisers and six destroyers to respond to any threat, and Ulysses was sure that peace hadn't softened their resolve to ensure that the station was defended. But it was the Ring Field that was the great strength and biggest potential weakness of Chelsea Station.

The warp ferries were based on the original design for the Alcubierre-White-Lupei Drive, more commonly called the "AWL drive" or even just "warp drive," which consisted of a single wide donut-shaped ring built around the core of the ship itself. It was this ring which made warp travel possible. Ulysses didn't have a firm grasp on the physics, but he knew that the ring essentially took the matrix of space-time, the very substance of the universe itself, and created a pocket where that matrix was thinner in front of the ship and denser behind the ship. In essence, this drive subverted traditional Einsteinian physics by having a pressure wave of space itself propel the ship forward.

The ship would not move faster than light in the traditional sense. A beam of light emitted from a source inside the warp bubble would always move orders of magnitude faster than the most advanced ship imaginable. The trick was that this warp bubble could move faster than a beam of light *outside* the bubble, resulting in the bizarre Doppler phenomenon Ulysses witnessed when his ferry left New Gateway Station back in the Solar system.

But when designing warp drives for military use, ship designers encountered a problem. The rings were a huge tactical vulnerability, and the technology was sensitive enough that it wouldn't take an unreasonable amount of damage to render them unusable or, worse, unstable. Instead of building the rings around the ship, naval planners had the ingenious solution of creating separate warp rings that would dock with warships and attach with extendable clamps. Warp travel was of limited use inside the limits of a star system anyway due to dense areas of gravity disrupting the operation of the drive. The warp stations were created to house these removable rings until they were needed.

During the war, Ulysses proposed sending a strike force to attempt to sabotage the rings to either disable them completely or force them to send warships on uncontrolled jumps that would result in their ultimate destruction. Because of the sheer scale of the rings and the highly classified nature of their construction, the plan was deemed too difficult to engineer. But Ulysses still considered the Ring Fields to be the gap in the armor that could ultimately cripple something like Chelsea Station.

Not that he would want that now, of course. Now he was a civilian. If he kept telling himself that, he may eventually believe it.

It took three more hours for Ulysses to disembark and find his way through the passenger station. Some of the passengers had brought their own ships as cargo, the only way that private transports could make their way from one star system to another, and followed the signs for the station's valet service.

Ulysses didn't have a ship, but he did have one rather large bit of luggage that had been waiting for him upon his arrival. The metal chest was almost as big as he was and was too heavy to move without the use of built-in rollers. There was no way some third-rate rock-jumper stuffed with passengers was going to have the juice to take him and his cargo as far as he wanted. He needed a real ship, a genuine transport. Fortunately, he had someone in mind.

As he walked through the baggage claim, he spotted a family engaged in a joyful reunion. An older couple welcomed a young man, who Ulysses assumed was their son, with a handwritten sign that read: "Welcome Home, Giovanni." The hugs and handshakes were interrupted, however, when two men in khaki uniforms emerged from an unseen alcove and took the young man under the arms. The young man's parents screamed in protest.

The old man took a step forward to confront the khaki-clad men, but one of them turned back and smacked the old man with a wooden baton. Blood flowed from the man's mouth and nose and he crumpled to his knees. His wife ran to his side and knelt by him, wrapping her arms around his neck.

Ulysses felt his hands ball into fists. He forced himself to breathe. This wasn't his problem. This wasn't his fight. He was here for a new start. He couldn't get himself thrown into prison only hours after arriving in the system. He watched helplessly as the young man was dragged through a door by the uniformed men.

No one else stopped. No one else even seemed to notice the old couple on their knees in the middle of the promenade. No one else seemed to hear their sobs.

Ulysses moved to the old couple. He pulled out a small cloth handkerchief from his pocket and offered it to the old man. "Here. Use this to wipe up the blood."

The man kept his head down, but the old woman looked at him. Tears filled her eyes, but there was anger in her words as she spoke. "Get away from us."

Ulysses raised his hands. "Sorry. I just wanted to help."

"Save your pity for someone who asked for it," the woman spat. "It's foreigners like you who corrupted our son and got him in trouble with the Kempeitai." She turned to her husband. "Come on. Let's get you out of here."

Ulysses watched them go, a hollow feeling in his stomach. Then he moved on, following the signs through the maze of shops to a circular kiosk in the center of the arrivals hall. The kiosk consisted of a waist-high counter that surrounded seven attractive young women in short green skirts, starched white button-up shirts, and green sweaters. The emblem of the Eternal Dragon Empire, a yellow serpent coiled around a spherical starfield, was stitched above their hearts. Behind the girls, and thus ignored by most of the men who walked by the kiosk, were screens that showed a loop of informative tourism videos.

The one playing when Ulysses approached showed muscular, fit men in their early twenties running across a field in unison. The men wore khaki uniforms with green trim on their collars and the hem of their sleeves. They wore high leather boots and had sidearms visible on large holsters on their belt. They were the same uniforms as the men who dragged that young man to an unpleasant fate just a few minutes earlier.

Words began to appear on the screen. "Dedication. Honor. Justice." The scene transitioned to a lush tropical landscape, and the men moved with precision. "The Kempeitai are the hand of the Eternal Dragon made manifest."

The men stopped at once, then pivoted on their heel to face the camera. A single officer, notable for his short-brimmed khaki hat, stepped forward and gave a curt bow from the waist. The chyron on the bottom of the screen read: "The Imperial Office of Internal Security respectfully welcomes you to our glorious system. Always remember: the Kempeitai are here for you."

Rage filled Ulysses at the double meaning of the implied threat. His thoughts turned to the young man who had been dragged away by those same Kempeitai agents. What had he done to warrant such attention from the self-proclaimed hands of the Eternal Dragon?

One of the young women spotted him and inclined her head as a gesture of respect. "Welcome, traveler. Is this your first time in the Eternal Dragon Empire?"

Ulysses adjusted the bag on his shoulder. "Uh. Yeah. Seems real nice, so far."

The girl was apparently immune to sarcasm. She giggled. "That is kind of you to say, sir. May I offer you assistance?"

"Yeah. There's a couple things you can help me with. First, I just need a shuttle reservation to take me starward."

"Absolutely, sir." There was a brief pause as she worked on a hidden computer beneath the counter. "Were you going to Yu-Kiang? Or did you have another destination in mind?"

Ulysses smiled. "Well, that was the second thing. I was wondering if you had any way that I could find someone who lives in this system. I'm trying to drop by unannounced. It's a surprise for his birthday."

"That depends, sir. While we do keep travel records of citizens of the empire, we do not allow just anyone to access that information."

Ulysses pulled out the small plastic business card he had been handed on the warp ferry. "My name is Akash Kulkarni. I'm an executive asset specialist on assignment."

The young woman must have recognized the logo on the card, because her already perfect posture went rigid. "Of course, Mr. Kulkarni. We are always happy to assist our friends from Centauri. I do have to warn you, however, there may be limits to the information I can provide. Is this person a member of a sensitive position? We cannot reveal the locations of any military personnel, either Centrality or Imperial, without written authorization from a superior officer." The girl had shifted to a formal tone, indicating that this was part of a script the girls all had to learn.

"No." The vac bag started to slide again, and Ulysses had to release his grip on the waist-high metal chest he had picked up from baggage claim in order to catch it. "Nothing like that."

The girl frowned. "Do you need help, sir? I can contact a porter who can take your luggage to one of our transports."

Ulysses waved her concern away. "Thanks, but I'll manage. Gravity's just a little different on the station than it was on the ferry and I'm still readjusting." In fact, the gravity settings had been the same, roughly .8 g, an intentional choice by the ferry's captain to allow the passengers to acclimatize to the standard gravity on all government-run stations in the Tau Ceti system.

The girl turned her attention back to her screen. "Very well, sir. Can I have the name of the person in question?"

"Val. Val Tanner."

CHAPTER FOUR

ASTEROID t-242 had no formal name, but the locals knew it as "Port Tew." It was named not for the number but for the infamous pirate Thomas Tew back on Earth. Legend had it that Tew helped start a pirate kingdom off the coast of Africa, and the name was chosen to acknowledge that legacy.

Though, Val observed as he walked past another drunk strewn face-down in one of the station's narrow corridors, this was hardly a kingdom worth claiming.

The asteroid was less than three kilometers long but saw a great deal of traffic because of its location in a stable portion of the asteroid belt known as the Rampart that bisected the Tau Ceti system. It labeled itself as a "free port," meaning that neither the Eternal Dragon Empire nor the Centrality had any involvement in the operation. That made it a popular spot with anyone who didn't want the secret police breathing down their necks. It also meant that the loose assortment of scoundrels who ran the place were under no obligation to keep their equipment well-maintained.

"You smell that?" Charity asked. She hopped over an uneven spot of deck plating. "Air recycler must be going bad. You get that charcoal smell when your system starts breaking down."

"It's not all bad," Val said. He ducked through a chokepoint where the rock walls jutted into the path. The small size of the tunnels carved into the asteroid meant that he was forced to walk at a constant crouch. "At least it covers the smell of everything else."

Charity smirked. She could walk upright and her hair barely touched the roof of the tunnel. "Hey, *you* wanted to come here. I was perfectly happy to go back to see my parents on Yu-Kiang. You know my father likes you."

"He likes my ship."

Charity shrugged. "Same thing. I'm sure he could get you some work."

Val chuckled. "I'm not that desperate, sweetheart."

"Of course not. Remind me," she tapped on her chin. "Did Savimbi say he was going to break your *fingers* or your *hands* if you didn't have his money? I need to know which splints to buy."

They passed a T-junction and Val stopped to examine the map on the wall. Satisfied that they were headed in the correct direction, he took the right turn. "Look. Bailey has always been good for work when I needed it. And Savimbi's a businessman. He wouldn't throw away a tool like me when I can still be useful."

"Oh, you're a tool, all right," Charity muttered. Val tossed a dirty look over his shoulder. His wife beamed in reply. Val shook his head, a grin threatening to overcome his dour expression.

The narrow corridor opened to a wide room that was roughly fifty meters on each side. The ceiling was nice and high, allowing Val to stretch out. Artificial sunlight poured into the space from hidden lamps set deep in the rock. Big water tanks took up one side of the room, with several species of fish visible through glass panels. Rows of plants grew in nutrient channels along the top of the tanks, a welcome spot of life in this dead rock.

A series of stalls were set up in front of the tanks. Each stall was made of cheap, collapsible aluminum rods that snapped together to form a skeletal framework. Sheets of pressed metal slid into the gaps for support and to advertise the various products for sale. Behind each stall was a small tent that stretched from the entrance of the stall to the rock walls of the chamber. Vendors at each stall shouted out their wares to anyone wandering close. If you wanted stale bread or used electrical parts in Port Tew, this was the place to be.

Val walked up to one of the closest stalls and spoke to a young boy no older than ten or eleven Earth-standard years old. The stall had a crude painting of a fish on the front and a small sampling of grilled fish on a plastic plate. "Hello, Neb."

The boy rolled his eyes. "Only my mom calls me that."

"Is she here?"

Neb sighed and leaned back in his chair, pulling back on a black curtain at the back of the stall. When he did, Val could see a tight little prep area complete with a compact, battery-operated electric grill on a collapsible table and a refrigeration unit tucked underneath that stored this tiny shop's rationed supply of fish from the aquaponics farm behind them. A blond woman in a blue and grey smock stood over the grill, keeping an eye on the tilapia she was cooking.

Neb called out, "Mom. Val's here."

The woman looked up from the grill and Val saw the same weary expression worn by her son. She waved for him to come into the tent, then stepped forward into the stall. "Val. Ain't seen you around here in while."

"I tried the gambling scene out around Parson," Val replied. "Local color reminded me that I should stick to places where I've got good friends who I can trust."

Bailey Evans snorted. "And, what? You thought you'd stop by on your way to find these so-called 'friends' of yours?"

Val spread his hands. "Bailey. After all we've been through? That hurts."

Bailey smiled, then looked past Val. "Well, at least you brought Charity with you. Maybe you ain't as stupid as you look."

"Hey, now." Val adjusted his vest. It was a different one than the one Charity had been forced to tear on Parson, colored dark blue with red buttons. "No reason to get nasty."

Charity extended her hand and Bailey shook it. "Nice to see you again, Bailey. My husband," she said, bumping into Val with her hips, "thought you might have some work for us."

Bailey's eyes darted around the room. There were a dozen people gathered around other stalls, but she wasn't going to take any chances talking in the open. "Come on back."

Val and Charity stepped behind the stall. It was hardly large enough for the three of them to fit at once. When they were inside, Charity picked up a skewer of grilled fish from the plate and took a bite. Val shot his wife a look. Charity shrugged and said, "What? She can take it out of our pay. I'm starving."

Bailey smiled. "Call it a bonus. On the house."

Val's eyes lit up. "Oh. Can I have one, too?" He reached for a skewer.

"Sure. And I'll take five percent off your payment." Val's hand froze. Bailey shrugged. "Suit yourself. It's good fish."

Charity took another bite and groaned with contentment. "It really is."

Val growled. "You had a job for us?"

"Right." Bailey pulled open the curtain to let Charity and Val walk into the back area. "Keep an eye out, Neb. Let me know if there's trouble."

"Yes, ma'am." The boy stepped away from the grill to return to his position in the stall. When he did, Bailey slid into the tent.

It was a simple setup. Just the table, grill, and cooler with a single folding chair off to the side. Or, at least, that's how it appeared. Bailey walked to the chair and moved it, then popped a hidden latch in the deck plating. A trapdoor roughly a meter wide swung open on concealed hinges. Bailey propped it open, then descended the hidden ladder to the true heart of her operation.

The room was scarcely larger than her stall a deck above. Shelving lined every wall, with each shelf covered with boxes and containers made from wood, synthetic ivory, titanium, and even a glass cylinder approximately five centimeters long. "What's that?" Val asked, reaching for the glass tube.

Bailey smacked his hand. "Don't touch." She browsed through the selection until she found what she had been looking for: a black box the size of Val's closed fist. She offered it to him, but when Val reached for it she pulled it out of his grasp. "I have a buyer lined up on Ranginui who's offered me ten thousand for this. Here's the deal. You deliver it for me and you get twenty percent."

Val frowned. Two thousand scales wouldn't pay off his debt entirely, but it would show Savimbi he was making progress. Another job and he'd have this burden off his back for good. At least until he had to take out another loan.

There was just one problem. "Do you think it's a good idea to show up on Ranginui before you have Savimbi's money?" Charity asked. "He might just think you were trying to run a scam on him and gut you on the spot."

Bailey shook her head. "Sorry, Val. That's all I got. The rest of this junk's collecting dust until the right buyer comes along."

"Meaning someone who will accept your outrageous price," Val said. Bailey grinned. "We'll take it. I'm sure Savimbi won't even know we're there."

Charity opened her mouth, but a child's voice rang out from the deck above them. "Trouble!"

Bailey sighed. "What now?" She grabbed the rungs of the ladder and started to climb. "Stay here. I'll be back and we can work out the details." When she reached the top, she started to close the trapdoor. "Sorry about this. Never had a reason to install any lights down there. I'll be back as soon as I figure out what spooked the kid."

The deck plating clanged shut, leaving Charity and Val in total darkness. Val reached out and grabbed his wife's hand, rubbing his thumb along her palm. "I told you this would work out. Bailey always comes through for us."

"I don't know, Val. Savimbi's not going to be happy that you don't have the full payment."

"Yeah, well, I'm sure he'll understand. Two thousand is still some decent coin, and it should at least buy a—"

"—stay of execution?" Charity finished the thought.

Val sighed. "I was going to say, 'buy a little goodwill.' But, since you want to look on the dark side of things, fine. Yes. Savimbi's more likely to play ball and let me walk away from the meeting if he can get two thousand scales for his trouble. It shows him I'm serious about getting the rest."

"Oh, Val. I love how naïve you are," Charity whispered. "It's cute."

Without a warning, the trapdoor flew open, exposing them to the light once more. But it wasn't Bailey's voice that called out, "You're gonna want to see this."

A heavyset man in a grey jumpsuit appeared at the edge of the opening. "I've got two more down here." He directed his attention down to the hidden room. "You down there. Come up slowly. I'm not asking again."

Val looked at his wife. Charity shrugged, then raised her hands. Val followed her lead. "We're coming up."

They ascended the ladder and emerged from the secret compartment. Both Val and Charity kept their hands raised as they stepped into the prep area and were careful not to meet the gaze of anyone else in the room. Val tried to keep the black box out of view as best as possible without looking like a threat.

Four men in matching jumpsuits surrounded them. None of them carried visible firearms, but they had the look of men unafraid to get physical if the situation called for it. Each man sported matching tattoos on their neck, a sideways V with a circle inside it. Val didn't recognize it, but from the way he felt Charity tense beside him he guessed that it wasn't good.

Two of the men were skinny and had more tattoos visible on the backs of their hands. The final man had a thick red beard and was only a centimeter or so taller than Charity. The knife in his hands, however, was no less threatening due to his height. He had it pressed against Bailey's kidney with his hand over her mouth. Bailey's eyes were wide with terror.

"Who are you?" the heavyset man asked. A sewn patch on his jumpsuit read *Irwin*. "Why were you hiding?"

"My name is—"

"We're just passing through Port Tew and dropped by to see an old friend," Charity interrupted. She bowed her head. "We apologize. We have nothing but respect for the Parvel Guild."

Val recognized the name and his blood ran cold. Jordan Parvel was one of the three administrators who ran Port Tew, and his guild was responsible for all merchant traffic into and out of the asteroid. Which meant that they would not take kindly to smugglers hiding valuable goods under their noses without paying the proper "licensing fee."

"Can't you speak for yourself?" Irwin asked. "What kind of a man lets his wife speak for him?"

"The kind of man who doesn't want any trouble," Val said. "Where's the kid?"

"Ran off," Irwin sneered. "Just like his father. He'd better be careful. One of these days he might find himself tripping out of an airlock like his old man, too."

Bailey let out a stifled scream, but the bearded man twisted the knife against her smock. "Now, now," he growled. "Let's not get carried away. I wanna have some fun with you first."

Val lowered his hands. "I'm sure this is all just a misunderstanding. There's no reason to hurt anyone."

Irwin frowned and took a menacing step forward. He towered over Val, chest heaving with every breath. "I'm sorry. Were you trying to tell me what I can't do on *my* station?"

Val lowered his eyes. "No. Of course not. I just feel like we can come to an understanding." He pointed to the trapdoor. "Look. Take whatever you want. I know Bailey didn't mean anything by it. Times are tough, and she was just doing what it took to survive."

"When she signed up with the Guild," Irwin said, "she knew her limits. The Guild looks out for its own. *We* decide what it takes to survive."

He reached down and grabbed Val's chin, forcing him to meet his gaze. "And we don't tolerate anyone who disrupts our business. The Guild is the only thing standing between this station and anarchy. We protect our merchants. We ensure a fair marketplace. And no second-rate fishmonger is going to stand in our way."

Irwin's hand moved from Val's chin to the black box in his hand. He opened it up to reveal a rock the size of Val's thumbnail. The rock glittered with silvery flecks of light. "What's this?" He held it up for inspection. "Whoa-ho-ho." He showed his men. "Where'd you get your hands on newtonium? You could run a whole ship with that sliver. A few of these could make someone rich enough to retire. If the Centrality didn't catch you and put a slug through your brain, that is."

Irwin's smile turned cold. "It's a shame you never came to us for approval." He stared Val in the eye as he slid the crystalline rock into one of his many pockets. "I hope you got payment in advance on that."

A pulse of rage stormed through Val, but he forced himself to breathe. "We're just trying to make a living, sir."

"No," Irwin corrected. "You're acting out of greed. Greed can get you killed out here." He looked at Bailey and a cruel smile crossed his face. "I think it's time for a demonstration."

At that, the bearded man lifted the knife to Bailey's throat. Her eyes went wild with horror and she struggled to break free, but the bearded man's thick hands were too strong. The blade broke the skin just below her jaw and a bead of blood pooled around it.

"Let her go."

Every eye in the tiny shop turned in unison to the black curtain, which had been tossed aside to reveal a lone man standing just inside the stall. He wore black pants and a gray shirt under a blue-and-gray flight jacket. The thumb of his left hand was hooked in his pocket while he held the curtain open with his right. His blond hair hung low over his forehead where it wasn't shaved on the sides. There were hard lines at the corners of his green eyes.

The stranger stepped into the tent, letting the curtain fall behind him. The bearded man looked at Irwin, silently asking his boss if he should, in fact, let Bailey go.

Irwin's face went from blank shock to rage in the blink of an eye. "I don't know what you want here," he growled. "But this is none of your business. Move along."

"I've decided to make it my business," the stranger said. He stepped up to Irwin as if daring the heavyset thug to look him in the eye. The two men sized each other up for a silent moment.

Val's breath caught in his throat. There was something familiar about this stranger. The details of his appearance were wrong, but there was something about the way that he moved. The way that he talked. The way that he walked into a room full of hostile thugs and acted as if they should be afraid of *him*.

The air in the tent was tense. Silence reigned. Everyone kept their eyes on the stranger, anxious to see what he was going to do.

Which meant that no one was watching Charity.

Everything happened at once. Charity slid behind the bearded man and stabbed him in the ear with a wooden skewer stolen from the grill. The man roared in pain and swatted at her, but Bailey managed to squeeze out of his grip. She drove a kick into his stomach for good measure, knocking the squat man to the ground.

At the same instant, the stranger slammed the heel of his hand into Irwin's jaw, clacking it shut and forcing the big tough to stumble backward. The stranger kept at it, delivering quick strikes intended to keep Irwin in pain and unsteady. None of them did any real damage, but Irwin was unprepared for the ferocity of the attacks and found himself retreating to the edge of the tent.

That left Val to face the two remaining Guild enforcers by himself. They came at him with sweeping punches, forcing Val to duck backward to get out of reach. As he did so, he tripped over the bearded man's extended leg and plunged to the deck.

Dazed by the impact, Val decided that it was time to stop playing by the rules. He reached into his vest and pulled out a small triangular piece of sharpened metal with a tiny, two-fingered grip. He slid the punch dagger into place between the fingers of his right hand and surged at the two tattooed thugs.

One of the men took a slash across the chest that tore through his jumpsuit and left a trail of blood. It hadn't been a deep cut, but it had to hurt all the same. Val kept up the pressure, blocking another heavy punch and responding with a jab of his own. The punch dagger came back covered in crimson and the first Guild enforcer looked down at his bloody chest in shock.

While Val's attention had been on the first man, the second maneuvered behind him and wrapped his arm around Val's neck. Val thrashed in the man's grip, but the enforcer had superior leverage. Val could do little but attempt wild stabs behind him with his dagger. None of his strikes found their mark. Spots danced at the edge of his vision and he felt his legs go weak.

Then the arm around his throat loosened. Val fell to his knees and sucked in precious oxygen. He turned around to see the enforcer go down under a vicious assault by his wife. She wielded the folding chair in her hands like a medieval mace. She kept at it, smashing the chair down once, twice, three times on the man's collapsed body before releasing her weapon.

Val watched as the stranger dodged an awkward backhand from Irwin, then caught the Guild thug by the arm. He used Irwin's own momentum against him, twisting him off-balance. The stranger grabbed Irwin by the back of the neck and pressed his face against the hot grill. Steam seared, flesh sizzled, and Irwin shrieked in pain.

But the big thug wasn't done yet. He reached into one of his many zippered pockets and pulled out a handgun no bigger than ten centimeters. But it didn't have to be large to be lethal, and he brandished the weapon like a holy symbol that would save him from damnation.

Irwin pointed the gun at the stranger's head. He likely would have killed him if Bailey hadn't appeared with the battery pack for her grill. She had torn it open to expose conductive wires and shoved them against Irwin's jumpsuit.

Against the same pocket where he had stored the stolen newtonium.

Newtonium was one of the most unique elements mankind had ever discovered and had become the key to modern space travel. Despite being the rarest naturally occurring substance in the known universe, it was found in every major spaceship, space station, and settlement on worlds and moons too small to hold their own atmospheres.

It had such value because, when a sufficient electrical current was applied to a given amount of newtonium, it began to generate enormously powerful gravitational fields.

The exposed wires snapped with electrical energy, and when they contacted Irwin's pocket the entire room imploded. It only lasted for a second, and the surge drained the battery pack completely, but it had a profound effect.

Men and women were knocked off their feet. The chair, grill, and refrigeration unit all flew toward Irwin. And the gun, held in an unsteady grip, snapped out of Irwin's hand and clattered to the deck.

The tent itself didn't fare any better. The fragile structure couldn't take the stress and the entire tent assembly collapsed in a tangle of fabric and bodies.

Val was the first to emerge from the chaos, removing himself from a pile of enveloping nylon. As the others started to break free, Val saw that there were a dozen other faces all staring at them. He gave them a hesitant wave, then straightened out his vest. His punch dagger was gone, lost in the jumble that had once been a ramshackle fish shop.

Bailey was the last person out of the wreckage. She had a green backpack slung over her shoulder. She started moving deeper into the market, but Val pulled on her sleeve. "Come on. I've got a ship. I can get you out of here."

Bailey shook her head. "Not without my boy. Don't worry about me. I can smooth things over with Parvel. But you need to get out of here."

"But—"

"Go!" Val released her and she stepped away. Before she disappeared into the crowd, she turned back to face him one last time. "No offense, but next time you feel like stopping by, go bother someone else instead." With that, she was gone.

CHAPTER FIVE

THEY reached the docks without incident a few minutes later. Either Parvel's thugs hadn't recovered from their ass-kicking or the merchant guild was slower to react than Val would have expected. But he wasn't going to turn down a run of good luck.

Not that he expected that luck to last. They hadn't prepared for a quick exit and the *Lucky Rabbit's Foot* was cold. It would take several more minutes to run through the start-up procedure before they would be ready to take off. Anything could happen in those minutes, and Val was done with surprises for the day.

When they reached the open space of the docking slip that housed the *Lucky Rabbit's Foot*, the stranger hesitated near a large metallic crate. Val kept running until he noticed that Charity, too, had stopped. He pivoted on his heel. "What are you doing? Those guys are going to call Parvel any second and I do *not* want to be standing around when that happens."

"I don't have a ship," the stranger said.

"You can come with us," Charity offered. "You saved our lives back there. It's the least we can do."

"I didn't want to assume." The stranger placed his hand on the crate. "I tried finding you here earlier, but the docking attendant said you had gone into the station on business. I left the crate here in case you came back. You see, I need a transport."

Val rolled his eyes. Oh, it was *him*, all right.

"No way," Val said.

"Of course," Charity said at the same time. They both exchanged a look.

"Uh. If you guys need a minute..."

Val looked at the stranger. "We don't have a minute." He sighed and rubbed the bridge of his nose. "Fine. Get this thing on board. We need to keep moving before the Guild shuts down the whole hanger."

Val and the stranger pushed the crate up the ramp while Charity ran inside to start the launch procedure. Once the crate was secured inside the ship, Val climbed into the cockpit. The stranger followed at his heels.

Val slid into his custom leather seat on the right side of the cockpit and ran his hands over the controls. "Toggle the gravity drive for hot-start," he said.

Charity was busy at her own console on the left side of the cockpit, but she looked up with surprise when the stranger stepped forward and flipped a pair of switches. He smiled at her, then stepped back and took a seat at the rear of the cockpit.

"That was a lucky guess," she said.

"Val's the lucky one," the stranger said. "I happen to have a little experience with these ships."

"'Val?'" Charity raised her eyebrows. "Do you two know each other?"

"We used to."

Val clenched his teeth. "Can we stow this conversation until we're not running for our lives?"

"Sorry," Charity rolled her eyes and completed her start-up checklist. "Engineering is 'Go.'"

Val sighed. "You don't have to say that every time."

Charity grinned. "I know."

Val pressed a button and the ship rumbled to life. He pulled back on the yoke and the *Lucky Rabbit's Foot* rose off the deck.

The ship's comm board lit up. "Station Control to vessel T-J194, we've detected engine start-up. Is everything okay?"

Val tapped another button on the arm of his chair. "Uh, yeah. We're requesting an emergency departure effective immediately. We have a dangerous reactor malfunction and we need to get away from the populated area of the station to take a look at it."

"Confirmed, T-J194. Provide your SI code and we can slave your computer to our remote system."

Val grimaced. "Uh, negative, Station Control. Simulated intelligence program is offline. We have to make a manual departure. Request emergency depressurization and departure."

The voice on the other end of the line was quiet for a long moment. "Understood, T-J194. Set your vessel on the following course and we will send a shuttle to pick you up while a drone examines your vessel."

Val gripped the control yoke and looked at Charity. "That's probably as good as it's going to get."

Outside the ship, in the *Lucky Rabbit Foot's* individual docking slip, yellow warning lights blared to life to indicate that the slip was being depressurized. Once that was finished, the large metal doors that separated the docking slip from the vacuum of space began to slide open to allow the ship to depart.

Charity kept an eye on the external feed. "Looks like they bought it. Bay door is opening now."

Val sagged in his chair. "We made it. I was worried for a second."

"Yeah, I..." Charity frowned. "Wait. Something's happening. The door stopped."

"What?"

The stranger sprang to his feet and looked over her shoulder at the feed. "She's right. There's a gap right now, but it's a tight squeeze."

"Give me the feed." Val looked at his console as Charity connected him to the same images she was receiving.

"T-J194, please hold," Station Control's voice came over the comm. "An engineering party is standing by to assist you. Please power down and allow station personnel to board."

"Dammit," Val muttered. "Hang on."

He yanked the yoke back to his chest with his right hand while rapidly tapping out a sequence on a keypad built into his chair with his left. The *Lucky Rabbit's Foot's* engines swiveled and fired, launching the ship in full reverse toward the gate. The thruster wash from the sudden burn turned the limited remaining air outside into a miniature tornado within the docking slip. The force of the engines ripped several metal grates from the bulkhead.

"The door is closing," Charity called out.

"Parvel must have gotten to them," the stranger said.

"Everybody shut up," Val growled. "And hang on to something. This is going to be close."

Charity strapped into her crash webbing while the stranger raced to his seat and did the same. Even with the burst of acceleration, the ship's artificial gravity system had been able to compensate for most of the stress that such a maneuver should have placed on their bodies. But if they crashed into that docking bay door, the artificial gravity wouldn't save them.

"Vac suits?" the stranger called out. Every ship carried a supply of airtight suits that could be donned quickly and protected the user from the effects of vacuum exposure, though they only contained an air supply of roughly two hours.

Charity shook her head. "There's no time." To her husband she said, "You have twenty-five meters of separation."

"I know, I know." Val's face was tight with concentration.

The numbers counted down. The impact sensors started to activate, but Val reached across his console without looking and turned them off. They were picking up speed, but the door was still closing.

"Twenty meters."

They were almost clear of the docking bay now. These slips had been designed to receive larger ships and dwarfed the relatively small *Lucky Rabbit's Foot*, but they were coming to the point of no return.

"You have fifteen meters of separation."

"Val. Stop. We won't make it," the stranger said.

Val let out a wordless cry and yanked on the yoke, kicking the transport up onto its side. Outside the viewport, the massive docking bay door came within centimeters of the *Lucky Rabbit Foot's* hull. Then they were through and the viewport showed the whole asteroid ahead of their nose as they raced at full reverse away from it.

Val kicked the pedals underneath his console, sending the ship into a barely controlled spin using the forward thrusters. He adjusted the thrusters to kill the spin, then shoved the throttle to the red line.

"How long until the gravity drive is ready to jump?" Val asked.

The stranger looked at a small display built into the side of the cockpit. "Forty-two seconds."

"They're launching interceptors!" Charity yelled. She consulted her data display. "Looks like two Mark One Copperheads."

Val didn't allow any emotion to register on his face. Copperheads were military-grade tech, even older generations like the Mark Ones. They were basically cockpits strapped to engines with a few guns bolted on to give them teeth. His transport could outmaneuver them, but they had the advantage in speed. Still, it wasn't the fighters themselves that had Val worried as much as the possibility of—

"Missile launch!" Charity's voice was strained.

The stranger, by contrast, seemed unnaturally calm. "Thirty seconds."

"Charity, prep countermeasures."

"We don't have any. We had to sell them off for fuel, remember?"

"Who made that dumb decision?" Val asked.

"You did, when you refused to sell your vests," Charity replied. She was trying to sound relaxed, but Val could hear the panic in her voice. "Another missile launch!"

Val shook his head. "Damn. Okay." He ran his left hand through another sequence. "Let's hope this old AKER still works."

The forward thrusters fired again, flipping the ship around on its vertical axis to face the oncoming missiles. Val thought he could see the tiny engines burning against the void of deep space, but it had to be his imagination. He moved his right thumb to a red trigger built into the side of the yoke. His console emitted a pulsing tone as the Auto-Kinetic Emergency Response system activated.

The AKER system was standard on most civilian vessels in known space. It combined sophisticated sensor data processing with auto-cannon turrets that could be used to track and destroy incoming debris or meteoroids that threatened vessels in deep space. It was also useful against ordnance, though tracking such small and fast-moving targets would tax the system to its limit.

Beep. Beep. Beep.

The missiles were coming in fast. If one of them hit, it could tear the ship open like an overripe fruit. Even without a direct hit, the shrapnel would cripple them, leaving them at the mercy of Jordan Parvel's goons.

"Twenty seconds."

Beep. Beep beep.

Val needed to wait for a solid tone. Military ships would have flooded the area with hundreds of rounds to saturate the target, but the *Lucky Rabbit's Foot* didn't have those kinds of ammunition reserves. Not anymore.

Beep beep beep.

"Ten seconds."

Now Val could see them, small bits of purple light burning angrily against the dark shape of Port Tew's diminishing form. He kissed the first two fingers of his left hand, then placed them gingerly against the side of his console. "Come on, baby. Be good to me."

Beeeeep.

Val pulled the trigger and a burst of 35-mm armor-piercing high-explosive rounds sailed out of the chin-mounted turrets beneath the cockpit. He held the trigger down for less than two seconds, but even that brief shot emptied their reserves. He wouldn't have a second chance if he missed.

Without waiting to see the result, he kicked the ship back over to face in its direction of travel. The gravity drive would send the ship in whatever direction the nose was facing, and if a ship was moving through space at a different angle it would cause a drift in the final jump. Many pilots used those drifts to navigate around dangerous regions of space, but it was a difficult technique that called for more preparation time than they had available.

"Five seconds to jump."

Charity hovered over her display, consumed by the tracking data on the incoming missiles. "Splash one!" She pumped her hand in the air.

"What about the other one?" Val asked.

"Uh." Her voice dropped. "No joy. It avoided the rounds and is still gaining on us."

"Well, we gave it everything we had."

The red light on Val's board turned green. Metal panels slid across the viewports, encasing the cockpit within a cocoon of composite armor. Val closed his eyes.

The tiny missile with its deadly warhead got within fifteen meters of the *Lucky Rabbit Foot's* rear engines when its proximity trigger activated. The missile exploded, filling the space around it with deadly shrapnel intended to shred any vessel into pieces.

And it would have done just that if the *Lucky Rabbit's Foot* hadn't surged forward in a burst of incredible speed that sent it hundreds of kilometers away in mere seconds.

Val sagged in his chair and wiped the sweat from his forehead. That had been too close.

The stranger unhooked his crash webbing and walked over to Val's chair. He clasped a hand on the pilot's shoulder, and Val was too tired to fight it. "That was an amazing bit of flying, Val. You've still got it."

"Maybe. Though some days I'm not sure I still want it." He looked at the man standing above him. "I still can't believe it's really you. Didn't the CIP sentence you to four life sentences at Venus for what you pulled?"

"Six, actually. Though the Council of Inner Planets was just reading from a script written by some Centrality flunky."

"Heh." Val folded his arms. "So, how come you aren't stuffed in some floating coffin or sucking down clouds of sulfuric acid?"

"I got out. Good behavior."

Val shrugged. "Sure. I guess there's a first time for everything. What's up with the new look?"

"Tired of all the autograph hounds."

Charity leaned back in her chair and studied the two men. "Is someone going to tell me the story here?"

Val rested his head on the back of his chair and closed his eyes. "Charity Tanner, meet Major Ulysses Walden. The most dangerous Martian ever born."

"Wait. You mean *the* Ulysses Walden?" Charity asked. "The war hero?"

"Not according to the Centrality," Ulysses said. "They wrote the history. Turns out I was a terrorist the entire time. My deception was so dastardly, even *I* didn't know."

Ulysses leaned against the bulkhead. "Also, as far as the rest of the system is concerned, my name is Chico Wallach. 'Ulysses' is fine on the ship, but I don't want anyone with a grudge coming back to haunt me."

Charity turned to her husband. "Why didn't you tell me about this?"

"I did," Val argued. The ship's simulated intelligence had control during a grav jump, so he was free to ignore the controls until they reached their destination. "Remember all those times I said, 'I don't want to talk about it?' That's everything you needed to know."

Charity pouted. "That's not fair."

Val shrugged. "Probably." He leaned back and kicked his boots onto the console. "What are you doing here, Yule? Come to start another revolution? Storm the Imperial Palace on Yu-Kiang? I think you'll find even fewer willing idiots out here than you did back home."

Ulysses sighed and returned to his seat. "Nothing like that. I'm a businessman now. I'm looking to get into the salvage game."

"Hmm," Val nodded. "Good work, if you can get it. But it takes some serious coin to get started."

"I made some contacts on my way here. I bought an EVA suit. That's what's in the case below deck." He gestured to the ladder. "And I met a man on the ferry who said he knew a good place to get started. He said he knew about a big load of scrap just waiting to be salvaged out near Bakuwana."

"Okay," Val said. "You've got the suit and you've got a scoop. But you've also got a problem. Where's your ship?"

Ulysses smiled and spread his hands, indicating the *Lucky Rabbit's Foot*. "I was hoping that we could be partners in this."

"No," Val said. He rose to his feet. "No way. I am not going into business with you."

"Just hear me out," Ulysses said. "It doesn't have to be a permanent partnership. I just need some help getting started. Take me to the coordinates and help me secure some goods to sell. I don't have any money after paying for the warp ferry and the suit, but once I make some money I can pay you more than what the journey is worth."

"Absolutely—"

"—an interesting idea," Charity said. "If you'll excuse my husband and I for a moment, we have some things to discuss. We'll meet you in the mess once we've made our decision."

Ulysses nodded his head once. "Okay." He moved to the ladder and disappeared to the lower deck.

Val spun around to face his wife. "'An interesting idea?' You can't be serious."

Charity rose to her full height and stared up at him. "I was going to say the same thing to you. Since when have we been able to afford turning down a paying job?"

"Charity, that man is dangerous. They don't put just anyone in orbital prison around Venus, and they certainly don't let any of those inmates go for 'good behavior.'" Val looked at the ladder. "He's up to something. Why come all this way for salvage work when there's plenty to be done back home?"

Charity shrugged. "He has a reputation. Maybe he's afraid no one in the Solar system could give him a fair chance."

"Maybe he doesn't deserve one."

"Val." Charity put her hands on her hips. "I know you don't want to talk about what happened during the war. But I also know a certain ragged pilot who spent the last of his money to escape to Tau Ceti for a new life. People didn't want to give him a chance, either."

She reached up and put her hand on his chest. "But he stayed. He met a girl acting out her rebellious years against her parents. And we built a new life. Why doesn't Ulysses deserve the same chance?"

Val sighed. "Charity, it's not the same thing."

"You're right. When you ran away from the Solar system, you had no one to help you. But Ulysses has someone. He has you." Charity stepped back. "And it's not like we don't need the money."

"We'll find another job."

"Where?" Charity began counting off on her fingers. "Bailey's off the table, Savimbi won't talk to you unless you have his money, Rothberg's up to his eyeballs in Kempeitai trouble. Do you need me to keep going?"

"There's always someone looking for a fast ship."

Charity gave her husband a slow smile. "You're right. There is someone I left off the list. My father."

"Hey, now," Val said.

"That's it. That's your choice. You can help your friend and make enough money to keep living independently or we can go to my father and you can be just another shuttle jockey. What'll it be?"

CHAPTER SIX

ULYSSES ran his hands along the crate, checking for any damage. The seal was still good. His investment was still safe.

He hadn't expected this much resistance from Val. Looking back, it shouldn't have surprised him. Val had built a new life here, and the only time he ever knew Ulysses was during the war. He had only ever seen that side of him, the commander leading men into battle. But Val wasn't the only one who had changed.

The ladder clanged as someone descended from the cockpit. Ulysses glanced up to see Val clamber down a rung at a time, muttering to himself all the while.

Val planted his feet on the deck, then looked to his former comrade. "You were supposed to wait in the mess."

"I got anxious. I wanted to hear the verdict as soon as I could."

"We have a couple of conditions."

Ulysses fought back a smile. "Name them."

"One," Val held up a finger. "We're not joining any mad crusade. If you came here to fight the Centrality, we don't want any part of it."

"Fair."

"Two. I want two-thirds of whatever you find, one for me and one for my wife. Without us you might as well try to flap your arms and get to your salvage haul that way."

Ulysses rubbed his chin, then shook his head. "That's too much. I'm paying you for transport work. It's my suit, my spot, and my ass on the line if it goes sideways."

Val crossed his arms. "Fifty-fifty, then."

Ulysses nodded. "Anything else?"

Val stepped toward Ulysses, getting within his personal space. "Yeah. If you do anything to hurt my wife, I'll kill you myself."

"Then it sounds like we have a deal." Ulysses stuck out his hand and Val shook it. "Congratulations on the wedding, by the way. She seems like a real firecracker."

"Yeah." Val looked up in the direction of the cockpit. "Yeah, she's wonderful. Keeps me and this old ship flying."

Ulysses walked down the corridor into the ship. As he did, he ran his hands along the piping on the bulkhead. "I didn't think I'd ever see this ship again. These Jackrabbits saved my life more times than I can count. The ships," he looked back at Val, "and the crazy bastards who risked their lives to fly them."

Val stayed where he was. "That was a long time ago, Yule. Things changed. I changed."

Ulysses snorted. "Please. I saw that look when we were escaping Port Tew. There's a reason you haven't gotten a safe job hauling freight between moons. You need the thrill, the challenge. You need to push yourself and your machine to its limits."

"Now you sound like Charity." Val placed his hand on the metal crate. "Will you need any help getting this to the cargo bay?"

Ulysses shook his head. "I should be fine. I know how to get there." The two men stood in silence for a moment. "It's good to see you, Val."

"Yeah," Val gave him a curt nod. "You, too." He looked up to the cockpit. "I've got to get back up there. We're about to come out of our jump soon. Once you get this stowed, come on up and we'll punch in those coordinates of yours."

"You've got it."

Val climbed the ladder and disappeared through the hatch. Ulysses turned back and walked to the crate. It slid easily, if not noiselessly, across the deck plating.

Every step flooded him with memories. He hadn't been on a *Jackrabbit*-class transport in almost a decade, but every corner still seemed intimately familiar.

He walked past the crew cabins, which were really nothing more than glorified sleeping pods. There were three on each side. During the war, Ulysses and his men had lived on this ship and "hot-bunked" due to the limited number of sleeping quarters. Val and Charity had likely converted most of them to extra storage now.

The ship's single crew toilet was on the port side with the single shower on the opposite side, both in cramped closets to provide a degree of privacy. Ulysses knew from experience that all the plumbing on the ship was designed to work in zero gravity in case there was an issue with the gravity drive.

A doorway separated the crew area from the rest of the ship. It was wide enough for the crate, barely, but Ulysses had to come around the front to guide it through. The hull began to flare out in this portion of the ship, providing a wider interior space for a communal mess and recreation area. A circular table was bolted to the deck, and a round bench surrounded it.

A small galley contained a refrigeration unit, electric stove, and pantry. A counter separated the galley from the rest of the space and allowed for food to be prepared. The galley area had a sink that hooked up to the ship's miniature water treatment system. No water could be wasted. Today's shower water was cleaned and re-used as tomorrow's sink water.

Above the table, hung as decoration, was an old breach-action shotgun. It was contained by tubular locks on the barrel and grip that would keep it steady when the ship was in motion. It gave the room a rustic flair, and Ulysses wondered where Val had found such an antique. Civilian ownership of firearms was strictly controlled, but such an old gun must have slipped through the cracks. Though it didn't look like the government had much to worry about. If the gun had ever been fired, it hadn't been for years.

A solid bulkhead blocked Ulysses's path forward, but he knew how to get past it. He released the crate and walked to a small panel on the side of the bulkhead. He really hoped Val hadn't installed some kind of code to lock unwanted intruders out. When the center of the bulkhead began to retract with the *hiss* of an air-tight seal, Ulysses realized he was almost disappointed. As he stepped through the blast door, he decided he would have to talk to Val about his security measures.

The cargo hold took up a little less than half of the ship's total interior space. It was incredibly modular. Stellae Shipyards, the company that built these transports, produced pods that converted the cargo hold into scientific laboratories, additional passenger berths, or even luxury accommodations complete with hot tub.

The *Lucky Rabbit's Foot* didn't have any of these modifications. Instead, the cargo hold was the same spartan, utilitarian design Ulysses had grown to expect from these ships. Steel-gray walls on the upper section gave way to a matte black finish on the lower third of the hold, a sub-deck slightly lower than the rest of the ship. A platform just beyond the blast door oversaw the whole hold, and a computer terminal there allowed a skilled loadmaster to operate all the equipment with a great deal of precision. The operations could also be managed by someone in the cockpit, though for delicate work a loadmaster on-site was be the far better choice.

The bottom of the cargo hold was made of armored plating that would allow the interior of the ship to be protected even when the exterior hull panels were retracted. Six thick extendable struts ran from the sub-deck to actuators on the inside of the hull, each capable of independent motion. The sub-deck could also be lowered flat or at an angle to provide a ramp. A yellow and black caution strip along the middle of the sub-deck highlighted where it could be opened down the middle, usually to receive and deploy cargo in the vacuum of space. In combat, it would also be opened to allow armored assault troops to egress rapidly by simply jumping out of the hold, trusting to either shock harnesses or ram-chutes to deliver them safely to the ground.

Ulysses rolled his crate onto the sub-deck and secured it with a length of chain. It was a crude but effective way of ensuring that the cargo would stay in place in the event of gravity loss. Once that was done, he walked to the edge of the sub-deck. Hidden by the black paint was a row of folding seats built into the wall. They were little more than metal slabs sturdy enough to support the weight of an armored soldier.

Ulysses pulled down one of the seats and sat on it. He leaned back and idly ran his hands along the thin crash webbing attached to the wall. How many times had he sat here, in this very seat, ready to leap into action? How many men had he joked with, laughed with, and prayed with before a battle? Good men, volunteers all, who sacrificed their fortunes and their futures against odds that would have driven lesser men insane. How many of those men had ever come home?

Damn few. Too few.

"Mr. Walden?" a woman's voice echoed in the empty cargo hold. "Are you all right?"

Ulysses blinked. He put a hand to his cheek and realized it was wet. He turned to the wall and rubbed the tears from his eyes. Once that was done, he turned to face the woman who had spoken. She had dark, shoulder-length hair swept back out of her eyes with a couple of clips. She wore mechanic's coveralls, but they were clean and devoid of any stains. Her face was wide and round, with features that belied an ancestry reaching back to somewhere in East Asia back on Earth. Her expression was one of concern.

"Um. Yes. Sorry. Charity, right?" Ulysses asked. The woman nodded. "Did you need something?"

"Val sent me to make sure you were okay."

Ulysses frowned. "Why would he do that?"

"We thought you were going to come back to the cockpit once you were done with your luggage."

"I was. I am."

"That was fifteen minutes ago."

Ulysses blinked in surprise. "Oh. I'm sorry. I guess I lost track of time." He swept a hand out to encompass the cargo hold. "This place, this ship, holds a lot of memories for me."

"Good memories?"

"Important ones. Ones I can't let myself forget."

"If you don't mind me asking," Charity bit her lower lip before she continued, "what was it like? The war?"

Ulysses leaned back in the seat. "I'm guessing Val hasn't talked about it?"

"His response is usually, 'War? What war?' I know I need to respect his privacy, but he drives me crazy sometimes."

Ulysses chuckled. "Yeah. He could be like that." He closed his eyes and considered how much to tell her. This was Val's ship. He should be the one to tell his wife about its history. But there were parts of the story Charity could learn on her own, even if it would be horribly distorted propaganda to justify the winning side.

"Well, you know that Val is from Aventine, right?"

"He told me he was from Jupiter, but he never delved into the specifics," she replied.

"I don't want to be giving away anything Val wants to keep private," Ulysses said, holding up his hands.

"No, please." There was a sudden desperation to Charity's voice that surprised Ulysses. "This is the first new information I've learned about my husband in three years. I only learned about his home planet because he had to fill out that information for our wedding certificate." She put her elbows on the railing and rested her head on her hands. "Please. I want to know."

"Well, okay," Ulysses said. "But you should really get the story from him sometime. I'm sure he tells it better than I do." He sighed. "Anyway. Val was born on Aventine, one of the seven orbital cities of Jupiter. Like he said, I'm from Mars. Back when I was a kid, that would have been enough to make the two of us enemies. There was a lot of bad blood between Mars and Jupiter back in those days after the collapse of the Solar Alliance. But it's funny how an invasion can make that feud seem so petty.

"When the Centrality sent its fleet into the Solar system, Mars wanted to stay out of it. But I've never liked bullies, and neither did a few hundred of the toughest Martians I've ever met. We volunteered to help Jupiter and her allies hold the line."

"How did you meet Val?"

"He was a transport pilot, one of the best. There was no drop zone too hot for him to land, no stunt too crazy for him to try." Ulysses grinned. "There was this one time when we had to land on Io to break the siege of the main settlement there. The problem was that there was this *Crusader*-class cruiser parked in orbit that would have turned us into dust the second we jumped into range. So Val locks us onto this tiny asteroid barely bigger than this ship, gives it the tiniest bit of thrust to get it moving, and we just sit there hoping we don't get blown up. No gravity, no power, no idea whether anyone knew we were there."

"Well, clearly you survived," Charity observed.

Ulysses held up his hand. "Wait. It gets better. We get within visual range of the cruiser, and these are massive ships, right? Suddenly Val decides that the only way to break the siege is to break the blockade in orbit. So he fires up the engines again for another burst, only this time he's headed dead-center for the cruiser. But he angles the asteroid between us and the big Navy ship, playing the thrusters to always stay in the rock's sensor shadow. To this day, I don't know why the captain didn't simply send a missile to obliterate the damn thing, but we just kept getting closer and closer."

"What happened?"

"Long story short, Val wound up sliding this ship right between the main engine nacelles at the back of the cruiser. We were filled with weapons to resupply the beleaguered defenders on Io, but our sapper Carlos, who was at least as crazy as your husband, repurposed all that ammunition into a big bomb. It took two hours and a miracle, but we placed that bomb in the sweet spot at the base of one of the nacelles where it fed directly into the fusion reactor."

Ulysses leaned forward. "I can only imagine the look on that captain's face when his Sensor officer told him that some Jovian light transport had suddenly appeared at point blank range. We were still well within minimum range for their missiles and none of their coilguns could get a target lock."

"Coilguns?"

Ulysses nodded. "Smaller versions of the big railguns. Instead of using direct electrical charges on the round, they drag them out with coils of fast-switching magnets. Smaller rounds means less recoil, which means they can fire faster without throwing the ship too far off course."

"Ah," Charity nodded.

"Anyway, Val was juking around so much that the inertial compensation crapped out and we were hanging on for our lives back here. A couple of the guys blacked out. But Carlos," Ulysses lifted his eyes to the ceiling of the cargo hold. "Crazy Carlos. He pressed that detonator like the war depended on it. Whole cruiser cracked open like an egg. We landed shortly thereafter and helped evacuate the garrison."

Charity's mouth was open. "That's amazing."

"Yeah. It was a wilder time."

"Thank you for telling me," Charity said. "Feel free to take your time in here. Our grav jump is almost finished. When you're ready, Val's going to need your information to plot a course."

Ulysses put his hands on his knees. "I'll be right there."

"Okay." Charity hesitated. "Mr. Walden . . ."

"Ulysses."

"Right," Charity nodded. She leaned on the railing that separated the walkway from the sub-deck. "I know Val can act like he doesn't care. But I know that having you here means a lot to him. I don't know what you have in mind for your new life, but I want you to know that you have friends here. You aren't alone."

"Thank you, Charity." He pointed to the crate. "I've got to prepare the suit so it will be ready to go when we reach our destination. After that, I'll come right up."

She gave him another curt nod, then turned back through the door. Ulysses watched her go, then allowed himself a slight smile. The war was over. But there were still good people on this ship. And that meant that there was still a reason for hope.

CHAPTER SEVEN

"THIS is hopeless."

Ulysses sank back in his chair. "Come on, Val. You're overreacting."

"Am I?" Val looked to his wife, who stood just over his shoulder at the pilot's console. "Honey, you've lived here your whole life. Were any battles fought in this area?"

"No. But—"

"And what about wrecks? Any famous ships go missing in this area?"

"Well, no. But—"

"Okay." Val ran his fingers over the keypad and a visual map of the Tau Ceti system was projected onto the viewport in front of them. The armored panels were still down, an automatic safety feature that would protect them against the deadly radiation pulses encountered when traveling at the extreme speeds reached during a grav jump. Despite the fact that they had returned to standard speed, the armored curtains were still in place for the next jump. As such, it made the display even easier to see than if the viewport had been transparent.

"I'll run the numbers again. Maybe I just mistyped something." Val glanced over his shoulder at Ulysses, who remained seated in the same chair he used during the departure from Port Tew.

Ulysses fed him the numbers again from memory. As Val typed them in, a cursor appeared on the map. The yellow dot started at their current location between the dense asteroid field that divided the Tau Ceti system and the capital world of Yu-Kiang. It shot starward until it was a short distance inside Bakuwana's orbit. The location was roughly as close to Tau Ceti's star as Mercury was to the Sun.

"And you're sure you remember this right?" Charity asked.

Ulysses nodded. "I had half a year to memorize it. Yes, I'm sure that's right."

Val swiveled his chair around to face Ulysses. "And you paid *money* for this information?"

"Well," Ulysses shrugged. "It was kind of a package deal with the suit."

"Uh huh." Val rubbed his chin. "I'm sorry, Yule. Your so-called 'friend' sold you a bill of goods." He pointed to the display on the viewport. "There's nothing out there. No shipping, no mining. Ships wouldn't go that close to the star without a good reason, and there isn't one. Even if there was a bad jump and a ship wrecked out there, the gravity of the star would capture it and drag it to oblivion in a matter of weeks. Any 'special find' that may have been there when you bought this information is long gone by now."

"Can we at least go check it out?" Ulysses asked. "If it doesn't work out, I can sell the suit and give you the money that way."

"But, Ulysses, what will you do without the suit?" There was concern in Charity's voice.

Ulysses shrugged. "I'll think of something. I'm a survivor." He looked at Val. "And I thought Val was a gambler."

"I only gamble when there's a chance I can win," Val replied. "I don't see any winning hand here."

"Come on, Val," Charity said. "It'll be an adventure. Just like the old days. Just like Io."

Val shot Ulysses an icy look. When he spoke, his voice was just as frosty. "You told her about Io?"

Charity nodded. "He told me how you and crazy Carlos blew up a cruiser and saved the garrison."

"Yeah. Crazy Carlos." Val shook his head. "Did he tell you that Carlos died six hours later? Some Centrality Marine lobbing mortars put an incendiary round into Carlos' backpack while we were evacuating the base. The backpack was filled with the remaining charges Carlos had rigged in case the first bomb only cracked the cruiser's armor. Eight men died, including Carlos. There wasn't enough of them left to bury in a footlocker."

The color drained from Charity's face. "Oh."

"Right. 'Oh.' There's a reason I don't want to talk about the past, Charity." Val sighed and closed his eyes. "Can you please go check on the gravity drive? I want to make sure we didn't take any damage during our escape from Port Tew."

"But—" Charity glanced at Ulysses, then back to her husband. "Fine." She clambered down the ladder to the lower deck. "But don't think this conversation is over."

"I wouldn't dream of it," Val called out as she left. Once she was gone, he stood and walked over to Ulysses. "Look. We'll check out this lead. But I don't want you telling war stories behind my back again, Yule. The past is dead. Leave it in peace."

"Deal. I'm sorry if I overstepped. She just wanted to know more about her husband."

"I love her and I trust her with my life," Val said. "That should be enough."

Gravity drives were the key to manned spaceflight within the confines of a star system. They were enormously complicated and relied on a core of newtonium to provide artificial gravity and some degree of inertial compensation. Those systems were distributed throughout the ship to ensure the gravity generated would be evenly applied in the desired direction.

The true miracle of the gravity drive, however, was its ability to generate a screen, of sorts, that reduced a ship's resistance to motion in a given direction. It did not generate any thrust on its own, instead relying on the ship's fusion engines to actually move the ship along the chosen path. Engaging a so-called "grav jump" also entailed a certain degree of risk, as any slight error in the navigational calculations could send a ship tens of thousands of kilometers off-course. There were some fail-safes built into the simulated intelligence of the onboard computer, but those were more to prevent ships from cracking open continents by flying into a planet than to protect the ship from a bad jump.

They were also famously fickle pieces of hardware. Val may have used the drive as an excuse to have Charity leave the cockpit, but that didn't mean that his concern was any less valid. The jump from Port Tew had been short and direct, but if a piece of shrapnel had damaged an engine or the gravity drive itself a longer jump could be suicide.

Fortunately for everyone on board, Charity returned ten minutes later, set a big wrench on her console, and gave the gravity drive a clean bill of health. With the coordinates set, they strapped in to their seats and Val engaged the gravity drive.

It was a quiet journey. Ulysses fell asleep a few minutes into the jump and his head dangled on his chest. Val and Charity exchanged no words, silently continuing to work at their respective stations.

They reached their destination two hours later. There was no "explosion" of stars like Ulysses experienced on journey into the system because the gravity drive, while allowing for speeds far greater than standard fusion engines alone, didn't allow the ship to reach anything close to the speed of light.

Once they returned to normal speeds, the armored panels slid back into the hull. Tau Ceti, the star for which the system was named, burned large and bright on their port side, and the viewports automatically tinted to protect the vision of the crew inside.

The three people on board the *Lucky Rabbit's Foot* all moved to the front of the cockpit to look outside, hungry for any sign of wreckage that could prove that Ulysses's information was genuine. After a quiet moment, Charity turned away and moved back to her seat. "There's nothing here."

Val sat down, too. But, instead of despair, he radiated anxious energy as he worked on his console. "We still don't know that for sure." For all of his talk against this hunt, he was not going to give up just yet. Not when they were already here. "Let me boot up the active sensors." He flipped a switch that was labeled *Act. Sen.* "It shouldn't take long to—"

Ulysses reached across the panel and flipped the switch back down again.

"Hey!" Val shouted. "What's the big idea?"

But Ulysses wasn't done. He moved systematically down the line, pressing a sequence of buttons and toggling every switch to *Off.*

The interior lights in the cockpit flickered off. The gentle hum of the engines died, too. Finally, the gravity drive powered down. Charity's wrench wobbled, then began to float away from the console before she caught it and slid it into her belt.

Val reached for his crash webbing and locked himself down. He looked at Ulysses, who had remained at the viewport and now hovered in mid-air. "Are you *crazy*?"

Instead of responding, Ulysses reached into his flight jacket and pulled out his tablet computer. Val caught a glimpse of the screen, and it showed a timer counting down.

It reached zero. And nothing happened.

"Come on," Ulysses muttered. He slid the tablet back into his jacket and scanned the space outside the viewport. "Come on."

"This is crazy," Val said. "I don't know if you finally snapped or if you were brainwashed at Venus or if this is some kind of elaborate suicide attempt. But don't think I'm going to just sit here while you . . ."

Val's words trailed off as a ship appeared in view. It was barely a speck through the viewport, but the visual scanner displayed it clearly. He hadn't seen a ship like that in seven years. Even after the war's end that silhouette made a shiver run down his spine. The ship was huge, half a kilometer long at least. Even from this distance, without the visual sensors, Val could make out the distinct slope of its armored prow. It was an older ship design, from an era before the modern composite armor and layered construction techniques that even decade-old ships like the *Lucky Rabbit's Foot* enjoyed.

The cruiser also featured wide fins toward the rear of the ship. These fins were radiators which allowed the warship to operate its engines and weapons without roasting the crew and melting all of its critical components. The *Lucky Rabbit's Foot* had radiators, too, but they were thin, retractable rods that could be withdrawn into the ship during combat.

The *Crusader's* answer to every problem was brute force. Need to stop radiation from cooking your crew? Build armored hulls two meters thick. Need to destroy your enemy? Just pull up beside them and unleash a hellstorm from the four railguns on either side. They weren't as long as the nightmarishly powerful railguns on the largest battleships, but a barrage from those railguns could knock whole settlements off the map. If anything survived, it would be atomized by the array of missiles, torpedoes, coilguns, and auto-cannons the ship carried with it. And did you need to actually move this spacefaring city through the cosmos? Just slap four enormous fusion engines to the back and watch it burn through reaction material as it paved its way across the stars.

It was not the most powerful warship ever built, but it was certainly the most iconic, built by an empire that no longer existed and now used to enforce the will of the largest political organization in human history. And it was sitting there, in plain view, waiting for the *Lucky Rabbit's Foot* to make the slightest mistake so it could blast them into eternity.

"Is that a Crusader?" Charity's voice was a harsh whisper.

Ulysses nodded. Charity gasped as she realized just how deadly the threat above Io had been. This wasn't a story of daring heroics. This was a desperate scramble to survive.

Val reached for the system controls. This was ridiculous. They needed to get out of here *right now*. He moved his hand to the primary generator switch.

Ulysses pinned his hand to the console with his foot, holding himself in place with both his hands on the viewport. "Don't." Ulysses said.

"Are you trying to get us all killed?"

"If we run now, that ship will light us up before we can engage a grav jump. The only option is to run silent and wait for it to pass."

Val's eyes went wide. "You knew this was going to happen. Didn't you?"

"Both of you, be quiet," Charity whispered.

Val was tempted to correct her. After all, the speech of three people in an otherwise undetected transport wouldn't set off the huge cruiser's sensors. But it felt *wrong* to make any more noise than absolutely necessary. Val kept his mouth shut. After all, why run the risk?

The cruiser loitered there for almost half an hour. Every minute was filled with unbearable tension, but no one dared speak or even move. It was the reaction of prey caught in the open. Their only chance of survival was that the predator didn't notice them.

The massive ship cruised past them, and Val couldn't believe he had ever been dumb enough to try to take these things on in combat. Of course, Io had hardly been a fair fight, and the *Lucky Rabbit's Foot* had been equipped with its full complement of weapons and ammunition. Now his ship had been stripped of most of its guns, and the auto-cannons it did carry were dry.

Running silent like this made it difficult, but not impossible, for a military ship to find them. Worse, they were blind, and the first sign of trouble would be the sight of missile thrusters careening toward them. If the cruiser spotted them, a single missile would be able to destroy the light transport before they could even activate the engines. Not that running would help. Missiles had every advantage in microgravity due to their vastly superior thrust-to-mass ratio. And, without any ammunition or countermeasures, the AKER system would be useless.

Without a warning, the cruiser's engines flared. It surged forward, faster than the eye could follow. No one moved. Finally, once they were certain that the big ship was truly gone, Val let out a deep breath. He started to run through the abbreviated warm-up checklist.

"Okay. I'm getting us out of here," Val said. Ulysses, still floating, reached over and flipped the active sensors switch. Val looked at him, rage beginning to boil inside of him. "Are you insane? *Now* you want to run the sensors?"

"Yes."

"Why the hell would you—"

A soft *ping* rang from Charity's station on the port side of the cockpit. She examined her display, then turned to Val. "Four new pieces of debris."

Ulysses was already moving toward the ladder behind Charity's station, pushing himself off the bulkhead to get him there before the artificial gravity came back online. "Not debris," he stated. "Data cores. Get us close."

"You son of a bitch," Val snarled. "You knew about this the whole time?"

Ulysses began to pull himself down the ladder. Val wasn't going to let it go that easily. He unhooked his own crash webbing and kicked off after Ulysses.

"I guess I'll wait here," Charity called out after them. She shifted to Val's seat and took over the controls.

Ulysses had a good head start. He was moving through the crew quarters toward the rear of the ship. "Ulysses, stop," Val demanded. The other man didn't respond. "I said 'stop,' dammit." Val pulled himself along small handholds on the ceiling, slowly building up speed.

He finally caught up with Ulysses by the galley. Val managed to get a hand on the back of Ulysses's jacket and tugged. Ulysses twisted backward as his momentum suddenly shifted, but Val maintained his grip.

"Let go, Val."

"No," Val said. He held on with one hand and began pulling himself and Ulysses to the front of the ship.

He might have succeeded, too, if the gravity hadn't picked that moment to reactivate. The two men fell to the deck plating and landed hard. Both men wheezed as the breath was driven from their lungs by the impact.

Charity's voice came over the intercom. "Heads up, boys. Gravity is kicking back on."

"Hadn't noticed," Val groaned. He propped himself up on his elbows and stared at Ulysses. "You've gone crazy. I don't know what's happened to you the past seven years, but that doesn't give you the right to come on this ship and put us all at risk."

Ulysses rose to one knee. "I'm sorry, Val. I swear, I didn't know it was going to be that close. I thought we might be lucky enough to swoop in after the cruiser had moved on. But it was behind schedule."

"Behind . . ." Val's mouth dropped open. "What are you talking about?"

"This was the plan. The data cores."

Val rose to his feet. "Wait. *That's* what these coordinates are? Some kind of dumping ground?"

Ulysses nodded. "Navy dumps outdated or worn out tech here where it can be sucked into the star without endangering the ships themselves or wasting drones pushing trash into the hot zone."

"You want to pick up a data core, huh?" Val rubbed his chin. "Yeah, okay. I can see that. A wiped data core could pull in some serious scales with the right people. I'll have Charity keep an ear on the comm ripper. If we pick up any transmissions from any Centrality ships, we're out of here, cores or no cores. Do you understand?"

Ulysses nodded, then smiled. "You still have a comm ripper? Those are illegal now, you know."

"Right. Because you'd never break the law."

Ulysses walked to the keypad on the bulkhead and typed in the activation code. The blast door cycled open again and Ulysses stepped into the cargo hold. Val started to follow him through, but Ulysses held up a hand. "Wait. Stay out here. This might be dangerous, and I don't want you to get hurt."

Val rolled his eyes. "You need someone to help you into the EVA suit, Yule."

Ulysses blinked. "Oh. Right." He lowered his hand. "Come on in, then."

They clambered down the short ladder to the sub-deck. The EVA suit was there, fully assembled and ready to go. Before he could climb inside, Ulysses and Val walked over to a set of lockers. They each pulled out an orange one-piece garment. The vac suits were somewhat loose and intended to be worn over clothing as stripping down to undergarments would take far too long in an emergency.

With the vac suits on, they both activated their internal air pumps to high pressure. The idea was to check the suits for any leaks before they were exposed to hard vacuum. Val went over Ulysses's suit first, examining the seams carefully. When he gave Ulysses a raised thumb to indicate a good seal, Ulysses turned around and gave Val the same once-over.

Satisfied that the vac suits were stable, they reduced their air tanks to normal pressure and stepped toward the EVA suit. Unlike the vac suit, which was constructed from a soft rubberized material with small tanks around the waist to provide breathable air and maintain pressure, the EVA suit was a heavy, robotic-looking creation. Its arms and legs were all motorized to allow a user to move in any gravity conditions, and a backpack built into the suit contained small thrusters that would allow the user to maneuver in microgravity. As a suit built for collecting salvage, it had several hard-points for attaching recovered scrap as well as a magnetic grapple line attached to a spool of thin titanium wire for recovering larger pieces of salvage.

Instead of donning the suit like a set of clothes, the rear of the suit was open so that the user would squeeze into the open arms, legs, chest, and head pieces as a single unit. Ulysses stepped forward into the suit and Val came in behind him to close it up. It was possible for a single user to close the suit in a pinch, but it was incredibly awkward and uncomfortable.

Once Ulysses was sealed inside the suit, Val grabbed the safety line from the suit's backpack and unrolled it. Once he had a good length of line unspooled, he attached the clamp on the end to a metallic ring on the side of the sub-deck. All EVA suits were required to have such a line, though daredevil spacewalkers were known to leave the line rolled up and unattached to allow unlimited range of motion. More than a few of these fools had faced embarrassing rescue by nearby ships when they realized just how "unlimited" their motion was and started to drift into deep space.

Val returned to the platform to operate the computer terminal. While he did that, Ulysses took the time to check out his new suit. He tested the arms first, moving each elbow, then moved each finger with care. The suit was designed to operate using small buttons inside the fingertips of the gloves which would let Ulysses utilize the thrusters and various tools, but they would be out of the way if he needed to clench his fists.

A heads-up display in the helmet gave Ulysses an augmented view of his surroundings, including an option to digitally zoom in on faraway objects. That was critical in deep space operations where the intended target could be a small sliver to the naked eye. While a vac suit had a small headlamp, the EVA suit had a powerful suite of lights on the helmet and backpack.

"Audio check."

The earpiece in Val's vac suit activated with Ulysses's voice coming through the throat mic in his own suit. The throat mics were designed to pick up any sounds generated by the user but could be adjusted to be more discerning using a dial on the vac suit's belt. "Sound is good, Ulysses. Any problems?"

The suit stood still.

"Say again, Ulysses," Val said. He adjusted the dial on his belt. "Do you have any problems with the suit?"

"Negative. Sorry. I guess you can't see me shaking my head in this thing, huh?"

Val rolled his eyes. "Nope. Everything's green up here. Let me know when you're ready."

"I'm ready."

The vac suits were on a closed-circuit comms system with the rest of the ship to allow anyone wearing them to communicate with someone in another part of the ship. It was a feature intended to allow spacers communicate with each other even while trapped in depressurized compartments, but it was generally useful even in mundane circumstances. "Charity, how are we looking up there?"

"Everything is good. We're in position for the first data core now."

"Perfect. Love you."

Charity laughed. "I love you, too. Now get to work."

"Yes, ma'am. Yule, stand by for depressurization and gravity loss."

"Copy," Ulysses replied. "Standing by."

Val stomped down, activating the magnetic pads on the bottom of his vac suit. Once he was sure he wasn't going to float away, he pressed a button on the computer terminal. Yellow lights began to flash, indicating that the compartment was being depressurized. It was a necessary step before the exterior hull panels could be retracted to prevent explosive decompression.

Gravity in the cargo hold shut down a few seconds later. Val felt the familiar nausea of sudden gravity loss for the second time in an hour, but his boots held him in place. Ulysses, however, began to drift. But a quick burst from his thrusters had him stable. He gave Val a thumbs-up.

"Cycling the door now," Val said. He manipulated the computer and watched the exterior feed as the hull panels began to slide open. Once that was finished, he slid his hand along the screen. The actuators hissed, still barely audible in the thin air that remained in the hold, and the sub-deck began to split open.

"All right, Yule. You heard the lady. Let's get to work."

CHAPTER EIGHT

"ADJUST your angle. A little more to the left," Val's voice came through the vac suit. Ulysses complied, teasing his thrusters just enough to drift in the correct direction. It had taken a few minutes of playing around to get a feel for the controls, but once he had gotten some practice they were rather intuitive.

It was harder to use the fingertip controls while holding the cylindrical data cores, though. The first time he grabbed one of the small metal rods on the outer layer of the core, he nearly shot himself into deep space. He soon learned that the key was subtle movements and generous use of the grapple line.

Ulysses fired another short burst of thrusters and came in for a landing on the edge of the subdeck. He stomped down to activate his magnetic boots, then proceeded to carry his newly acquired prize next to its companions. Small clamps latched onto the sides of the cylinder to secure it for travel. Once the data core was in place, Ulysses bent down and unraveled the titanium cord.

He looked toward the control platform to see Val give him a thumbs-up. "That's three."

"Charity, we've secured another core," Ulysses said.

"I copy," she replied. "Hang on. The last one is starting to drift faster than the others. It's going to be tricky to get into range."

Ulysses reached for a stubby handhold near one of the folded seats. "I'm secure."

"Same here," Val said.

"Okay, boys. Here goes nothing."

The *Lucky Rabbit's Foot* fired its engines again. Without any inertial compensation in the cargo hold, Val and Ulysses had to rely on their handholds and their magnetic boots to keep them from bouncing around. More than one poor spacer had been pummeled into jelly because they lost their grip during high-G maneuvers.

Ulysses had been through worse during the war, and his hardened EVA suit would protect him from the worst of any potential damage. But Val usually lived in the cockpit, and his vac suit wouldn't stand up to any real impact. Fortunately, Charity was taking it easy, pulsing the engines with small bursts of acceleration rather than simply racing for the final data core.

After two or three minutes, the ship drifted to a stop. Charity said, "Okay. We should be in range of the final core." An alarm began to chirp, the sound picked up by Charity's microphone.

"What was that?" Val asked.

"Checking," Charity replied. "Uh. Oh. Oh, no."

"Sounds like good news," Ulysses quipped.

"Stray slug inbound. It's travelling fast, too."

Ulysses groaned. Railguns were the among the most powerful weapons mankind had invented. The largest *Champion*-class battleships had twin railguns that ran almost the entire length of their hulls, and each was capable of throwing a fifteen-kilogram ferrous slug up to nearly one percent of light speed. They were incredibly destructive, each slug hitting with the force of the original nuclear bombs developed in the twentieth century.

The problem was that, if they missed, the slugs just kept moving until they hit something. If the target was thin enough, even a direct hit could only shave off a fraction of the slug's energy before it continued straight through the other side. It would eventually impact an asteroid or a moon or a distant star, but the slug would only stop when it ran into something it couldn't just punch through.

Cruiser-sized ships carried much smaller railguns that faced outward from the sides of the ships, which meant that they had much shorter barrels and thus far less energy. Those were generally considered no more of a threat to normal space travel than meteoroids. But a stray slug from a battleship would tear a ship like the *Lucky Rabbit's Foot* apart and not even slow down.

"Can we make it?" Ulysses asked.

"I'm not sure. It's at the distant edge of our sensors right now, but all the computer models are showing it running right through this area. We could wait for a more precise model, but it might be too late to get out of the way."

"Understood. Just keep us steady." Ulysses stomped his foot down, releasing the magnetic grip of his boots on the sub-deck.

"What are you doing?" Val asked.

"I've got to get that last data core." Ulysses fired up his thrusters for a hard push. He felt the safety line whir behind him as he shot out of the cargo hold and into open space.

"Yule!" Val shouted. "Just leave it. We've got three cores already. Don't be stupid."

Ulysses grunted. Val didn't understand. Ulysses needed these cores, and he couldn't take the risk of letting even one get out of reach. He ignored Val and started to scan the region of space around him. The illumination built into the EVA suit was far more powerful than the small head lamps found on vac suits, but it was still insignificant compared to the vast darkness of space.

"Come on," he muttered. "Where are you?"

He cycled through data feeds on his heads-up display. Besides keeping him from drifting into oblivion, the safety line attached to the ship allowed Ulysses to patch into the computer of the *Lucky Rabbit's Foot*. Anything the ship could see, he could see.

As he scrolled through the sensor feeds, he watched as the computer models for the incoming slug began to converge. Charity had been right. The slug was barreling right toward them. With Ulysses outside on a spacewalk, Charity couldn't fire up the engines to escape the danger without either severing the safety line or, worse, dragging Ulysses behind the ship into the output of the fusion engines. Asphyxiate or burn alive. Neither sounded appealing. The smart play would be for Ulysses to return to the ship. There was a good chance the slug would destroy the data core, but at least they would be safe.

But Ulysses needed that core. He closed out the computer's analysis and kept digging through the data. There, finally, was the lidar contact for the final core. Ulysses used it to figure out the core's relative position, then engaged his visor's zoom to spot the meter-long cylinder drifting lazily through the void.

"I see the final core. I'm moving to retrieve it now."

"You're crazy," Val said. "I'm pulling you in."

The safety line began to contract, pulling Ulysses back to the ship. "No!" Ulysses shouted. "Damn it, I'm so close. Val, give me control."

"Why?"

"Because I can do this."

"Guys," Charity said, "you need to figure this out because this slug is coming in hard."

"Val. Trust me."

"Famous last words."

"Val . . ."

Val groaned but didn't reply. Then the safety line went slack again, and Ulysses could move. He fired the thrusters for another hard burn. He had been delicate with his previous retrievals, but he didn't have time for subtlety now.

Rather than take the time to wrap the data core with titanium wire and secure it to his suit, Ulysses killed the thrusters and reached out for it. Once his outstretched left hand wrapped around the metal casing, he shouted, "Val, pull me in *now!*"

The safety line jerked him backward, reversing his forward motion. The sudden jolt almost caused him to lose his grip on the data core, but Ulysses held on. He pulled the core in tight against his body, wrapping his right arm around the cylinder to keep it steady.

"Eighteen seconds to impact," Charity warned.

"Throttle up and get us out of here," Ulysses commanded.

"But—"

"Do it! I'll either make it or I won't, but if we wait around I'm dead, anyway."

Charity didn't respond. Because the safety line was pulling him in from behind, Ulysses wasn't sure how close he was to the *Lucky Rabbit's Foot.* He could only pray that he hadn't doomed them all.

Suddenly he saw the edge of the sub-deck shoot past in his peripheral vision. He landed hard on his backside, data core cradled in his lap.

"Go, go, go!"

The engines roared, more of a tactile sensation through the hull than an audible sound in the vacuum. Ulysses began to topple forward, tumbling toward the open cargo door despite the safety line.

A hand reached out and gripped Ulysses's shoulder. Ulysses turned at the waist to see Val struggling to hang on to his EVA suit with one hand while he gripped the base of the computer terminal with the other.

His fingers were slipping.

"Val, let go," Ulysses said.

"Not a chance," Val replied through clenched teeth.

The acceleration slowed, and the pressure on the two men dropped. They were both breathing hard from terror and exertion.

And, in Ulysses's case, anticipation.

"We're clear of the danger zone," Charity said. "Good thing, too. That could have been a direct hit. Everyone still on board?"

"We're okay," Ulysses said.

"I'm closing up now," Charity said. The thick panels of the sub-deck began to retract into the ship. Though Ulysses couldn't see it, he knew the exterior hull panels were closing, as well. "I figured that Val was a little busy."

"Thanks, sweetheart," Val said. He had released his grip on the terminal and floated limply next to Ulysses. Ulysses met his eyes through their respective masks. "You just *had* to go back for the last data core."

Ulysses shrugged, a gesture which did not translate through the thick EVA suit. "Thanks for trusting me."

"Well, I just hope it was worth it."

"Yeah." Ulysses considered the metallic cylinder in his grip. "So do I."

CHAPTER NINE

"ULYSSES has been in there for hours," Charity said.

Val nodded. He was back in the pilot's seat, watching the internal video feed from the cargo bay. The screen showed Ulysses Walden as he knelt beside one of the recovered data cores. "I told you. He's gone crazy. You saw what he did. He could have gotten us all killed."

Charity put a hand on his shoulder. She stood beside the pilot's console and had her eyes on the same video feed that Val was watching. Val reached up and wrapped her fingers in his. Her hand was trembling. He looked up at her. "Are you okay?"

Charity gave him a single curt nod. "I'm still coming down from the adrenaline dump. That's all."

"You did good, sweetheart," Val said. "You did me proud."

If Val hadn't known her as well as he did, he wouldn't have noticed the rise of color in her cheeks. "Thanks. It wasn't that hard. You just make everything seem more complicated than it has to be."

Val chuckled, then pulled her hand to his mouth and kissed it. "That's probably true."

He released her hand and she walked back to the co-pilot station. "What do you think he's up to in there?"

"Checking them for damage, I'd bet," Val said. "The navy isn't usually too concerned with some minor dings when they're tossing these things into space to be consumed by a star. But, if there's significant damage, it could compromise their storage capacity."

"Which would mean less money for us."

Val pointed to his wife to acknowledge her answer. "Bingo."

Charity removed her arms from the back of the chair and slid into the seat. "What do we do now?"

"I already put the word out to a couple of contacts," Val said. "But we both know Savimbi's going to have the most to offer. Even after we settle my debt, our half of this haul will let us fully restock the *Lucky Rabbit's Foot*. Maybe I can even pick up some new vests."

"Because you clearly don't have enough as it is," Charity rolled her eyes. "But I meant with him." She pointed to the image on the screen.

"He gets his half," Val said. "I know a couple guys on Ranginui who might be interested in selling him a used ship at a decent rate. He's actually pretty good at this whole 'salvage' thing. God knows he has enough practice jumping out of ships like this. At least now no one's shooting at him."

Charity frowned. "You're just going to let him go? Just like that?"

Val shrugged. "Why not? He's an adult, Charity. He'll survive just fine out here. Hell, this might be the last place in settled space his whole 'rugged individual' thing would let him get ahead."

"I'd just hoped that the two of you . . ." Charity's voice trailed off. "What I mean to say is that you two went through a lot together. You were friends. It's a shame to have fate bring you together again just to steal some data cores and then go your separate ways."

"War's over," Val said, a bitter edge in his voice. "I just don't know if Ulysses knows that. If he wants to make a new life here, I wish him all the luck. But it's more likely he's going to try something stupid and heroic, at least in his own mind. I don't want to get dragged into another one of his disasters when he does."

Charity pulled her legs up to her chest and wrapped her arms around them. "What exactly happened between you two? Ulysses seems to have nothing but respect for you, but you keep treating him like he's got an infectious disease."

Val rubbed his eyes. "Because he's got hope. Hope that things will be better. That the Centrality will topple. That the planets of every system will be free to chart their own destiny. Hope can spread more quickly than any disease, and the results can be far deadlier. He already dragged Mars into a war that was none of his business. I don't want him destroying us, too."

"Do you really think he would do that?"

"Who knows? Maybe he's right. Maybe he has changed." Val's tone became icy. "But that's one gamble I can't afford to make."

The *Lucky Rabbit's Foot* rumbled as it ended its grav jump near the planet Paikea. Paikea was almost double the size of Earth and was the third planet in the Tau Ceti system. It was separated from the inner planets of Bakuwana and Yu-Kiang by an asteroid field similar to the one that divided Mars and Jupiter, known locally as the Rampart.

If the field in the Solar system served a purpose like the Rio Grande on Earth, providing a natural dividing line between two separate nations that were on more or less equal footing, then the asteroid field in Tau Ceti was more akin to Hadrian's Wall. The starward side of the asteroid field was properly civilized, even a hot-house jungle world like Bakuwana. The outer planets, meanwhile, were where the barbarians lived, and woe to anyone who would dare travel to those worlds.

At least, that was the official story.

Despite the warnings from the Imperial Palace about the dangers of associating with the "criminals" of the outer planets, all ships coming into the system from Chelsea Station had to make a stop at one of the settlements to take on food and fuel for the trip to the capital. That made a moon like Ranginui a popular stop for tourists of all stripes, especially those who found the admonitions of the Eternal Dragon Empire to be more intriguing than frightening.

It also made the whole region a popular spot for piracy. With all these scales moving in and out of the system, it was only natural for enterprising criminals to try to cut in on the action. Few incidents of piracy ended in any form of bloodshed. The pirates were smart enough to know that pressing too hard would scare the lucrative shipping away. The tourists, for their part, were often thrilled at the chance to encounter and survive a genuine pirate attack. It was a form of theater played out on a grand scale, with every person involved playing a role in the dance.

Well, almost every person. There were a few idiots who took to the idea of a bloodthirsty corsair a little too well. One of these gems of humanity stumbled onto the *Lucky Rabbit's Foot* as it skirted around the normal lanes of spacefaring traffic. It hovered in the transport's path, cutting off their approach to Ranginui.

"Surrender your cargo and prepare to be boarded." The voice was male and gruff, but in a way that told Val the speaker was far younger than he was trying to sound. "We *will* open fire if you will not empty your entire cargo hold in the next ten seconds."

The voice was coming from the pilot of a small semi-circle of a transport that looked like the centuries-old flying wing design. The visual scanner showed Val that it had been covered in paint and graffiti with no discernable pattern. It carried a pair of forward-mounted auto-cannons built into the "wing" structure, but at its current relative angle there was no way they would be able to hit the *Lucky Rabbit's Foot*, which was positioned in front of and slightly above the pirate vessel.

Val pressed the button for his comm. "Listen, idiot, most cargo holds take about thirty seconds to cycle. Even if I was going to surrender, which I most certainly will not, you're threatening me with a physical impossibility."

"Um. Well," the pirate sputtered. "If you do not surrender immediately, we will be forced to open fire."

Val sighed. "Look, kid. Check your scanner again. Not only do you have no shot, I have twin auto-cannons pointed at your cockpit right now. If you so much as twitch in our direction, I will pull the trigger and blow you to hell."

Charity shook her head. "Let's just hope he doesn't realize we don't have any ammunition for those guns."

"Quiet, you," Val said. He pressed the comm button again. "So, kid, what's it going to be?"

"Hey! You can't threaten *me*," the pirate complained. "That's not how this is supposed to work."

"Kid, I'm telling you that this is not a fight you want to start. Just let us pass."

"I can't." The young pirate sounded defeated. There was fear in his voice, but it wasn't fear of Val or the *Lucky Rabbit's Foot*. "As an emissary of Commodore Buti Savimbi, I am duty-bound to collect a tax from any incoming vessel I select."

Ulysses, who stood behind Val in the pilot's chair, raised an eyebrow. "Emissary?"

Charity looked to her husband with the same puzzled expression. "Commodore?"

Val rolled his eyes. "Kid, we're here to see your boss. This cargo is for him."

The pirate's voice lightened. "Oh. Why didn't you say so in the first place?"

"Because you started this conversation with 'Surrender your cargo and prepare to be boarded.'"

"Oh. Right. Sorry. Uh, you may proceed."

"Thank you for your generosity," Val's voice dripped with sarcasm. The pirate ship drifted away to harass someone else. Val throttled forward.

The *Lucky Rabbit's Foot* rocketed toward the mottled grey sphere that was Ranginui. The night side of the moon was awash with bright lights. Unlike its twin, the desolate orange rock known as Papatuanuku, Ranginui had few pockets of valuable natural resources. Despite that, the moon had adapted very well to the terraforming process and had been a booming settlement during the first wave of colonization.

Then the First Interstellar War broke out and Paikea, the world that Ranginui orbited, became a battlefield. The conflict was brief but destructive, and much of the original colony on Ranginui was lost. Following the war, the government of Tau Ceti reformed into its current form by Emperor Hideyoshi, the Eternal Dragon himself. The government, bloodied and nearly bankrupt, withdrew to the "safe worlds" inside the Rampart to rebuild their strength.

But, while official support for the settlement vanished, the few survivors on Ranginui found new benefactors. This collection of investors all had one thing in common: they despised the collectivist economic policies of the Eternal Dragon Empire. There was no central government here, only a loose confederacy of corporations who effectively had free reign of the place.

The *Lucky Rabbit's Foot* flew in low over ArgoTech City, ducking between the vast industrial towers at the edge of the settlement. The general glow of light visible from orbit became a dizzying array of pulsing flashes in every imaginable color. A storm had come in from one of the vast man-made lakes on the southern half of the moon, drenching the city in a torrent of rain. The falling water caught the light and refracted it, a million tiny prisms sparkling in the night sky.

The city itself was a sprawling affair, all stark illumination and deep shadows. Imposing glass and steel structures dominated the skyline, separated by wide streets filled with vehicles. The largest of these skyscrapers at the very center of the city bore the scarlet logo of ArgoTech Industries, but dozens of smaller companies and subsidiaries were represented. As the *Lucky Rabbit's Foot* dipped in to the bustling spaceport, Val spotted a maglev train as it departed the station to take new arrivals downtown. The silver train shimmered with reflected light as it moved into the city.

The spaceport itself was an enormous circular set of structures nestled in the low hills to the west of the city itself. The entirety of Port Tew could have fit within the boundaries of the spaceport with room to spare, but it wasn't a vast, empty space. Every square meter was packed with ships, cargo, and passengers.

The airspace around the spaceport, too, was crowded with ships waiting for their slot in the landing pattern. Val slid the *Lucky Rabbit's Foot* into the designated spot and began to follow the circular path provided by Traffic Control. The ship's SI took over the pattern, leaving Val free to rest and stretch out for a couple minutes before he took the ship in to land. He could have just hovered in place, but it would have burned through a lot more fuel without speeding up the process.

Val leaned back in the chair and crossed his hands behind his head. "And now we wait."

"How long does this usually take?" Ulysses asked.

"It depends," Charity replied. She consulted the screen on her console which showed the position of all the ships spiraling around the spaceport. "It doesn't seem too busy today. Maybe two hours?"

Ulysses blinked. "And that's *not* busy? Remind me not to come during peak season."

Charity shrugged. "I like it. It lets you get a nice view of the city."

"Is this where you grew up?" Ulysses asked.

Charity laughed. "No. I'm a capital girl from New Changsha on Yu-Kiang. My grandfather was an early supporter of Emperor Hideyoshi. The empire has rewarded my family for their loyalty, and I grew up in a beautiful home on the edge of the city. But I like it better out here."

"Is this anything like where you grew up?"

"In some ways. New Changsha is a much larger city, obviously. But it's too . . . structured. Everything, and everyone, has a place and they do not deviate from it. It's orderly, but it has no soul."

She pointed out the viewport at the sparkling cascade of lights below them. "Ranginui, by contrast, is pure chaos. Everything is in flux. Everything is for sale." Charity shrugged. "It may not mean anything to the two of you, but the fact that the empire allows this place to exist at all amazes me."

"All that tax revenue must be a decent incentive," Ulysses commented.

"It's more than that," Val added. "Ranginui is wild, unfettered capitalism with all the dangers that come with it. The Imperial Palace can point beyond the Rampart and tell misbehaving children that, unless they find their fit in the social order, they will be condemned to this unstructured madhouse."

"And that works?"

Val shrugged. "Sometimes."

"And, when it doesn't, it gives rebellious adolescents somewhere to go instead of festering unrest on Yu-Kiang," Charity said.

Val reached across the cockpit. Charity reached back and took his hand in hers. "And thank God for that."

Charity smiled. "Ranginui can be the pressure valve that keeps an uptight, rigid society like the empire from collapsing. It allows dangerous ideas to be shunted to the outer planets before they have a chance to spread to the general population."

"But what happens when someone with those ideas tries to come back?" Ulysses asked. "It seems to me that gathering all the discontented members of your society in an 'anything goes' environment will only strengthen those rebellious tendencies."

"The Kempeitai keep a close eye on the place, that's for sure," Charity said. "There are all kinds of rumors about labor camps on Papatuanuku and secret torture facilities hidden among the corporate towers. Just because the Eternal Dragon turned his back on supporting the outer planets doesn't mean he has no desire to control them."

Val opened his mouth to say something, but the *Lucky Rabbit's Foot* suddenly banked hard to the right. Because they were within the gravity well of the moon, the ship's artificial gravity systems were turned off to conserve power. As a result, the sudden turn threw everyone hard against their restraints.

"What the hell was that?" Ulysses asked.

"Wasn't engine failure," Charity said. "My board is still green."

Val ran his hands over the instruments. "It was the computer. Traffic Control changed the pattern." He gave his wife a concerned look. "We just got moved to the front of the line."

Charity pursed her lips. "Savimbi?"

"Has to be."

The ship levelled off and flew directly to the spaceport. On final approach, the computer returned control to Val. He guided the ship into the designated landing site, a private docking slip on the eastern edge of the spaceport.

"Private pad?" Charity asked.

"I think he's trying to show off," Val replied. He ran the ship through its shut-down cycle. The engines went from a dull roar to a low hum, then cut out completely.

"Who is?" Ulysses asked.

"Buti Savimbi," Val said. He unhooked his crash webbing and hopped to his feet. "He's a pirate, or at least he used to be. Now he's got the largest fleet of ships on Ranginui and appointed himself as their 'security consultant.'"

"Basically, he's been extorting the corporations into giving him unchecked power," Charity added.

"Right. He's extremely dangerous, but he's also got tons of cash and he's willing to throw it around." Val glanced at Ulysses. "He's our buyer for these data cores, so I expect you to be on your best behavior."

"You know me," Ulysses said. "Always the diplomat."

CHAPTER TEN

ULYSSES looked out the window of the maglev as the dark, shapeless forms of the hills blurred into the bright, indistinct shapes of buildings. The train was moving too fast to pick up out any details, but it was a hypnotizing view. The watery world of Paikea was enormous in the night sky, but it reflected little light from the distant star.

The winding hills were covered in a green-grey moss. There were relatively few trees on Ranginui, but these mosses had taken to the moon like they were genetically engineered for it. Herd animals, in turn, ate the mosses and provided the people of Ranginui with enough food to be a self-sustaining settlement.

"Next stop: Guriev Square." The voice from the overhead speaker was soft, feminine, and almost certainly computerized.

"That's our stop," Val said. He was seated beside Ulysses on the train, but he had been more focused on his fellow passengers than the view outside.

"Are you sure we should be going without Charity?" Ulysses asked as they stood. "She said she wasn't feeling well when I asked."

"She'll be fine," Val said. "She's never been fond of Savimbi's style. She's better off sticking with the ship."

The train came to a stop inside a simple concrete structure. Dozens of people were crowded around the tracks waiting for the train to arrive, and once the doors opened Ulysses had to struggle to get through them. Once he was through the mass of humanity, he found Val standing near a set of stairs that led to a lower level.

"I'm surprised that a man like Savimbi operates from the city," Ulysses said as he followed Val down the stairs.

"He doesn't," Val said. "He has a compound on the outskirts of town. He's sending a car to pick us up."

They reached the bottom of the stairs and Ulysses's jaw went slack. What appeared to be a plain block of concrete from the train concealed a wide marketplace that stretched for a kilometer in any direction. Wide banners proclaimed all manner of goods and services. Colorful streamers and pulses of neon caught the eye, attracting potential customers. Small kiosks and multi-level storefronts alike competed for Ulysses's attention, and the sheer amount of noise and light was enough to leave him speechless.

The area was washed in light from bright advertisements on every flat surface large enough to carry them. The colors inside the marketplace shifted as the displays changed. ArgoTech, naturally, featured prominently in many of the advertisements, but dozens of other companies selling every conceivable product had paid good money for their chance to promote their latest innovation.

Then there were the people. There were hundreds of them gathered there dressed in anything imaginable. Women in vibrant kimonos chatted and laughed with men wearing slim-fitting business attire. The people shopped, ate, drank, laughed, and talked. The sounds of hundreds of simultaneous conversations drowned out the soft tones of music playing from concealed speakers.

Money changed hands constantly. Even though Ranginui was technically not part of the Eternal Dragon

Empire, the currency was Imperial scales like the rest of the system. Scales were small chits made out of hard plastics that contained minuscule computer chips to prevent counterfeiting. Each denomination had a different color, escalating from blue to black to white to red to gold. Large transactions were performed electronically, but cash was harder to track and thus had a certain appeal to an underground market like this. A whole rainbow of currencies flowed as customers passed scales to merchants and merchants passed scales to one another.

Among the chaos and swirl of activity, a man in a turban and five-button suit appeared beside Val and Ulysses, a computer tablet in his hand. "Good sirs, a moment of your time."

"We're kind of busy," Val said, nudging Ulysses forward.

The man kept walking after them. "It will only take a moment. I represent an organization that wants to ban the use of railguns by the military. Errant railgun slugs are capable of vast destruction, and the possible loss of life years or even centuries after they have been fired makes their use immoral."

Val snorted. "Ban the primary weapons of the entire fleet? Good luck with that."

The man extended the tablet. "I'm here to collect signatures to bring to the office of the Ministry of Warfare on Yu-Kiang. The war is over. These horrible weapons can be tossed in the dustbin of history. Can I count on your support?"

Val opened his mouth, but Ulysses stepped toward the man and took the tablet in his hand. "Sure. I'll sign your petition. I'm no stranger to how deadly these things can be."

The man's face lit up with excitement. "You will? That's great!" He took the tablet back from Ulysses after he signed his name. "Thanks a lot, Mr. . . . ." he flipped the tablet around and looked at the list. "Mr. Wallach."

"No problem, son." He watched the young man run off to find more signatures. Val stood behind him, shaking his head. "What?" Ulysses asked.

"Oh, you did it now," Val said with a smile.

"Did wha—" Ulysses's tablet began to buzz in his pocket. He pulled it out to see the screen covered in advertisements and donation requests from charities across the system.

Val wrapped an arm around his old friend's shoulders. "You don't give anything away on Ranginui. Someone is always watching, tracking for patterns. If there's a way to collect data on you, you can bet any one of these corporations is going to do it." Val pointed to a thin man in a khaki jacket. Ulysses recognized the uniform from Chelsea Station. "And if the mega-corps don't use that data, you can bet that the secret police will."

"Don't give away anything," Ulysses nodded. "Got it."

Val pulled his friend away from the Kempeitai agent and into the throngs of shoppers clustered around the marketplace. They hadn't made it ten meters when another young man, this one pale and sunken-eyed, emerged from the crowd. He wore a thick black coat with oversized lapels and skinny denim pants. Instead of carrying a computer tablet, he held honest-to-God paper leaflets in his hand. Ulysses hadn't seen genuine paper since his university days.

"Mr. Wallach, I presume," the man said with a droning accent that marked him as a foreigner in the system. "As such a socially conscious person, you must be a patron of the arts, am I correct?" Ulysses opened his mouth, but the stranger continued. "Of course you are. That's why you should come see the live performance of my new drama: *The Slopes of Olympus.*"

"Oh, boy," Val muttered. He started to pull Ulysses away again, but Ulysses ducked out from under his arm. He stared at the paper in his hand, then his eyes shifted to the man in front of him.

"'A riveting story of love, betrayal, and heartbreak on the slopes of Olympus Mons?'" Ulysses read. "What is this?"

"Chico," Val said. "We need to go. We have an appointment, remember?"

"In a minute." Ulysses stepped toward the dramatist, towering above the younger man's smaller frame. He glared at the man. "What. Is. This?"

"I . . . I'm so glad you asked, sir," the dramatist stammered. "It's a historical drama that tells the story of a young Martian officer who finds out that her lover deserted to join their sworn enemies of Jupiter. I take the audience through her grief, and then showcase her strength when she finally faces him in combat during an attempted coup by his so-called 'Martian Volunteers.' Righteousness triumphs in the end, but only when our hero learns that even true love must be sacrificed for the greater good."

Ulysses crumpled the paper as his hands balled into fists. Val stepped forward between the two men. "Okay, kid. We're all for the arts, but we have to keep moving."

"Sir, if you'd like a preview, I can upload it to your tablet," the dramatist said. He punched some information into his own tablet, which he had concealed in his coat, then looked up. "There you go."

"Do you think this is a joke?" Ulysses asked. His face flushed crimson. "Do you even know what happened on Olympus Mons?" He surged forward and grabbed the dramatist by his lapels. "Do you know how many people died?"

"Whoa," the dramatist held up his hands defensively. "Calm down, man. We did some interviews with the Martian Marines who put down the insurrection there. We took some liberties with the characters, of course. It's called creative license. It's an allegory. Relax. It's not like this was anyone you know."

Val pried Ulysses's hands from the dramatist's coat. "Walk away," he warned the younger man. "Right now."

"But—"

Val met his eyes. "Now."

The dramatist dusted off his coat. "Everybody's a critic."

Ulysses surged toward him, but Val put a hand on his chest. "Chico. Remember who you are. Remember *where* you are. And who may be watching."

Ulysses blinked. "Right. Sorry. It's just . . ." He sighed. "He has no right to demonize the dead like that. It's beyond slander. It's despicable."

"I know."

Ulysses glanced at Val. "How could you know? You weren't even there."

Val didn't have a response. The two men stood there in silence for a moment, a lifetime of grief going unsaid between them. Then Ulysses spotted a man in a black turtleneck sweater who gave them a quick wave. "I think our ride is here."

Val nodded. "Look, Yule . . ."

"It's 'Chico,' remember?" Ulysses straightened his jacket and took a step toward the man in the turtleneck. "Ulysses Walden died a long time ago. Let him rest in peace."

The ride to Savimbi's compound wasn't very long, but the silence made it almost unbearable. Ulysses stared out of his window, unwilling to even look at Val. He knew his anger was irrational, but it was there all the same.

Savimbi's stronghold was situated on the top of one of the highest hills surrounding ArgoTech City. It was enclosed by an octagonal stone wall with watchtowers on each corner. The facility was large enough to encompass the entire hilltop, with a private landing pad and four buildings within the stone walls.

It was difficult to say for certain how many men were working inside the compound. From his quick study while they approached, Ulysses saw a dozen men making the rounds in the moss-covered hills leading to the facility itself. He suspected that security was at least as heavy once they were beyond the wall.

As they got to the gate, he counted at least four men at the gate station alone. Each man carried a military-grade mag rifle on a three-point sling with more traditional chemical propellant sidearms in drop holsters. Every man had reflective visors over their eyes, which were meant more for intimidation and linking video feeds than protection from light generated by the system's star, which barely gave enough light at this distance to allow for photosynthesis. They also wore padded body armor in a grey-green camouflage pattern with rigid plates over their chests.

Three of the buildings were standard pre-fabricated aluminum structures that gave away no hint as to their true purpose. Based on what little he knew of the man, Ulysses suspected these were support buildings for his operation, but whether they were armories, living quarters, or remote drone stations remained a mystery. What Ulysses did know was that Savimbi himself wouldn't be inside any of them.

No, the self-proclaimed "commodore" would be found in the fourth building. It was unlike anything Ulysses had ever seen. It was a pyramid constructed of smooth black stone with no apparent joints whatsoever. Small windows placed around the sides of the pyramid glowed an eerie crimson. A single vast blast door, like something found on a naval ship, was the only visible entrance. As the car approached the compound and was waved through the security checkpoint, the massive door began to split open.

The car slowed down and stopped in the paved courtyard in front of the pyramid. The driver got out first, then opened the door for Ulysses and Val. The two men nodded their thanks to the driver before he returned to his seat and drove the car to the far side of the pyramid.

Ulysses and Val stood in the courtyard waiting for someone to arrive. The rain had stopped, but the pavement was still slick with water. The small pools reflected the red glow from the pyramid.

"Cozy," Ulysses said.

"Yeah," Val said, eyeing a passing guard. "Savimbi likes to entertain guests here. All this security is part of his act. These guys aren't the stereotypes of wild pirates. They're disciplined, focused, and professional. But make no mistake. They're killers, every one of them."

"Fantastic."

The blast door rumbled to a stop. Bright light washed out from inside the pyramid, blinding Ulysses to anything within. Three figures emerged from this light. Ulysses examined them as the details became visible, and all three were a study in contrasts.

The figure on the right was a blond woman, tall and lanky, in a conservative white business suit. She had sharp, hawkish features, and her only ornamentation was a pair of elaborate gold earrings that dangled from each ear. Her heels clicked on the pavement as she walked, providing a brisk staccato to accompany her movement.

The man on the left wore flowing blue trousers and a matching jacket with extremely wide sleeves. A simple white belt was tied around his waist. A curved sheath was thrust through the belt, and the grip featured an interlocking diamond pattern. The man's jet-black hair was tied in a topknot secured with a single black cord. His entire appearance was that of a traditional Japanese swordsman except for his shoes. He wore black boots of a more modern style, probably to take advantage of the magnetic grip while operating in space.

But it was the third man who truly captured Ulysses's attention. He was a huge man, easily a head taller than anyone else around him. His blue eyes stood in stark contrast to his dark skin and shaggy black eyebrows. His shoulders bulged with obscene muscle, and his bare forearms showcased a jagged crisscross of scars. He wore a fur cape around his shoulders and a black leather vest with elaborate patches over a simple brown shirt. A red beret rested on his wide head with more patches sewn into it. He sported two gold rings on the fingers of his right hand, each with a different gem set in the middle. Olive-green cargo pants and heavy combat boots completed his ensemble.

The three figures approached Val and Ulysses. The man in the center stepped forward while his companions held back a few steps. The big man spread his arms and a grin lit up his face.

"Val! So good to see you again. I was afraid you were avoiding me." He clasped Val on the biceps and squeezed. Val ground his teeth but said nothing. The larger man then turned his attention to Ulysses. "And who's your friend?"

Ulysses stuck out his hand. "Chico Wallach. I presume that you are this Commodore Savimbi I've heard so much about."

The big man's hand dwarfed Ulysses's own as he shook it. But, once he was done, he didn't release his grip. He leaned in close and studied Ulysses's face. "No."

Ulysses hesitated. "Um. No?"

The big man shook his head. "No. You don't need to lie to me." He released Ulysses's hand. "I know who you are. A man like Major Ulysses Walden needs no introduction."

Ulysses's blood ran to ice. "Sir, I believe you have me confused with someone else."

Savimbi stared at Ulysses. "There's no need for that here, Major. We're all friends. I've got no more love for the Centrality than you do. You are welcome here." His tone dropped. "But it is rude to lie to your host. I suggest that you accept that you can trust me and stop with this deception before I begin to take it personally."

"What gave me away?"

"I knew you were alive the moment I heard of your death." Savimbi said. His comment drew perplexed expressions from Val and Ulysses. "What I mean is that I knew a man like you wouldn't die from a catastrophic decompression in a cell above Venus. You'll have to tell me how you pulled that off, by the way. I read the report and I can't figure out where you switched places with the genuine corpse."

"Trade secret, I'm afraid," Ulysses shrugged. "Let's just hope the Centrality believed it more than you did."

"They lack our imaginations," Savimbi said. "They rely on machines to think for them.

"But how did you know *I* was Ulysses Walden?"

"You didn't make it easy. Different eyes, different hair, and you even had microsurgery on your fingerprints. Very clever. But you never changed your handwriting."

Ulysses's eyes went wide. "The petition. That was one of yours?"

Savimbi shook his head. "Not directly. But I'm plugged into every network on this moon. All these corporations just care about what they can sell you. I'm more interested in who you are."

"About those data cores . . ." Val said

Savimbi clapped his hands together. "I never discuss business on an empty stomach." He gestured to the pyramid. "Please, accept this invitation into my home. You are my honored guests for the evening. Once we have finished dinner, we can discuss our arrangement."

Ulysses nodded. "Lead the way."

CHAPTER ELEVEN

THE interior of the pyramid was lavishly decorated. Ulysses, Val, Savimbi, and his companions sat at a long table made from dark wood. Tapestries hung from the walls, rich greens and reds and purples that depicted stylized predators on the hunt. Lamps suspended from the walls provided illumination.

There had been armed guards on the lower levels of the pyramid as they entered, but none were visible inside the dining room. That said, Val didn't think for a second that men with guns weren't prepared to come running into the room if Savimbi snapped his fingers.

The walls and ceiling were flat, rather than sloped, leading Val to guess that there was extensive armor plating between the exterior and interior walls. He had never been inside Savimbi's stronghold, having previously only done work for the commodore through intermediaries. It was not what he had expected from a man with Savimbi's reputation.

A man in a white jacket set a plate of food in front of Val. It was genuine steak, not the reconstituted meatloaf they had to eat on the *Lucky Rabbit's Foot*. All the food was fresh, which meant that it had been sourced on Ranginui rather than brought in from off-world. It made sense. There wasn't a lot of farmland on Ranginui, but a few big agribusinesses were based here. They had learned over the years how to get the most out of limited space.

The wine, on the other hand, was a '29 Cabernet Sauvignon imported from Dulcinea. The dark, full-bodied wine had been chosen by Savimbi's private chef as the perfect complement to the meal. As Val took a sip, he had to agree.

Savimbi sat at the head of the table, with Ulysses seated on his right side and the woman in white on his left. Val sat next to Ulysses and directly across from the man in the traditional Japanese robes. "This meal is very generous, Commodore," Ulysses said.

"Think nothing of it," Savimbi said, waving his fork around for emphasis. "It's a rare honor to dine with such infamous company."

Ulysses gave their host a weak smile. "Yes, well, the feeling is mutual, I'm sure." He glanced at the man and woman seated across the table. "Forgive my manners. I don't believe that we've been introduced to your companions."

Savimbi grinned, and his teeth shone all the brighter in the depths of his thick black beard. "They are not important."

"I find that hard to believe," Ulysses said. "Besides, I feel that it is only right that I know the names of my dining companions for the evening."

Savimbi sighed. "Fair enough. The man with the eccentric sense of style is Hikaru Shimada, my bodyguard." He gestured to the woman. "And that is Isabella, my second wife."

Ulysses's eyebrows quirked upward. "Is that a fact? Are you a widower, Commodore?"

Savimbi tilted his head. "I don't understand."

"If I may ask more bluntly, what happened to your first wife?"

"She is likely in her chambers," Savimbi said, confusion evident on his face.

Val leaned over to Ulysses. "Isabella is his second wife. He has four altogether."

"Really?" Ulysses placed another slice of steak in his mouth. "Will your other wives be joining us for dinner, Commodore?"

"Why would they?"

Ulysses frowned. "I had assumed you would like to dine with your wives."

"No. They talk too much without understanding what is truly important. Isabella is my secretary. She is simply here to assist us with our business transaction after our meal." He looked to his wife. "At least one of my women has a brain in her head."

"Thank you, my love," Isabella said. It was the first thing she had said since they had arrived. Her voice was sweet and soft, not at all what Val had expected from her coldly professional demeanor.

Ulysses opened his mouth to say something else, but Val gave him a subtle shake of the head. This was not the time or place for this conversation. Ulysses took another drink of wine and sat back in his chair.

To change the topic, Val said, "So, 'commodore,' is it? When did that happen?"

The grin returned to Savimbi's face. "Do you like it? I think it suits me."

"It certainly does," Isabella commented.

"Was this a title you gave yourself?"

The grin never wavered, but something dangerous crept into Savimbi's eyes. "I will assume that you meant no offense, but take more care with your words, Tanner."

Val held up his hands. "I misspoke. I only meant that I didn't realize Ranginui had a recognized military."

"It does now. It has *me*."

Val put his hands on the table. "I see. You know, we ran into one of your, er, 'soldiers' when we were entering orbit. Gave us quite a scare."

"Oh, I doubt that Major Walden scares that easily. Maybe you should learn to be more like your friend."

"Yeah." Val frowned. "Maybe."

Savimbi picked at his vegetables. "Just how did the two of you meet, anyway?"

Val let out a nervous chuckle. "It's kind of a boring story."

"I'll be the judge of that. You seem like such an unlikely pair. And I'm always interested in hearing old war stories. I never had a chance to fight myself, you know. The Eternal Dragon rolled over with the arrival of the first battleship. I need to hear about people who really had a chance to cause those Centrality bastards some pain."

Val shifted in his seat. "Well, the trouble started when the Centrality sent a fleet of warships into the Solar system. We had no warning and then *boom*." He clapped his hands together. "Gateway Station was gone and Neptune was staring down a dozen cruisers with only a couple orbital stations to defend itself. They called on the mutual defense pact they had with Jupiter, which is how I got involved."

Savimbi leaned forward. "You were a combat pilot?"

Val shook his head. "Hell no. I flew cargo. It's the one thing I've ever been good at. But I went with the first wave of Jovian ships to relieve the men at Neptune."

"And you've had your ship all this time? The," Savimbi looked to his wife, "what was it called?"

"*Lucky Rabbit's Foot*," Isabella supplied.

"Yes." Savimbi snapped and pointed at Val. "That."

"Well, no," Val said. "My first ship was the *Master's Loom*, a dry hauler that had been commandeered to resupply the fleet. It took a coilgun round to the gravity drive and went out from under me less than twenty minutes after we arrived. And thank God it did. If I'd lost the ship an hour later, the surviving Jovian ships would have been too busy fleeing to bother picking me up."

"Incredible." Savimbi glanced at Ulysses. "And where was Mars in all this?"

Ulysses sighed. "The official position of the Council of the Inner Planets was that the conflict at the edge of the system was none of our business. If some madmen from Alpha Centauri wanted to fight the madmen from Jupiter, Mars wasn't going to waste lives trying to stop them. I told them that they could shove their pacifistic attitudes up their asses, assuming they had room in there next to their heads. The war was coming for Mars one way or another."

"That would explain the charges of desertion and terrorism that we've heard so much about," Savimbi said. "But what brought the two of you together?"

"A few hundred Martians volunteered to resign their commissions and join the fight against the invading fleet," Ulysses said. "We had a few patrol boats to our name, mostly used for interdicting smugglers coming through the asteroid field. But the problem was that we didn't have any skilled pilots who could fly the things."

"Meanwhile, the encroaching fleet had the brass in the Jovian Navy rattled," Val said. "They planned to meet the Centrality ship for ship, engaging them in a series of bloody battles that would prove that the invasion was too costly to go on. When the Martian Volunteers arrived, they didn't know what to do with them and let them work independently of the main fleet. The navy didn't have a replacement ship for me to fly, and I didn't have the training to crew up on a capital ship."

"So you took the job of flying a transport for the Martian Volunteers?"

Val nodded. "More or less. It was that or find myself serving hot meals on some Jovian frigate."

"Tell me." Savimbi leaned forward. "What was it like to kill so many Centrality soldiers? Did it satisfy you to punish these men who had invaded your home?"

Ulysses stared into his wine glass and did not speak. Val pursed his lips. "I'm sorry, Commodore. That's not really . . ." He searched for the words. "It's difficult to explain to someone who wasn't there."

Savimbi nodded. "I see. But you must have enjoyed it."

"We did what we had to do," Ulysses said. He didn't meet Savimbi's eyes as he spoke.

"And here you are, all these years later, back together again. What kind of trouble do you have in store for the universe this time?" Savimbi laughed.

"No trouble," Ulysses said. "War's over. We're all just regular folks trying to get by."

"Ah, yes," Savimbi said with a knowing smile. "Just businessmen now. Like me." Ulysses didn't respond to that. "Well, now that we are on the topic of business, I believe it is time for us to get to the reason for tonight's meeting." Savimbi made a circle in the air with his right hand. Unseen attendants emerged and removed the plates from in front of the assembled diners, but the wine glasses remained.

Once the table was cleared, Isabella produced a data tablet and handed it to Savimbi. He consulted it for a moment, then set it on the table. "The two of you got your hands on some Centrality data cores. There must be a story there."

Ulysses and Val shared a look. "Not really," Val said.

"Boring salvage work," Ulysses added.

Savimbi smiled. "Compared to the things you did in the war, I'm sure the bar for excitement must be high for you." He placed his elbows on the table and steepled his fingers. "I'm glad you came to me with this. As it turns out, we're expanding our data-mining operations. The extra processing power could be extremely useful."

"You were the first one we thought of," Val said.

Savimbi's smile took on a predatory edge. "And the fact that you owed me a great deal of money never crossed your mind?" Val squirmed again in his seat but said nothing. "After this I'd say all is forgiven. For four data cores, after balancing your outstanding debt, I'd say twenty thousand scales should be more than fair."

"It's a generous offer," Ulysses said. "Unfortunately, there are only three data cores for sale."

"What?" Savimbi's head whipped around to face his wife. "You said there were *four*." He slapped her across the face with the back of his hand.

Ulysses started to rise out of his seat, but Val held a hand up in caution. The man in the Japanese robes also moved, his eyes locked on his employer and his hand going to the sword on his belt. There was deadly intent in his eyes. If Ulysses had gone for Savimbi, Val was certain the swordsman would have cut him down.

What was less certain was what Ulysses had in mind. What did he mean, there were only three data cores for sale? He had risked his life, all of their lives, to retrieve that fourth data core. Why would he do that if he wasn't going to make a profit on it?

"It's not her fault," Ulysses said. His body language still radiated tension, but his voice was smooth and calm. "It was probably an error in the transmission. We believed that we had found four data cores, but only three were recoverable."

"I see." Savimbi's malicious gaze lingered on his wife another moment. One of the rings on his finger had caught her cheek, and a drop of blood fell from a cut beneath her eye. It splashed on her suit, and the perfect white suit emphasized the scarlet stain.

Savimbi straightened his vest. "Well, that is unfortunate. I'll have to drop the price to thirteen thousand. Will that be acceptable?"

Val could see the rage burning behind Ulysses's eyes. They could have probably negotiated up to fifteen, but Val was afraid of what Ulysses would do if Savimbi had another outburst. It was better to leave the table while you were ahead than to get greedy and lose it all. "I think that sounds fair, Commodore."

Savimbi's expression softened. "Excellent." He handed his wife the tablet. "See to it that these men get their money."

Isabella never met her husband's eyes. "Yes. At once." She started typing on the tablet. A minute later, the tablet in

Val's pocket vibrated. It was letting him know that money had been transferred into his account.

"It was a pleasure doing business with you, Commodore," Val said. He stood and reached across the table to shake the muscular man's hand.

Savimbi shook the offered hand without rising. "The pleasure was mine. All expenses were worth it for the chance to meet someone even more infamous than myself, which is a rare opportunity these days."

Val allowed himself a slight chuckle. "I can see how that would be a challenge."

"Thank you for your hospitality, Commodore," Ulysses said. He rose to his feet to join Val. "We will return to the ship right away and get those cores ready for you."

"Sit." Savimbi said the word with a smile, but there was no mistaking the command in his tone. "My men will retrieve the cores from your ship. There is no reason our evening needs to conclude so soon."

"That is most generous," Ulysses said. "But we really can't abuse your hospitality any more than we already have."

"Oh, but you can," Savimbi said as he picked up his glass of wine. The smile was gone. "I insist."

Out of the corner of his eye, Val watched as a pair of armed guards slipped silently into the room. They moved toward Ulysses with their weapons raised.

That was their mistake.

Ulysses pivoted on the ball of his foot, snatching the mag rifle out of the hand of the first guard. He kicked the man away, then swung the gun like a club to strike the second guard under the jaw. He followed it up with an ankle sweep that knocked the stunned guard to the carpeted floor.

The first guard recovered his balance and moved in to subdue the unruly Martian. Ulysses wrapped the sling around his elbow and allowed the rifle to dangle. He stepped forward and delivered a series of quick strikes to the guard's armpits and neck where the padded armor provided no protection. He finished it by flipping the rifle up and slamming the butt of the gun into the guard's face, shattering the tinted visor and sending the man sprawling to the ground.

Ulysses spun to point the rifle at Savimbi.

And stopped when cold steel touched his neck.

Val stood in stunned silence. The entire exchange had taken fewer than five seconds. Now Ulysses stood, a gun to the head of his host, with the blade of an ancient katana pressing into his flesh. Hikaru stood on the table, arms outstretched but relaxed. A single twitch would result in a bloodbath.

Savimbi hadn't moved a centimeter. He took a casual sip of his wine and gave Ulysses an expectant look.

Val cleared his throat. "Ulysses. That's enough."

Ulysses stood frozen for another moment. He took his finger off the trigger and held his hand up. Hikaru withdrew the katana a centimeter to allow Ulysses to set the gun on the table without slicing his head off in the process.

A slow grin spread across Savimbi's face. He set the wine down and started to applaud. Isabella joined her husband, though her heart clearly wasn't in it. "Well done. I never thought I'd get to see a Martian commando in action. I must say it lives up to the hype."

He stopped clapping and gestured toward Hikaru. "But I have a relic of my own who is quite capable of stopping you. I understand that he's dedicated his entire life to the study of the blade. He has been teaching my men how to fight hand-to-hand, and none of my toughest men can touch him. But you might stand a chance. I'm tempted to see who would win if you two went head-to-head. That's a fight I would pay to see. Maybe I could sell tickets."

"That's enough, Savimbi," Val said. "You win. We'll stay here. But only until the cores arrive and you've had a chance to verify them. Do we have a deal?"

Savimbi nodded. "Agreed." If he was unnerved by having a rifle shoved in his face, he wasn't showing it. He never even shifted in his chair. He snapped his fingers and the white-coated attendants reappeared with trays of sugary confections.

"Now." Savimbi showed his teeth. "How about dessert?"

CHAPTER TWELVE

CHARITY leaned back in the pilot's chair of the *Lucky Rabbit's Foot*. The technicians for the spaceport were gone, and she could finally relax and enjoy the solitude. In addition to topping off their fuel reserves, Charity had put in an order for more ammunition for their auto-cannons as well as replacements for the ship's original countermeasures. Four drums of 35mm rounds were safely stowed away in a compartment below the cockpit. That little expense had essentially wiped out their accounts, but Charity knew Savimbi's money should be coming in soon enough that it wouldn't matter.

She loved her husband more than she ever could have imagined, but it was nice to have some time to herself. They lived in cramped quarters on this ship, having to share a single toilet and shower like they lived in the slums.

But Charity didn't mind. She would gladly live in the slums of her own will than live out the careful plan arranged by her parents. She loved them both and held them in high regard, but this was her life. She had to make her own mistakes and forge her own path.

She never felt any attachment to her family's wealth and privilege. They were still "new money," as much as they tried to deny it. The old way of doing things had been more like Ranginui: free markets and rapid growth at the expense of the common workers who had turned Yu-Kiang from a second-tier backwater into the jewel it had become. Charity didn't feel guilt or shame about what her grandfather had done during the rise of Emperor Hideyoshi. She only felt regret that their push for freedom only trapped them in new bondage, the burden of responsibility replacing the chains of oppression.

Val had been her escape from all that. The filthy, desperate Jovian pilot who had fled to Tau Ceti hoping for a fresh start all those years ago captured her imagination in a way that all the morality lessons and society functions of her youth never could. He was a man with nothing but his ship and his grit. Charity fell in love with him the minute she saw him in the market in Guriev Square. She ran away with him and never looked back.

Her parents had forgiven her over the years. She hadn't been lying to Val on Port Tew. Her father had a genuine affection for his son-in-law. He was the kind of scrappy, hard-working man that could forge any destiny he chose, exactly the sort of man who could bring great success and status to the family enterprise. But there had been genuine terror in her heart when she gave Val her ultimatum.

What if he had chosen to work for her father? She shuddered to think. Oh, they would be financially secure and physically safe, but she knew that their souls would shrivel and die. Without her soul, how could she still love? Without love, how could she live?

Val was fond of the phrase "Thank God." Charity's family had never been spiritual, let alone religious. The state religion, if you could call it that, called for veneration of the Eternal Dragon above all others. Charity didn't buy that, either. She liked to think she was rational and open-minded. But the God that Val referenced had been kind to her, and she would always be thankful for that.

The console beeped. She looked up from her reverie to see an alert on the comm unit. She pressed a button. "Hello?"

"Mrs. Tanner?" It was a male's voice with a rich baritone. "The commodore sent us to pick up his merchandise."

Charity frowned. The plan had been for Val and Ulysses to return to the ship and prepare the cores to be moved to Savimbi's compound. Had something changed? She consulted the clock on the corner of her screen. Despite the fact that it was night in ArgoTech City, it was around noon Universal Time. Universal Time was the Earth-standard twenty-four-hour day still used to keep all of humanity on a consistent clock despite the vast differences in how local times were measured. That meant that Val and Ulysses had been gone for three hours already. What was taking them so long?

The comm beeped again. "Yeah, yeah," she said. "Keep your shirt on." She pressed the button. "I'm sorry. I was expecting my husband."

"Mr. Tanner and Mr. Wallach are still eating dinner with the commodore. We were sent to pick up the merchandise so they can conclude their deal."

Charity sighed. Typical. Val and Ulysses were enjoying Savimbi's expensive cuisine while she sat in the ship chewing on stale protein bars. Not that she envied the company. She couldn't stomach the idea of trying to enjoy food around a man like Buti Savimbi.

"I'm opening the cargo ramp now," Charity told the man on the comm. She worked the controls and the sub-deck to the cargo bay lowered as a ramp to allow the men outside the ship to board. "I'll meet you in the hold to help you load the data cores."

She rose from her seat with a groan and worked her way back through the ship. She cycled through the blast door at the same time three muscular men in sleeveless shirts ascended the ramp. The man in front had a shock of bright green hair, and when his eyes met Charity's she saw nothing but sadism and boredom.

"Ah, Mrs. Tanner," the man said. His voice matched that of the man on the comm. "Thank you for letting us on board your ship."

"Yeah, well, the sooner you get these cores, the sooner we can get out of here."

The man gave her a sinister smile. "Of course."

Charity climbed down from the control platform to the sub-deck itself. "Do you boys need help?"

The green-haired man shook his head. "We can each take a core and be out of here in no time."

Charity shook her head. Buti Savimbi liked to pretend that he was some smooth operator, but his men were still little more than dumb pirates. "Uh, okay. But there are three of you and four cores. Are you sure you don't want help?"

Savimbi's man went rigid. He examined the cargo hold more closely to see that there were, in fact, four data cores tied down to the sub-deck. "You said there are *four* data cores?"

"Count them yourself," she replied. She did not add "you idiot" to her comment, though the thought ran through her mind.

Green-hair looked to one of his men. "Go get a cart." The other man nodded and walked down the ramp. "I've got to contact the boss and let him know about the change."

"Fine," Charity said. "Go right ahead."

Green-hair put a hand to his ear to activate a hidden earpiece. "Yeah, put me through to the boss." He glanced at Charity. "Tell him I've got some news for him."

"Let go of me!" Charity shouted. She kicked and scratched at the man who held her arm in an iron grip, but nothing she did had any effect.

Charity trembled as the massive blast door to Savimbi's pyramid opened in front of her. It was raining again, and Charity's hair and clothes were soaked by the time she was dragged in front of Savimbi's fortress. The damp clothing only made the pervasive chill that much worse. But it wasn't a simple chill that made Charity shiver uncontrollably.

She had heard stories of people who had made Savimbi angry, and none of them had ended well. She knew something had happened. The sudden change in attitude from the green-haired thug aboard the *Lucky Rabbit's Foot* made that clear.

But the worst part was that Charity couldn't figure out what was going on. Last she had heard, everything was going well. Then Val and Ulysses didn't come back from Savimbi's compound, those goons stomped all around her husband's precious ship, and she was dragged off along with the data cores like some kind of prize.

Or a hostage.

A woman in a white business suit stepped out of the pyramid. As Charity studied her, she noticed that the woman had a cut under her eye and a single drop of blood had stained her suit. The woman didn't seem to notice, instead consumed with the information on a computer tablet in her hands.

The thug holding Charity finally released her, tossing her to the pavement. Charity caught herself on her hands and knees, and when she pulled them back her palms were scraped and bloody.

"Who are you?" Charity asked. "Where is Savimbi? What did you do with my husband?"

"Charity Tanner?" the woman asked. She didn't bother looking at the woman on the ground at her feet.

"Depends on who's asking," Charity said.

"Your husband is inside."

Charity's eyes went wide. "Is he okay? Is he hurt?"

"Your husband is alive," the woman replied. "For now. But his continued well-being depends entirely on the answers you give me."

Charity was tempted to tell the woman to go jump off ArgoTech Tower, but she stopped herself. Mouthing off would only get Val in more trouble. She would have to control herself.

She nodded once. "I'll do my best."

The woman in white looked away from her tablet at that. "Your best? My dear, I hope for your husband's sake that you can manage a little better than that."

Charity growled in response, which elicited a chuckle from the woman. "Very well, Mrs. Tanner. Let's start with an easy one. Do you know why you are here?"

"Because your goons dragged me off my ship and tossed me onto this ugly slab of concrete," Charity replied.

The woman pursed her lips. "Technically correct, I suppose. But do you know *why* they did that?"

Because your boss is a sick bastard who hurts people for fun, Charity thought. "No. Your men came on the ship to pick up the data cores we brought to sell you. There was some confusion about how many we were selling. And then this sack of meat back here dragged me into a car." She tilted her head to the big goon who had gripped her arm. "And here we are."

The woman typed something onto the tablet. "You mentioned confusion about numbers. Exactly what do you mean?"

"Your thugs said they were there to pick up three data cores when there were clearly four cores sitting right there in the cargo hold."

The woman raised her eyebrows. "So you admit that you were able to salvage four data cores with your husband and Major Walden?"

Charity's jaw dropped. How did they know about Ulysses? Had one of them slipped up? Or did Savimbi's network run so deep that no secret stayed out of his reach for long?

"I'm not 'admitting' anything," she said, trying to keep the fear out of her voice. "We had an arrangement with Savimbi to sell him four recovered data cores. Now, instead of treating us like business partners, you're acting like we're prisoners. If you think you can intimidate us into handing over the data cores without their full price, you and your boss can go suck exhaust."

"Charming," the woman sneered. "Do you know why Major Walden claimed that only three data cores had been recovered? He said that the initial estimate of four had been revised because one of the cores had been unrecoverable. Do you know anything about that?"

Charity frowned. "No. Why would he say that?"

"That's precisely what we would like to know. Did you have another buyer lined up? Did Major Walden express any desire to split the sale between two or more buyers?"

"Why would we? Savimbi's got deep pockets, and we had no reason to try to double-cross him."

The woman lowered the tablet, then looked Charity in the eye. "Do you truly know nothing of this deception?"

"I think you're full of crap, lady," Charity said.

The woman sighed. "Very well." She glanced to the goon who loomed over Charity. "Bring her inside."

The big man grabbed Charity by the arm and yanked her to her feet. "Hey!" she shouted. "You bitch! I told you I don't know anything!"

"Yes," the woman said. She turned around, then glanced back over her shoulder. "If it helps, I believe you." She began walking away. "But you can still be useful in getting the others to admit to their lies. Let's go."

As Charity was frog-marched into the pyramid, she found herself grateful for the rain. At least all this falling water would conceal her tears.

CHAPTER THIRTEEN

VAL stumbled as he was shoved into a small room, devoid of any furnishings and little more than a closet. He had to catch himself to avoid falling over. He spun around on his heel to face the man who pushed him, but a steel door slammed down in front of his face before he had a chance.

Val pounded on the door. "Let us out of here!"

"It's no use," Ulysses said. He sat against the far wall with his legs crossed. "Just relax and take a deep breath."

Val turned and stared at his friend. "Ulysses, I swear to God I will throttle you if you don't tell me what game you're playing."

"I can't," Ulysses said. "This isn't the time or place for that conversation."

"I knew it," Val muttered. He jabbed a finger at Ulysses. "I knew letting you back into my life was a mistake. Charity and I didn't have much, but we were happy."

"I know. I'm sorry. This isn't what I wanted."

"Well, once again, your good intentions mean nothing." Val hammered on the steel door again, each impact sending a clang echoing in the tiny space. "Open this door!"

The door opened. Charity burst into the room. She looked dazed and her jumpsuit was water-logged. Rough abrasions coated her hands. "Val?"

"Charity?" His heart soared to see his wife and he wrapped her in his arms. Then the weight of her arrival hit him. "What are you doing here?"

"Savimbi's men came for the cores. Apparently, there was a mix-up and they thought there were only three."

Val shot Ulysses a look. "Yeah. Wonder where they got that idea."

"Savimbi had his men take me. Some woman tried to get me to talk, but I told them I didn't know anything. What's going on?"

"I don't know, but we'll figure it out." He pulled her to close to him and kissed her.

"Truly touching," Savimbi said. He stepped inside the doorway followed by the swordsman. "What genuine love you two share. It's an inspiration to us all." He looked over his shoulder to Hikaru. "Kill the woman."

Val's stomach dropped, but he moved his body to shield his wife. "Don't you touch her!"

Hikaru didn't move. "Sir, I am your bodyguard." They were the first words the swordsman had said all evening, and his voice was gruff. "This woman is no threat to you. Find someone else to be your executioner."

Savimbi's growl was a low, rumbling thing. "Fine." He pulled a thick revolver out of a shoulder holster under his vest. It was an ancient model noted for its reliability and ease of use, and the rounds it fired were even deadlier than those of a mag rifle at close range. "I'll do it myself."

"No!" Val tried to interpose himself in the shot, but Savimbi slapped him down.

"Then talk," Savimbi said. He leveled the gun at Charity. "You have three seconds."

He thumbed back the hammer. "Three."

"Goddamn it, I don't *know* anything," Val said.

"Two."

"What do you want from me?"

"The truth, Tanner. For once in your miserable life, be useful. Tell me what I want to know." Savimbi put his finger on the trigger. "One."

Val closed his eyes and turned his head. He couldn't bear to watch. Savimbi's finger pulled back on the trigger.

"Wait."

Val opened his eyes and looked up. Ulysses was on his feet, arms outstretched and palms open in a gesture of surrender. "I'll tell you why I lied. But only if you put the gun down."

"You don't command *me*, Walden," Savimbi said. "I'm the one with the gun. I'm the one making the rules." But he lowered the gun and decocked the hammer. "Don't lie to me again."

"I won't," Ulysses said. "I swear."

"Then talk."

"It wasn't an accident that we found those data cores. My escape from Venus wasn't something I arranged by myself. There is a resistance movement in the Solar system that orchestrated the whole thing. They had a mole on a Centrality cruiser who was slipping them information, but the cruiser was reassigned to the Tau Ceti system and they lost contact. They needed someone to come here and pick up where they left off."

Val glared at him. "I knew it. I knew you weren't here to start a new life."

"That part was true," Ulysses said. "They wanted me to lead a new rebellion, but I'd had enough. The resistance promised that they could get me a new identity and a passport to another system, but only if I did them this favor in exchange. I came here to pick up one final message from the mole and relay it back to the resistance."

"And the message is on one of those data cores?" Savimbi asked. "Wouldn't it simply have been erased when the core was wiped?"

Ulysses shook his head. "No, the message was a dead drop left for me at Chelsea Station, along with the EVA suit. I relayed the information via encoded message that was sent with the warp ferry when it returned to the Solar system.

"But I discovered something else. The data cores were the prize at the end of a long trail. The mole had discovered something weird. Something that had spooked the Centrality brass but no one would talk about. I don't know what it is, but it is contained somewhere in the vast amount of fleet sensor records on that last data core. He managed to get the core slated for destruction and altered the records to show that it had already been wiped when it had not been."

"Sensor records?" Savimbi asked. The anger in his voice was fading, replaced by surprise. "Are you saying that last data core has the sensor records for the entire fleet?"

Ulysses hesitated. "Well, the records from a period ranging from two years ago to six months ago."

Savimbi stroked his beard with his free hand. "Outdated or not, my data-mining operation will be able to recreate Centrality patrol routes from this data. If we know where they'll be, we'll know where we can avoid." He tilted his head. "Why not sell me this information? An unwiped data core from the Centrality Navy could be worth a million scales."

"And what if I sold you the core and promised you that the data was viable? What if it turned out to be false or altered in such a way as to lead you into a trap? You would have killed us," Ulysses said. "I couldn't take that risk. Not until I had a chance to test it myself."

Savimbi tapped his chin. "A good story. Unorthodox but believable." His expression shifted. "But you are still lying to me."

"Commodore, I—"

Savimbi held up a hand. "I will give you a final offer. Tell me what you are trying to hide from me and I will spare your lives. Refuse and I will kill you all. Now that we know to check, my technicians will have the information by the morning, anyway. That is your deadline."

"I admit my mistake, and I accept the consequences." Ulysses pointed to Val and Charity. "But let the two of them go. They did nothing to you."

"Maybe not. But I know your type, Walden. You think nothing of sacrificing yourself, so threatening you will get me nowhere. But if I threaten your friends, you will tell me what I want to know. Or they will die."

Savimbi stepped out of the room. Hikaru lingered for another moment, then followed his master. Before the door closed, Savimbi said, "The choice is yours."

The steel door slammed shut. Val held his wife protectively in his arms and shot a look of pure rage at Ulysses. "What are you doing? You spent hours with those cores after we picked them up. I know you must have examined the data. Why won't you just tell him what he wants to know?"

"You don't understand," Ulysses said. He leaned against the wall. "What I found . . ." He shook his head. "A man like Savimbi can't be trusted with that kind of information. He's a tyrant now, but if he discovers what is on that data core he could become a true monster."

"Spare me the drama," Val said.

"Hey. Stop that." Charity's voice was quiet. "This isn't his fault."

Val scoffed. "And how do you figure that?"

Charity pulled out of his embrace and walked to the door. "We could have sold those cores to half a dozen other people who weren't noted killers, but we chose Savimbi because he paid the most. We all made mistakes here. Instead of assigning blame, let's figure out a way out of here."

Ulysses stepped toward her. "What do you have in mind?"

Charity reached into one of her pockets and pulled out a thin metal case. "They made the mistake of not patting me down when they dragged me in here. Savimbi's a chauvinist and probably never considered that I would bring in a weapon. In this case, he was right."

She popped open the case, revealing a small set of tools. "I'm no gun-toting commando. But give me a wrench and a screwdriver and I'll be your worst nightmare."

She ran her fingers around the doorframe. There was no set of door controls on this side, which made it an obvious choice for a makeshift prison cell. But, within seconds, she seemed to find what she was looking for and pulled a narrow blade from the tool set.

As she began cutting through the insulation around the doorframe, Ulysses asked, "What's the plan?"

"Well," Charity said, brow furrowed in concentration, "I'm no master strategist like you. But, the way I see it, Savimbi locked a skilled mechanic, an ace pilot, and a Martian commando in the same room. His mistake. Once I get this door open, you can take out any guards he has stationed to watch this room. Then we make a run for the courtyard."

"To what end?"

Charity paused her work long enough to glance at her husband. "Do you still have your lucky charm?"

Val lifted the small totem from his pocket. "Always."

Charity nodded. "Hit it now. It's going to take a while for the *Lucky Rabbit's Foot* to cycle through the start-up procedures without us."

Ulysses recognized the device for what it truly was. "A remote caller? That's a nice trick."

Val pushed the button. A small red bulb lit up. "It'd be nicer if it worked. Savimbi must have a jammer up around his property. We'll have to get out of its range to activate it."

"And there's no chance we're simply out of range ourselves?" Ulysses asked.

Charity shook her head. "The *Lucky Rabbit's Foot* could pick up that signal from Paikea. Jammer's the only thing that makes sense."

"Okay. That just makes it more important to get out of the compound. Once this door opens, things are going to happen fast," Ulysses said. "I want you to be ready. Val, if I can get you a weapon, do you think you can use it?"

"Do I have a choice?"

A smile crept across Ulysses's face. "None whatsoever."

It took several minutes of work, but Charity finally accessed the door controls. Something sparked in the doorframe. The door shot up and locked in place. "Hey!" A man's voice carried into the room. The green-haired henchman stepped through the door and saw Charity with her tools in hand. "Why you little—"

Val smashed the man's face into the wall. The thug slumped over, dazed but conscious, and Val pulled a pistol out of the man's waistband. He tossed it toward Ulysses. "Yule!"

Ulysses caught the gun in mid-flight. By reflex, he checked the magazine. Like most handguns, it used ammunition with chemical propellants instead of the miniaturized coilgun technology that made mag rifles work. The recoil was stronger due to the pressure of the escaping gasses and the guns were more prone to jamming, but they didn't require the heavy power packs built into the butt stocks of modern military mag rifles.

"Let's go," Val said. He moved through the open door, followed by Charity.

Green-hair was already staggering to his feet, but Ulysses pistol-whipped him as he ran through the doorway. The thug went down and stayed there.

Once the three of them were out of their makeshift prison, they found themselves in a long hall with a spiral stairwell at the opposite end. They appeared to be on the lowest level of the pyramid as the stairwell only went upward. A series of unmarked doors ran the length of the hallway, and a few meters to their left a T-junction led to another hallway. The walls were cold black stone, and the floor was comprised of red ceramic tiles.

"Which way?" Val asked.

Charity bit her lip. "I think they took me this way," she said, pointing in the direction of the T-junction.

"Oh, this is a great plan already," Val rolled his eyes.

Charity put her hands on her hips. "If you want to go back into that cell and wait for your execution, go ahead."

"Less arguing, more fleeing," Ulysses said. He held the pistol in a two-handed grip and led the way. They made it to the T-junction to discover that the hall ended in a set of double doors.

Ulysses raised the gun and crept toward the door. He put a little of his weight against the steel surface. The door was hinged and not automatic like the one in their makeshift cell. It opened smoothly and silently as Ulysses pushed. He peered into the room, edging the door open by increments to avoid exposing himself to anyone he couldn't see.

The room was roughly twelve meters to a side and had the same black stone walls and red tiled floor as the hallway. Most of the room was filled with advanced computer equipment that Ulysses didn't recognize. He saw no displays or input consoles, so these weren't simply workstations. Maybe this was the data-mining center Savimbi had talked about?

A man in white coveralls stepped into view and Ulysses froze. The man had a tablet in his hands and bent down to examine something just out of Ulysses's vision. When he was sure that the man hadn't spotted him. Ulysses took a chance and pushed the door a little more.

The data cores were there against the opposite wall. They were in a metal mesh cage with thick cables running from the data cores to the computer network that filled most of the room. The technician was paying particular attention to the data core on the far right, running his tablet over the connection and typing in a sequence of information. That had to be the core Ulysses had tried to keep out of Savimbi's hands.

His failure stung, but Ulysses wasn't going to let anyone else get hurt for his mistake. He swung the door closed slowly to avoid attention from inside the room. When it was shut, he turned to look at Val and Charity. "Looks like a computer room. But it doesn't look like there's another way out."

"Okay," Charity said. "Pick another door or try going up the stairs?"

"I'd rather not blunder into Savimbi while he's on the toilet," Val said. "I saw windows on the upper levels while we were outside. We can at least orient ourselves that way."

Ulysses nodded in agreement. The three of them moved to the stairwell and began ascending. The stairs were a metal mesh attached to a central steel column. The steps were wide enough that the three of them could stand next to each other, though Ulysses stayed a few steps ahead of the others.

As they climbed, Ulysses heard someone speaking on the floor above them. He held up his hand in a balled fist. Val stopped immediately, but Charity took a few more steps before she got the message.

They crouched on the open stairwell. Ulysses felt horribly exposed, but he didn't dare move forward until he knew what was happening. He listened, trying to determine whether the voices were getting closer or farther away.

"—not the honorable thing to do," Hikaru's gruff voice carried across the tile.

Savimbi scoffed. "When will you understand that I don't care about your precious 'honor?' I care about results, and the only reason I didn't shoot *you* downstairs was because I think you can still be useful. Don't prove me wrong."

The voices weren't moving, which told Ulysses that they had stopped to have their little chat. He crept forward another step until he could just barely see through the gap to the floor above. The stairwell was surrounded by a waist-high glass enclosure that would prevent anyone from accidentally plummeting to the floor below, but it allowed Ulysses to see Savimbi scowling at his bodyguard. Savimbi was half-hidden in the doorframe of a room about five meters down the hallway, but Hikaru was clearly visible as he faced his master.

"You promised that they had until morning to make a decision," Hikaru said.

"It wouldn't have made a difference if I had promised them two years," Savimbi replied. "Men like Walden, men like you, are too arrogant. They believe they are righteous and honorable." Savimbi made the last word a sneer. "Threats will not make him talk. Only action."

"I still don't think—"

"You don't get to think," Savimbi said. "You act. Or you get replaced."

Hikaru bobbed his head once. "Yes, sir."

Savimbi, apparently mollified, crossed his arms. "Good. And don't be concerned. Your honor will emerge intact. I promised them that I would not kill them before the morning. I said nothing about torture. Bring me Tanner first. I doubt he knows anything, but that man has been a thorn in my side for years. Perhaps his screams will motivate the others."

Hikaru grimaced. "It will be done."

Savimbi put a meaty hand on Hikaru's shoulder. "I know. You will not fail me again."

Ulysses lifted the handgun and prepared to fire. He wasn't sure if the round would punch through the glass, but he doubted that even a man like Savimbi would install bullet-resistant glass in the interior of his personal residence. Just two rounds, placed correctly, would eliminate the two greatest threats in the building.

Hikaru turned at that exact moment and locked eyes with Ulysses. He froze, his eyes wide. Savimbi, who had been withdrawing into the room beyond the doorframe, noticed his shift in expression.

"What is it?" Savimbi asked.

Ulysses put a finger to his lips with his left hand and kept the gun trained on Hikaru's head with his right. Hikaru turned to his master and said, "I simply do not see the need to kill these people. They lied, yes, but is that worth execution?"

Savimbi sighed. "They lied to *me*. Besides, this isn't about business any longer. These are the first casualties in a war long overdue. Perhaps history will even remember their sacrifice."

Savimbi stepped back and the door slammed shut. Ulysses climbed to the second level, his gun never wavering from its target. He signaled for Hikaru to step forward until they were out of earshot from Savimbi's door.

"You didn't have to come all this way," Hikaru said. "I was on my way to get you."

"Yeah, I heard. I'm not interested in spending my last few hours on Savimbi's torture wheel."

"It's a triangular rack, actually," Hikaru said. "The commodore is fond of triangles."

Ulysses stared at the swordsman. "I don't care what he likes. I only care about finding the exit."

Hikaru took another step toward Ulysses. Ulysses stepped back. "Hey. I'm not interested in playing 'dodge the katana' today. As a matter of fact, put the sword on the floor." Hikaru hesitated. "Do it!"

The swordsman sighed, then slowly pulled the sword, still in its sheath, out of his belt. He set it on the red tile with reverence. Ulysses never moved. "Val. Get the sword."

Val scurried up the remaining steps, then reached for the sheathed blade. Hikaru frowned, but Ulysses kept him back. Val took the sword and tucked it under his arm. "Cool. We got a souvenir. Can we get out of here?"

"You will not make it through the front door alive," Hikaru said.

"And they said we'd never survive a war against the Centrality, either," Ulysses said. "But here we are."

"After losing that war."

Ulysses scowled. "The point is that we're tougher than we look."

"Perhaps," Hikaru said. "But there is an easier way. Return my sword and I will tell you how to get out unseen."

"How about this?" Val asked. "You show us how to get out, and once we leave we'll return the sword. Deal?"

"Oh, come on, Val," Ulysses said. "As soon as we turn around he's going to blow the whistle on us. No way."

"Ulysses," Val said. "I have no idea how to get out of here. Do you?"

"We'll figure it out. I wandered around inside a Centrality battleship for two days until my team learned how to destroy it."

"And how many of them made it off that ship alive?" Val asked. Ulysses's scowl deepened, which was the only answer Val needed.

Val held the sword just out of Hikaru's reach and said, "We're not enemies here. We just want to be allowed to leave in peace. Your boss has what he wanted. If Savimbi asks, you can answer honestly. When you went to our cell to check on us, we had already escaped."

Hikaru tapped his chin. "Okay. Once I show you how to escape, the rest is up to you. I will not betray you, but I am also not responsible if you make a mistake and get shot."

Val nodded. "I can live with that."

"Let's go," Hikaru said. He nodded to the stairwell. "Up to the third level. And hurry. The commodore will not stay in his quarters forever."

They followed the swordsman up the stairs. Ulysses stayed directly behind him, ready to put a bullet in him at the first sign of betrayal. Charity was next, and she stayed low to avoid attracting any attention. Val brought up the rear, the sword in his hands still sheathed but held in a ready position.

It turned out the third level was still two floors above them. Based on that, Ulysses understood that the computer room and holding cell had been in a basement sub-level. The third floor was close to the top of the pyramid and the angle of the walls became apparent. As with the previous floors, there was no one in sight. Ulysses said, "I expected to see more guards out on patrol."

Hikaru glanced over his shoulder. "Why? This is the heart of the commodore's operation. He has an army outside these walls, guards at every exterior door, and a security team at constant readiness. Even if someone who wanted to harm the commodore got past all those men, he would still have to deal with me."

"It didn't take much effort for us to take you off the board," Ulysses said.

"Only because I have chosen not to play." He gestured to a triangular window of red glass built into the stone wall. "We are here."

Ulysses kept the gun pointed at Hikaru as he glanced through the window. It was tough to see through the rain and the tinted glass, but the window did lead to the exterior of the pyramid. It was a steep slope, but there didn't appear to be any obstructions on the way. If they were careful, they should be able to slide the ten meters or so to the mossy ground.

Ulysses stood there for another minute, watching for patrolling guards. He didn't see anyone. The wall surrounding the compound was only a few meters from the edge of the pyramid. The pyramid was placed directly between two of the watchtowers, providing a slim gap in coverage for anyone keeping an eye for intruders or escapees.

"Okay. I think this might work." Ulysses backed away from the window. "Val, give me the sword."

Val handed the sheathed blade to Ulysses, then looked up in surprise when Ulysses handed him the pistol in return. "Yule . . ."

"Take it," Ulysses said. "You lead the way and make sure the path is clear. If you run into trouble, try to find cover and pin them down. If you stumble onto the guards, I'll come down right after you to back you up. Otherwise, Charity will follow you and I'll bring up the rear."

Val nodded and took the gun. Ulysses unsheathed the katana and used it to slice through the rubber insulation that connected the glass to the stone. When the window was loose, he pried it toward him so that he could gently set it on the tile floor without it shattering.

Rain poured into the opening. Val tucked the handgun to his chest and climbed through the narrow hole. He gave his wife a nervous smirk. "Here goes nothing."

Val slid feet-first on his backside, gun held away from him to prevent an accidental discharge. Val picked up significant speed as he skimmed along the rain-slicked stone. He landed in the soft moss, knees bent to absorb the impact, but the force of it still sent him sprawling on his face.

No one breathed beside the window as they watched Val. He popped up to one knee, gun extended, and looked around for any guards. No one sounded an alarm at his descent, and when he looked back at the window he raised his thumb in an all-clear signal.

Ulysses and Hikaru helped Charity through the window. Before they released her, Ulysses said, "Don't wait for me. I'm right behind you, but you need to get out of this jamming field as soon as you can."

Charity looked back, her eyes half-closed to keep the rain out of them. "What are you saying?"

"I'm just covering your back. I'll be fine."

Charity frowned, but she nodded. As she slid down the pyramid, Hikaru whispered, "You are not a talented liar."

"No," Ulysses admitted. "Perhaps not."

He watched as Val caught his wife at the base of the pyramid. They had a brief conversation and Val looked up at Ulysses. It was tough to see his expression through the storm, but he nodded once and turned to the wall. The stone was slick from the rain, but Charity helped boost Val until he could pull himself up by his fingertips. Once he was on the wall, he lay flat and reached down to pull his wife to safety. Charity hopped to the other side and disappeared. Val looked to the window one final time, then he slid to freedom.

Satisfied, Ulysses stepped away from the window. Hikaru frowned in confusion. "Why not join them?"

"Someone's bound to notice that we're missing and come looking for us," Ulysses said. "There's nothing but open hilltop for a kilometer in any direction. They aren't going to get very far without a distraction."

As if to emphasize his point, a shrill alarm sounded from outside. A moment later, another alarm went off inside the pyramid. Spotlights swept across the open ground of the compound.

"Pressure sensor on the wall," Hikaru said.

Ulysses pointed the katana at the other man. "You mean you knew about this and didn't tell us?"

"I told you that I would lead you to your best hope for escape. The only alternative would have been the front gate, and I doubt they would have fared any better. At least they were able to make it out of the compound this way. I have fulfilled my obligation." Hikaru held his hands out, palms open. "My sword please."

Ulysses took a step toward Hikaru and glared at him. Then he sighed and flipped the katana back into its sheath. "You kept your word. I have to live up to mine." He placed the blade in Hikaru's hand.

Hikaru immediately snapped his fingers around the grip and drew the sword in a smooth motion. The blade leapt toward Ulysses. Ulysses stood unmoved, accepting that this was the way things had to be. He closed his eyes and wondered what death would feel like.

Something crashed to the tiled floor behind him and his eyes sprung open. He pivoted on his heel to see an armed guard, the same one whose visor he had crushed in the dining room. His mag rifle lay on the ground just beyond his reach, and his grey-green camouflage was ruined by a bright red stain spreading across his chest. The guard crumpled and collapsed face-first, his blood the same scarlet as the tile.

Ulysses looked at Hikaru, who still held the katana in outstretched hands. Blood dripped from the blade, but the swordsman didn't move.

"What?" Ulysses blinked. "I don't understand."

"You have shown courage and a willingness to sacrifice," Hikaru said. "You have shown honor and lived up to your promises, even at the risk of your own life. I will not see your sacrifice wasted."

Confusion blossomed into hope in Ulysses's mind. "Are you saying you'll help me?"

Hikaru nodded. "I am saying we can both die with honor. The storm will hinder drone operations, but with the compound on alert it is only a matter of time before patrols are sent out to retrieve your friends." A predatory smile spread on his face. "That is, unless they find themselves faced with a greater threat inside these walls."

Ulysses picked up the mag rifle and pulled two spare magazines out of the dead guard's pockets. His feral grin matched Hikaru's. "Savimbi said he wanted to see a fight. I say we should give it to him."

CHAPTER FOURTEEN

FOUR guards waited inside the elevator at the center of the pyramid. They were the best men Savimbi had on his security detail, ready to kill on command. An alert had been activated and the stronghold was under attack. This was what they had been waiting for. Each man was heavily armed and prepared for a fight.

It did them no good.

The elevator doors slid open silently. The leader of the security detail put his hand to his ear to activate his headset. "Team One arriving—"

A mag rifle round impacted his chest above the armored plate, blowing a ragged hole through flesh and bone. The men behind him raised their rifles in immediate response to the ambush, but they hadn't expected to engage an opponent in close quarters.

Hikaru slid into the open elevator, katana in hand. Ulysses lost sight of him as he shifted position. He raised his rifle and kept moving toward the elevator. He kept his eyes on the stairwell to his right, as well. If Hikaru failed to secure the elevator, Ulysses could find himself boxed in and exposed.

There were no screams, no cries for help. By the time Ulysses reached the elevator, Hikaru stood alone amid a circle of bodies. Each guard had a savage slice across their neck, chest, or femoral artery, and the folded-steel blade in Hikaru's hand gleamed red.

"Let's go," Hikaru said, wiping the blade clean on one of the dead guard's uniforms. "We need to get to the ground floor. The security office is there. All comm traffic for the guards is routed through that office. If we can disable it, we can effectively cut the guards off from one another."

"Okay," Ulysses nodded. He stepped over one of the guards before the elevator doors closed. "And I need to get to the basement level."

Hikaru frowned. "Why? They will trap you down there."

"The data cores are in the computer room. Whatever happens, Savimbi can't get the information on that last core."

"You really are insane," Hikaru said. He pressed a button and the elevator began descending. "If you want to die for this, so be it. I will take the security office." He reached down and pulled a handgun from the holster of one of the guards. He turned the gun toward himself.

"What are you doing?"

Hikaru responded by pulling the trigger. The round tore a gash through his jacket, but there was little blood. The round merely grazed Hikaru's abdomen. "There. Stay out of sight when the doors open. I'll tell the guards that you set up an ambush and that the elevator is a kill-box. I barely made it out alive." He smirked. "They'll move up the stairs to take you out, which should give you enough time to ride the elevator to the basement."

"Pretty sneaky for such a staunch traditionalist."

Hikaru rolled his eyes. "'Honorable' doesn't mean 'stupid,' Major Walden. Guile and deception are often the key to victory."

The elevator stopped. Ulysses pressed himself against the corner of the elevator and thought invisible thoughts. Hikaru slumped and tossed the gun aside. Before the doors opened, he gave Ulysses one final glance. "Good luck."

Ulysses nodded silently. The doors opened and Hikaru stepped out. Ulysses heard voices, but Hikaru shouted them down. "No! The elevator is a trap. He's set up a nest on the third level. We need to get—"

The doors closed. Ulysses was alone. He pressed the bottom button on the control panel. While he rode to the basement, he pulled out his computer tablet and made sure that it was still functional. Everything had happened so fast, Savimbi's men never thought to take it. They never expected that it could hold information of any real value. They were wrong. It would be crucial to what had to happen next.

The elevator stopped once more. Ulysses tucked the tablet into his jacket and raised the mag rifle to a ready position. The doors opened on a vacant hallway. Ulysses remained in place, partially concealed by the corner of the elevator. Once he was sure no guards were coming, he stepped into the hallway.

The elevator was directly across the hallway from the double doors that led to the computer room. Ulysses crossed the distance at a jog, not wanting to stay in the open any longer than necessary. He stopped at the double doors and edged them open again to get a peek inside.

Two technicians were still inside the room, but there was no sign of Savimbi's guards. The only man on duty on this floor must have been Green-hair, and he was still unconscious in the makeshift cell. The technicians themselves barely seemed to notice the alarm which continued to blare throughout the compound.

Satisfied that he wasn't walking into an ambush, Ulysses kicked the door open the rest of the way and pointed the mag rifle at the two technicians. "Get on the ground!"

The two men, both wearing matching white coveralls, raised their hands and got down on their knees. One of the men, a young redhead with freckles, said, "Okay. Okay. Just don't hurt it."

Ulysses frowned. "It? Don't you mean 'us?'"

The other man, who was older and had thinning black hair, said, "Yes." He gave his fellow technician a significant look. "He did."

Ulysses shook his head. "I don't have time for this." He gestured to the data cores. "Get me into that cage."

The younger technician frowned. "We can't."

"We don't have access to the cage. Only our boss and the commodore's personal staff can get inside."

"Is it EM resistant?" Ulysses asked.

The older technician shook his head. "This whole room is EM resistant to external sources, but the cage is just to keep the data cores in place."

"Perfect." Ulysses walked up to the cage. He held the rifle in one hand and pulled his tablet out with the other. He placed the tablet on top of the cage above the last data core, the one that he assumed contained the sensor records.

The older technician scoffed. "If you're trying to hack it, good luck. You'd need hours to gain access. I'm guessing you don't have that kind of time."

"You would be right," Ulysses said. He began typing out a sequence on the tablet. "That's why I built myself a backdoor into the system before we landed here."

The smug expression on the technician's face faded. "Who are you?"

"You don't want to know." Ulysses finished typing and a status bar appeared on the screen. Even without having to access the core itself, this was going to take too much time.

While his back was turned to them, brief as it was, the older technician made a break for the door. Ulysses snarled and pivoted, raising his rifle toward the man's back. But, despite everything he had endured, Ulysses wasn't a cold-blooded killer. With a grunt of frustration, he lowered the rifle.

The technician burst out through the door and began shouting. Ulysses knew that any chance of getting out of this room undetected had vanished. He just hoped that Val and Charity had made it out of the jamming field by now. They still had their share of Savimbi's payment, so they had at least come out of this disaster with something to show for it. Ulysses just wished he could reach out to them one last time to say he was sorry for dragging them into his mess.

Ulysses studied the room, looking for any points of cover he could use. Banks of computer towers took up most of the space, forming a silicon hedge maze. An open row in the middle of the room provided access to the door, and the technicians had been in that open space when Ulysses had surprised them. The cage with the data cores was just off-center to the left, which still left Ulysses exposed to fire from any guards who were sure to be coming.

He moved to the closest computer tower and pointed his rifle at the door. A full minute passed. Nothing happened. It was possible that Hikaru's distraction had worked better than they thought and there were no guards remaining on the lower levels.

Then the door exploded.

Smoke billowed from a sudden hole where the door had been. It was far more than the shaped charge should have produced. Ulysses realized that the guards had popped smoke grenades to conceal their approach into the room. Magnetically accelerated rounds poured from inside the smoke, and Ulysses had to drop to one knee to avoid the torrent of incoming rounds. He began returning fire, but it was impossible to make out any clear targets.

"Stop shooting!" the younger technician stood and began waving his hands. "You idiots! You're going to ruin every—"

One of the guards must have been startled by the sudden movement because he put two rounds through the technician's torso. The young man fell to his knees and looked at the holes in his chest with surprise. He put his hand on one of the computer towers as he died.

Ulysses fired again into the spreading cloud of smoke and heard the satisfying grunt as a guard was hit. He moved down the line of towers at a crouch and came around the outside corner. As he did, a half-dozen rounds tore apart the computer tower he had been using for cover and chewed into the tile floor.

The smoke was beginning to dissipate. As Ulysses moved to flank the incoming guards, he saw that there were three surviving guards who were taking up their own positions behind computer towers on the opposite side of the room.

Ulysses leaned out from cover and fired at the guards, but he didn't have a clean shot and the shots went wild. The computer towers were taking a beating in the exchange, their once clean and bright housing now punctured with sparking holes.

Ulysses moved again, shifting along the bank of computers to try to get a better angle. The guards spotted the move and poured fire into the computers. Only a few rounds punched all the way through, but if Ulysses had been standing upright they would have gone through his skull.

The guards were moving their own positions, trying to leapfrog to cut Ulysses off. Ulysses came around the corner and saw one of the men charging forward. Ulysses fired a shot from the hip and ducked back into cover before the other guards could reply in kind.

Over the hum of the computers and the shriek of metal piercing metal, Ulysses heard a faint pulsing buzz. He looked to the data cores and saw that the screen on his tablet was flashing. His program was finished, but it waited for his final command. But to get there, he would have to expose himself to the guards.

Ulysses took a deep breath. They were closing in on him, anyway. If he didn't get to that tablet, this would have been for nothing. He clenched his teeth and ran for the data cores.

Mag rounds poured at him, but the guards hadn't been prepared for the suicidal blitz. Ulysses had no plans to stop to give them a clean target. Instead, he snatched his tablet from the cage and pressed down on the illuminated button on the screen.

The data core began glowing red and the acrid scent of burning electronics filled the air. Ulysses allowed himself a grim smile. Every naval data core had an emergency protocol that would slag it and render it useless in the event of a ship's capture. Savimbi would never get the answers that he wanted now.

Ulysses tucked the tablet under his arm and slid feet-first across the tile floor for the relative safety of another line of computer towers. A mag rifle round put a crater in the tile less than half a meter from his head and his face was pelted with superheated ceramic fragments. Ulysses winced in pain and lost his grip on his mag rifle, which skittered away across the floor out of reach.

Two guards descended on him at once. Ulysses held up his hands in surrender. Savimbi would be out for revenge for what he just did, but perhaps his interrogation would distract the pirate long enough for Val and Charity to get to safety.

The first guard put his finger on the trigger, but the second guard looked at him. "Boss wants this one alive."

The second guard hesitated, then nodded. Instead of shooting Ulysses, he moved in and kicked him in the gut. Ulysses double over in pain. The guard bent down and picked up the tablet. "What's this? What did you do?"

Ulysses gave the guard a grim smile. "I made sure your boss can never get what he wants."

The guard cursed and kicked Ulysses again. Ulysses coughed and droplets of blood came out. "You're going to regret that," the guard said. He looked to the other guard. "Tell the com—"

The words died his throat as he saw the end of a curved blade protruding from the other guard's chest. The blade withdrew and the dead guard dropped to the ground, revealing Hikaru standing behind him. His clothes were shredded and burned in places and he had several lines of blood on his arms and chest. A savage fire burned in his eyes as he faced the last remaining guard.

The final guard, to his credit, reacted quickly and raised his rifle to engage the sudden threat. Confusion was evident on the guard's face as his master's personal bodyguard and *de facto* head of security killed his own men, but his training kicked in and overrode the guard's desire for answers. Hikaru was too far away to reach the guard in time. The swordsman stood there in defiance of his own certain death.

The mag rifle snapped as its capacitors discharged. A single round penetrated its target with lethal efficiency.

And Ulysses Walden lay outstretched on the tile floor, hands wrapped around the weapon he dropped during his slide. His sudden surge of motion placed uncomfortable pressure on his wounded ribs, and his entire abdomen felt like it was on fire. But the final guard fell to the ground, a portion of his head simply missing.

Hikaru and Ulysses stared at each other in blank shock for a moment. Ulysses released the rifle and pushed himself to his feet. He snatched the tablet out of the guard's hand and placed it back in his jacket. Then he picked up another mag rifle and slung it over his shoulder.

"Thanks for the save," he said.

Hikaru looked down at the guard. "You, too."

"You look like you had fun," Ulysses said, pointing to Hikaru's damaged clothing.

"I trained most of these men," Hikaru said. "This is not *fun*. It is necessary."

"Right." Ulysses winced as he moved. "Sorry."

"There are more guards on the way." Hikaru said. "The command center is out of commission, but they will recover and return."

They made their way through the ruined door. "Any word on Val and Charity?" Ulysses asked. Hikaru shook his head. "Well, if they'd been captured I'm sure you would have heard something in the security office."

"That is true. And the commodore gave orders to take you all alive, if possible."

"Yeah." Ulysses paused and listened at the corner of the T-junction outside the computer room. "Lucky break."

"He merely wants to kill you himself."

Ulysses shrugged. "He can get in line." He stopped and considered their options. "Elevator's no good, and I've got to imagine they've got more people covering the stairwell."

"They *had* people covering the stairwell," Hikaru said. "But their casualties have likely been replaced by now."

"Right. So how do we get out of here?"

Hikaru pointed to an otherwise nondescript door at the opposite end of the hallway from the stairwell. "There. It leads to a tunnel that will take us beyond the compound."

Ulysses nodded. "Lead the way. I'll watch your back."

They reached the door just as more guards began to come down the stairwell. Ulysses's mag rifle snapped and snapped again as he fired. He didn't hit anyone, but the guards were forced to scramble for cover instead of advancing. It gave Ulysses and Hikaru a chance to slip through the door.

"Oh, crap." Ulysses said as he entered the room.

"Yes, yes," Hikaru said. "Very funny. Get in."

He held open a section of floor grating that exposed a tunnel barely wide enough for one person to fit at a time. Thick, brown-grey liquid ran through the tunnel and the smell was enough to make Ulysses gag. "You didn't say this was a sewer."

"You didn't ask."

Ulysses shrugged. "Fair enough." He hopped into the tunnel and the sludge came up to his knees. Ulysses had to crouch low to avoid scraping his head.

Hikaru lowered the grating and climbed into the tunnel. There were no sources of light, and when the grating shut it was pitch-black. Ulysses heard a splash behind him.

"Keep moving. The sewer ends four meters beyond the wall."

"Why didn't you just tell us about this exit in the first place?" Ulysses asked.

"I did not trust you. If you escaped and then returned through this same sewer to do my employer harm, I would have been responsible."

"So, instead, you kill your own men and wreck Savimbi's operation?" Ulysses shook his head. "That's some weird logic."

"As I said, I did not trust you. But when I saw that you were willing to sacrifice yourself to help your friends escape, I knew that my place was no longer with Savimbi but with you."

Ulysses gestured to the sludge around them even though he knew Hikaru couldn't see him. "This is the kind of place you end up when you decide to follow me."

It took the two men ten minutes of wading through semi-liquid muck, but Ulysses finally saw dim light ahead. "I think we're close."

The sewage pipe narrowed until Ulysses was forced to lay flat and half swim, half crawl his way forward. Finally, his fingers wrapped around the edge of the pipe and he began to claw his way out of the tunnel. His head emerged to see open sky. He took a deep breath of fresh air, then started to pull himself free.

The pipe let out onto a steep portion of hillside. Ulysses, slick with muck, had to extricate himself carefully to avoid taking a deadly tumble. Once he was out, he helped Hikaru. The swordsman's trousers and jacket were drenched in sludge, but he never complained. Ulysses wasn't sure if that was an indication of profound stoicism or if Hikaru lacked a sense of smell.

Behind them, the compound was ablaze with searchlights and flashing alarms. Above the general din and confusion, Ulysses heard the whine of engines. Two assault rovers, built wide with a low center of gravity to maintain stability on the relatively low-gravity moon, came racing over the hilltop. Even with the supplemental gravity that was found on any terraformed world, most ground vehicles were built to be useful in case the supplemental gravity systems failed or if they had to be used outside of the designated gravity envelope.

Unlike the car that had carried Val and Ulysses from Guriev Square, the rovers bearing down on their position were open-framed vehicles with mounted weapons platforms instead of a back seat. One of the drivers spotted the men emerging from the sewage pipe and shouted, "They're over there!"

Spotlights on the walls converged on their location. The rovers swerved toward them, and the gunners in the rovers pivoted their weapons toward the escapees. Behind the rovers, more guards were pouring out of the front gate on foot.

Ulysses lifted the mag rifle and lined up a shot. As the rover drew closer, his left hand adjusted on the side of the barrel to apply the correct degree of magnetic force based on range. Magnetic accelerator technology had come a long way since it was first introduced in the First Interstellar War, but it still took a split second for the capacitors to charge. These were the weapons of marksmen, not spray-and-pray automatic fire.

He pulled the trigger, and a metallic round fired from the mag rifle. It was a good shot, and the gunner on the closest rover slumped over his weapon. But the second rover was only a meter behind and the gunner decided that his boss could interrogate a corpse. Bullets poured from the mounted weapon, and Ulysses was forced to retreat behind the relative safety of the exposed sewage pipe.

"Damn," Ulysses muttered. "We have to move."

"There's no use," Hikaru said. "There is no other cover in reach, and we can't outrun them."

Ulysses looked at the pipe. "Back in the pipe?"

"To what end?"

Ulysses held out his hand. "Then it's been an honor."

Hikaru gripped his hand. "The honor was mine."

The assault rover whined as it raced up the hill above the sewage pipe. From that angle, the gunner would have a perfect shot at Ulysses and Hikaru. There would be nowhere to hide.

The assault rover exploded in a shower of flames.

The hilltop shook as something big and grey came soaring in from the south. The deep-throated roar of a ship's fusion engines nearly drowned out the steady metallic barrage of fire coming from the twin-linked auto-cannons beneath the cockpit.

Ulysses raised a fist in triumph. "Val, you beautiful bastard!"

"What is it?" Hikaru asked.

"It's our way out of here." Ulysses slapped Hikaru on the arm. "Come on. The ship can't settle down on this slope. We'll need to go to them."

The *Lucky Rabbit's Foot* came in low and buzzed Savimbi's compound. The auto-cannons never stopped firing, turning vehicles, watchtowers, and interior structures into flaming wreckage as it swept across the hilltop. A few rounds struck the pyramid itself, but the building's thick stone walls had been reinforced with armor and the rounds did little more than cosmetic damage.

Ulysses clambered up the steep incline on his hands and knees until the ground leveled off. He raised his rifle as he ran, picking off approaching guards who found themselves exposed on the flat, moss-covered terrain. Hikaru was right behind him, sword returned to his belt.

The engines of the *Lucky Rabbit's Foot* were pivoted down in hover mode, and the wash kicked up a cyclone of displaced air. The belly of the ship opened and the cargo ramp extended toward the rear of the ship while it was still twenty meters in the air. The guards were returning fire at the ship, but their mag rifles and sidearms were intended to obliterate human tissue, not armored hull plating. It was only a matter of time until they upgraded to heavier weapons. Time was not on Ulysses's side.

He tossed the rifle away and started to run at a dead sprint. The *Lucky Rabbit's Foot* was coming down on the road in front of the compound. By the time Ulysses reached the ship, the cargo ramp was still out of his reach, but he leapt up and managed to catch the edge by his fingertips.

"Hang on!" Charity called from inside. He felt her hands wrap around his, and together they pulled him up onto the cargo ramp.

Hikaru jumped up a moment later, taking advantage of the ship's continuing descent to vault onto the ramp without assistance.

"Oh, crap!" Charity screamed. She tried kicking Hikaru in the chest, but he casually deflected the blow. "We've got company! Ulysses, help me!"

Ulysses placed his hand on Charity's shoulder. "Relax, Charity. He's with us. He helped me escape."

He felt the tension leave her. "Oh."

The ship rocked and Ulysses nearly lost his footing. "Did we get him?" Val's voice came over the ship's internal speakers.

Charity scrambled up the ladder to the control platform and punched a button. The cargo ramp folded into itself and returned into the ship, followed by the exterior hull panels a moment later. "Clear. Go!" she shouted into a microphone built into the computer terminal.

"Hang on."

Ulysses ran for the folding chairs on the side of the cargo hold and sat down. He hooked into the crash webbing a moment before the engines thundered with increased power and the ship rocketed into Ranginui's atmosphere.

Hikaru, for his part, was unprepared for the sudden acceleration and was flung into the bulkhead behind him. He grunted in pain and his arms were pinned to his sides. Instead of fighting it, he tucked his legs to his chest, then kicked down to the wall behind him. He stomped his feet on the bulkhead, engaging his magnetic boots.

The *Lucky Rabbit's Foot* had gone completely vertical in its flight from Ranginui, and what had been the rear bulkhead of the cargo hold was effectively the floor. With his magnetic boots to stabilize him, Hikaru managed to walk "sideways" along the bulkhead until he reached the row of chairs opposite Ulysses. He reached above his head and got a grip on the crash webbing, then deactivated his magnetic boots and used the webbing to climb into a seat. It was no small feat given the gravitational force pushing down on him. He hooked the crash webbing across his chest, then gave Ulysses a nervous thumbs-up.

Ulysses saw dark spots at the corners of his vision from the extended hard burn. Charity had secured herself with straps beside the computer terminal, but the strain on her face was evident. Within minutes, however, the fusion engines throttled down. The interior of the ship shifted from high-g maneuver to microgravity in an instant.

"We've still got a few seconds until the gravity drive can come online," Val announced. "I'm pretty sure we caught Savimbi napping, but he's got his own armada in orbit. We may need some fancy flying to get us out of here. Stay locked down until we make the grav jump."

Ulysses sagged. His part in the escape was over. He found the darkness at the edges of his vision once more, this time not from lack of blood flow but from exhaustion. He rested his head back against the cold steel bulkhead and closed his eyes. He patted his jacket to feel the reassuring outline of his computer tablet in his interior pocket.

Against all odds, they had survived. Maybe there was hope left in the universe, after all.

CHAPTER FIFTEEN

"STAND down by order of–" the pirate on the open comm channel noticed the ship careening toward it from the moon below. "Aw, hell. Not you again."

Val rolled his eyes. It was the same kid who had accosted them on their way in. There were more ships closing in on his position, as well, but none of them were in auto-cannon range and it was unlikely they carried the kinds of military-grade missiles that would be a threat at that range.

Val activated his comm. "Look, kid, get out of my way or end up as a light show for the nice people on the ground. Your choice."

The flying-wing ship rolled on its axis to track the rapidly approaching transport. "The commodore said that all traffic off-planet was restricted until further notice. I can't disobey a direct order like that."

"I don't have time for this." Val brought up a firing solution and pulled the trigger. A short burst of armor-piercing rounds scraped across the port edge of the pirate's ship, scratching the hull but not penetrating it.

"That was a warning," Val told him. "Next ones go through your cockpit. Tell your boss you didn't see us until we were already out of range, but you doggedly gave chase until your ship was forced to withdraw when you took fire."

"That might work," the pirate said, to himself as much as Val. "But I have one problem. What's 'doggedly' mean?"

Val sighed. "Break off your attack vector or die."

"No," the pirate said. "That doesn't sound right. Are you sure that's what it means?"

"Oh, for the love of God," Val muttered to himself. "Move, kid. Feel free to tell your boss that, when he wants to talk, he can look for us on Port Tew."

"I guess that could work. 'I chased you like a dog.' That's what you said, right?"

Val rubbed his eyes. "Sure, kid. Run with that." The indicator light for the gravity drive turned green. They were out of Ranginui's gravity well. "It's been fun." He engaged the grav jump, and the *Lucky Rabbit's Foot* left the whole planetary system behind.

Val leaned back in his chair and wiped his brow. He hadn't done something like that in almost a decade. But the old habits were easy to slip back into, like a well-worn pair of boots.

That was what scared him. Ulysses had been back in his life for less than a week and Val was already making combat extractions from a hot zone. At this rate, he'd be making head-first attacks on Centrality cruisers by the end of the month.

Val shook his head. The madness had to stop.

If there was a bright side, Savimbi's scales had already been transferred into his account. Still, it was better to be safe than sorry. At their next port, he would pull everything he had out in cash in case Savimbi decided to pull strings to shut off his account access.

"Did I hear you say we were going to Port Tew?" Charity asked as she ascended the ladder into the cockpit.

Val turned his chair to face her. "No, I said that if Savimbi wanted to find us he could start looking there. Why would I want him to start looking where we'll actually be?"

"That's fair." Charity moved to her seat at the co-pilot's station. "I can't believe we made it."

"It was all thanks to your husband," Ulysses said. He clambered up the ladder and stood in the center of the cockpit. "I haven't seen flying like that since the war."

Val rose to his feet and slugged Ulysses in the jaw.

"Val!" Charity jumped up.

The blow sent pain racing up his arm, but he didn't care. Val stared at his old comrade. "He deserves worse than that for what he pulled."

He took a menacing step toward Ulysses, but Ulysses simply remained where he stood. "We had everything locked up, a nice ten thousand scales each lined up for the two of us. But then you had to play some game that nearly got everyone killed. Tell me you at least kept that kabuki prop. We might be able to sell a sword like that to a junk shop somewhere for some extra scales."

"Well, I did bring it on the ship," Ulysses said. "Along with its owner."

"What?"

Charity nodded. "I was coming to tell you. We picked up an extra passenger."

Ulysses held up his hands. "Now, before you get angry, let me explain."

"Sounds like the story of your life."

Ulysses nodded to concede the point. "Maybe, but Hikaru saved my life. He burned every bridge he had with Savimbi to get me out of there."

"And what if he's a spy?" Val asked. "What if he's here to report our location to Savimbi?"

"Why would he do that?" Ulysses countered. "He could have betrayed us at the first opportunity, but he didn't. Instead he risked his own life, and because of that we all survived. We don't have to keep him on board, but we at least owe him the chance to get somewhere safe."

Val felt the rage bleeding off of him like heat from a fusion engine. "Was it at least worth it? Did you achieve whatever crazy plan you failed to tell me about?"

Ulysses nodded. "I slagged the data core. Savimbi won't get anything else out of it."

Val sat back in his chair. With the tension draining, Charity did the same. "Oh, good. We could have made a million scales off that data core, but instead you have to nearly kill yourself just to keep Savimbi from getting his hands on outdated sensor data," Val said.

He began counting on his fingers. "We almost died. The auto-cannons burned through a whole drum of ammunition. The *Lucky Rabbit's Foot* picked a brand-new set of pockmarks that will cost a fortune to repair. But at least we did it all without any hope of profit. It's a wonder the Centrality didn't simply surrender when faced with such brilliance."

"I know things didn't exactly go according to plan," Ulysses said. "But I think I have a way that we can salvage this operation."

"Yeah, well, I want out," Val replied. "The war's over. This isn't the time for crazy plans and desperate measures. I have a business to run." He met his wife's eyes. "I have a family to protect. Thanks but no thanks, Yule. I want out."

Charity frowned but remained silent. Ulysses settled in his now-familiar seat. "I can't blame you. You didn't ask for this. You have something that I've lost." His head drooped. "You have something to lose. I can't be the man who takes that away from you."

The cockpit was quiet for a long moment. "Where will you go?" Charity asked.

Ulysses shrugged. "There were a few other survivors from the war who emigrated here. I checked up on them when I arrived in the system. None of them have their own ship, but I'm sure six thousand scales will get me a decent head start. I just have one final favor to ask."

Val narrowed his eyes. "It depends on the favor."

"Can you drop me off at Angel Station? Last I heard, Harry Lee was living there."

"'Hard Luck' Harry?" Val looked at Ulysses. "Of course. It makes sense that you'd want to recruit the one man in the universe as crazy as you are."

"Nothing like that," Ulysses said. "But he has experience in microgravity. I could use a man with his talents."

"You're both out of your minds. But at least you'll have each other to annoy instead of me." Val typed navigational data into his computer. "Okay. We'll drop out of the grav jump in twenty minutes and make the course correction to take us to Angel Station."

He leveled a finger at Ulysses. "But get this straight: I'm out. No more of your crazy schemes. I don't care if you're planning to invade Yu-Kiang or open a bakery. From now on, leave me out of it. Thanks for the reunion and the reminder of why I fled the Solar system in the first place, but it's time we parted ways once and for all."

"Val," Charity chastised.

"It's okay, Charity," Ulysses said. "He has a point. I've brought nothing but pain and chaos into your lives. You deserve better than that. I'm only sorry I couldn't help you like you helped me."

"We're seven thousand scales better off than we were when you came to us," Charity said. "Not to mention that our debt to Savimbi was erased."

"Yeah," Val added in a grim voice. "Now he just wants to kill us, not take all of our money."

Charity ignored him. "The point is that you've been good for us, Ulysses. I'm proud to have known you."

"Get comfortable," Val said. "It's four hours to Angel Station. But when we get there, don't expect me to be surprised when you change your mind."

"Oh, come on," Ulysses said as he settled into his chair. "It can't be that bad."

It was worse. Angel Station was one of the original resupply stations built during the first wave of colonization. Built on the edge of the Rampart, it was intended to support travel through the asteroid field. However, a rogue asteroid clipped the station decades ago and sent it spiraling, slowly but surely, out of the system. Within the next hundred years, Angel Station would be even farther from the star than Chelsea Station and thus no longer part of the Tau Ceti system. But it was unlikely that the structural integrity of the station would be able to hold out that long.

Despite its drift into oblivion, the station still saw a decent amount of traffic. Its current location, about halfway between Paikea and the Rampart, made it a useful stop for spacers who were heading starward. While no one claimed official ownership, the Eternal Dragon Empire kept a token force on board to keep the riffraff from entering the "civilized" portions of the Empire.

The station itself was comprised of four wide metallic rings around a central shaft. It was an old design that did not even incorporate artificial gravity systems but relied upon tried-and-true spin gravity in the rings. That meant that, from the perspective of people on the station, what appeared to be the sides of the hull was their "down."

As the *Lucky Rabbit's Foot* approached the station, Ulysses gasped in horror. One of the rings had a gaping hole in the hull that was easily a hundred meters long. "Was that from the asteroid impact?" Ulysses asked.

Val checked his visual scanner. "What? That?" He shook his head. "That's new. It wasn't there last time I stopped here."

Ulysses frowned. "Were they attacked?"

Val shrugged. "Who knows?"

"You're being awfully calm about this," Ulysses said. "Look at the size of that breach. That would have killed hundreds of people."

"You've never had to live here, Yule," Val replied. "I have. Trust me. The dead may be the lucky ones."

Station Control was sloppy. It took them an hour to find a clear docking slip for the *Lucky Rabbit's Foot*. When they did get an approach vector, the transport had to squeeze in between a bulk freighter and a drifting hulk that had once been a passenger liner on its approach. The hulk looked abandoned, simply another wreck that no one had bothered to clear, but Val's sensors were picking up energy readings. Out here, anything that held out vacuum and had marginally functional engines would find someone willing to claim it.

"Okay, Yule," Val said. "Station Control sent me a station map. I'm sending it to your tablet."

Ulysses checked the handheld computer. "Got it. From the information I gathered at Chelsea Station, Harry should be in something called Heaven's Gate." Val winced at the name. "What? Is that bad?"

"Heaven's Gate is a hostel on Ring 3," Val said. "Even at my lowest point, I never even considered getting a room there."

"That big breach," Charity said. "That was Ring 3. Are you sure your friend is even alive?"

"According to the records kept by the Eternal Dragon Empire, he was alive as of a few days ago. It's the best I can hope for."

Charity bit her lip. It was obvious that she wanted to say something, but she glanced at her husband and remained silent.

The ship settled into its slip, which was little more than an empty spot of deck plating where cargo could be unloaded. Thick armored windows allowed the interior of the station to be seen. A small crowd of people were gathered on the other side of the windows. A few looked at the new arrival, but most had their heads down and couldn't be bothered.

The slip wasn't even pressurized. Instead, robotic arms extended a pressure tent from the airlock that would form a seal around the airlock at the front of the *Lucky Rabbit's Foot*. Val watched as the grey tube extended from the circular airlock door built into the bulkhead.

An indicator panel on Charity's screen turned green. "We have a good seal."

Ulysses slapped his knees then rose to his feet. "Well, I guess that's my cue to leave."

Val nodded. He pressed a button on the internal comm. "Hikaru. We're docked. Come to the front airlock for debarkation."

Charity stood and took a step toward Ulysses. "Are you sure you want to do this? We can go starward and drop you off on Yu-Kiang or one of its moons. I'm sure my father could find work for you. Nothing as flashy as salvage," she joked, "but you'd be comfortable."

"Thank you. But this is something I have to do."

Charity took another step wrapped her arms around Ulysses. Ulysses blinked in surprise, then returned the hug. "I'm going to miss you," Charity said.

"I'm glad that I met you." Ulysses extricated himself from the hug. "Keep an eye on Val, will you? You know how he likes to get into trouble."

Charity laughed, but there were tears in her eyes. She wiped them away with the back of her hand. "You've got it," she sniffed.

Ulysses looked out the viewport at the ugly tower of titanium and steel. "Well. I guess I should be going."

"Yeah," Val said. His voice was flat. "I guess you should."

Ulysses opened his mouth to say something, then he decided better of it. He descended the ladder to the airlock. Charity gave her husband an angry look then followed after him. Val leaned his head against his headrest and sighed. He hadn't asked for any of this.

He stood and began climbing down the ladder. When he reached the deck below, Hikaru and Ulysses were already inside the airlock. A green indicator light beside the door meant that the exterior door could open without loss of pressure or atmosphere.

Hikaru had borrowed a set of Ulysses's clothes and discarded his sewage-drenched robe. The katana was slung across his back. Anywhere in the inner planets, the Kempeitai would have hauled him into some secret prison for openly displaying a weapon like that. But out here he was just another eccentric traveler trying to make his way in the universe.

The exterior door opened. "Thank you for granting me passage on your ship. May fortune smile on you." Hikaru gave Val a stoic nod, then stepped into the pressure tent.

Ulysses lingered another moment, then turned back to face Val and Charity. "Listen, Val—"

Val closed the interior door in his face.

"Val," Charity said. "That was cruel."

"No, it was simple self-preservation," Val said. Instead of returning to the cockpit, he began walking to the ship's mess.

Charity was at his heels. "You think he was going to threaten you? That seems out of character."

"No, I'm not afraid of threats," Val said. "I'm afraid that he's going to talk me into changing my mind. I'm afraid that he'll inspire me to follow him on one of his adventures. And then, only when it's too late to turn back, will I realize that I've killed us both by allowing that man to speak."

He sat down at the table and put his head in his hands. "Ulysses is a good man. Maybe someday we will meet again and I won't have this fear that he's about to lead me on a doomed crusade." Val looked up at his wife. "But you've seen him. He's reckless. He endangered our lives time and again without even telling us why."

Charity moved behind her husband and put her hands on his shoulders. "It's not like you don't know how addictive it can be to defy the odds."

Val reached up to touch her hand with his. He gave her a sad smile. "That's the problem with gambling. At some point, the luck runs out. The difference between me and Ulysses is that I've learned when to walk away."

CHAPTER SIXTEEN

ULYSSES walked away from the hanger bay and made his way through the cramped corridors of Angel Station. His focus was divided between his surroundings and the computer tablet in his hand. The tablet had a two-dimensional map of Ring 3 displayed. Ulysses studied it to determine the best route to the Heaven's Gate hostel.

It wasn't a simple desire to track his progress that kept Ulysses's head down. The station was a wreck, with gaps in the wall panels exposing wires that had been stripped clean of any valuable scrap. The overhead light panels flickered at odd intervals, sometimes going out for minutes at a time. The floor was a filthy shag carpeting, and the curve of the station made looking up a disorienting experience.

As decrepit as the station itself was, its denizens were even worse. It seemed to Ulysses that there were only two senses of style on Angel Station: thick, all-obscuring robes that only exposed its owner's eyes and hands or thin strips of fabric and plastic that left almost nothing to the imagination.

A young man, or at least that's what Ulysses assumed, bumped into Hikaru as they walked. The adolescent had fluorescent green hair cut into a spiral on his head. Oblong slivers of obsidian dangled from each ear, and his only clothing was a loincloth and thin strap of fabric around his chest that matched his hair. Tattoos covered his arms and torso without any apparent pattern.

The young man recoiled at the impact. Hikaru looked at him. "Forgive me."

"Yeah, watch where you're going," the young man slurred. "Freaks."

As they continued to move, Ulysses said, "You'd better check your pockets. I think that kid tried to rob you."

Hikaru smiled, but there was no warmth to it. "He is welcome to try. Beyond my sword, I have nothing of value."

Ulysses examined his tablet again. "According to this, Heaven's Gate should be up here on our right."

"I think I see it," Hikaru said. He pointed to a bright blue and yellow neon sign in the shape of a cloud with a golden gate. The sign was flashing, and Ulysses couldn't tell if it was an intentional way to attract attention or just another victim of the faulty wiring in this station.

The sign was above a rounded set of automatic doors. When Ulysses approached the double doors, only the one on the right moved. Ulysses ducked through the door to find a man seated behind a low desk. He was an older man with grey hair that had gone pure white on the sideburns and he sported a well-trimmed grey mustache. Thick glasses rested on his nose, and he pushed them up with the fingers of one hand to get a better look at the newcomers.

"Welcome to Heaven's Gate," the old man said. Hikaru squeezed through the half-open door. "Yeah, sorry. It does that sometimes. You just gotta smack it, you know?"

Ulysses stepped to the desk. "Do you know a gentleman named Harry Lee?"

The man behind the desk chuckled. "The name's familiar, but the description ain't."

Ulysses smiled. "He's here, then?"

The old man nodded. "Down the hall. Room C-11. One of the pricey ones. He insisted on a room with a view."

"Thanks."

Ulysses dropped a few scales on the desk. The old man scooped them into his pocket. "No, thank you."

Ulysses waived Hikaru forward. They stepped through a swinging door and into a long hallway. "Okay. We've got to find Hall C," Ulysses said. He walked down the hall, seeing A-1, then A-2. He looked to his right and the rooms were numbered B-1, B-2, and so on.

"I don't think it's a hall designation," Hikaru said. He pointed to the deck. There were a series of hatches built into the deck plating, each with its own number: C-1, C-2, etc.

"Well, it's an efficient use of space," Ulysses admitted. "Come on. C-11 should be this way."

They walked down the hallway. The hostel was in even worse shape than the rest of the station. Paint peeled off the walls, exposing the cheap aluminum panels underneath.

One of the C hatches opened as Ulysses was walking and he nearly fell into the sudden hole. He stared down into the open hatch and saw a room little larger than a coffin. The bed, such as it was, was a metal rack built into the bulkhead. There was space for a single footlocker beside it. The floor featured a small circular viewport which showed the empty vastness of space. That was what the old man had meant by "room with a view."

A woman popped up out of the room. Her stringy red hair was shaved at seemingly random intervals and she wore even less clothing than the spiral-haired man outside. She shouted, "Hey! Watch where you're goin'!"

"Sorry, ma'am." Ulysses used the bulkhead to steady himself as he returned to his feet.

The woman's face twisted in anger. "Ma'am? I ain't no one's 'ma'am.'"

Ulysses grimaced and adjusted his jacket as he kept moving. "Of course, ma'am."

They found themselves at a T-junction with an unmarked door. As they stood there, a man emerged from the door shaking water from his hands. Ulysses hoped that this was a communal toilet, otherwise he didn't want to know where that water was coming from. "C-11 should be on the left," Ulysses said.

He started to move in that direction. A man lay curled up in the fetal position and the hallway smelled like cheap booze and vomit. The man had a shaved head and a set of dark green robes that, for some reason, seemed so popular among the denizens of the station. Ulysses gingerly stepped over the unconscious man.

"Here it is," he said. Hikaru was trying to move around the drunk and gave Ulysses a silent thumbs-up as acknowledgment. Ulysses bent down next to the hatch labeled C-11 and rapped his knuckles against it.

Nothing happened.

Ulysses scowled and knocked on the door again. The sound reverberated in the narrow hallway, but there was no response.

"Perhaps he is not home," Hikaru said. "We could wait here for—"

The "unconscious" drunk lunged at Hikaru's back and latched on. He yanked on Hikaru's hair, exposing his neck. Hikaru reached for his blade, but the robed man's position on Hikaru's back prevented the swordsman from drawing his weapon.

"You screechers! I'll teach you all," the man screamed. He was frothing as he spoke, and flecks of spit flew with every word. "Just empty noise. That's right!"

Hikaru tried to pry the man's arms from around his neck him, but his wiry arms gripped with terrifying strength. Instead of pulling him off directly, Hikaru charged backward, slamming the bald man into the bulkhead. The man groaned and his grip loosened. Hikaru snapped forward at the waist. The throw sent the bald man arcing over Hikaru's head.

He landed hard against the deck and stared blankly at the men above him. The bald man blinked his blood-shot eyes, and Ulysses saw discoloration down the front of his shirt from where he had vomited at some point. It wasn't a fresh stain, either. While the man had no hair on his head, his face was absolutely covered in a thick red beard. It, too, had specks of spittle and other, less savory fluids in it.

His eyes regained some of their focus. They shifted to Ulysses and the man's entire demeanor changed. He rolled to his feet. Hikaru raised his hands defensively and Ulysses made sure his weight was evenly distributed.

But the bald man wasn't interested in launching another attack. His fingers reached out gingerly, nervously, and pressed into Ulysses's stomach with firm pressure. "Are you alive?"

"Ow." Ulysses stepped back. "Obviously I'm alive. What gives?"

"It's you," the man said. "It's really you." His head tilted. "You changed your eyes."

Ulysses mouth went slack. "Harry? Is that you?" He tried to look past the beard and the stench to see his old friend underneath. "What happened to your hair?"

Harry Lee ran his hand over his head. "I . . . I don't know." He gave Ulysses a nervous smile. "It's been a hard few years. I don't always have full control of myself. Past and present get really blurry."

"Well, I'm just happy that you're alive," Ulysses said.

The smile faded from Harry's face. "That makes one of us. When I saw you, I thought you might be like the others?"

"Others?"

Harry nodded. "The dead, sir. They . . . they won't leave me alone."

Ulysses gave Hikaru a look. Whatever had happened to "Hard Luck" Harry after the war, he had certainly lived up to his nickname. Hikaru coughed and Ulysses rubbed his hands together.

"Right. Where are my manners? Specialist Harry Lee, this is Hikaru . . ." Ulysses's voice trailed off. He knew that

Savimbi had supplied his last name, but Ulysses had been distracted during that dinner.

"Shimada," Hikaru finished. He stepped forward and offered Harry his hand.

"Good to meet you," Harry said. He didn't shake Hikaru's hand. "Shimada? Any relation to Daichi Shimada, the robot tycoon?" Hikaru didn't respond. "Ah. I can see you're a big talker. Well, any friend of Ulysses has got to have a screw loose, so you're in good company."

"Hey," Ulysses protested. He considered it and shrugged. "Okay, that's fair. But this wasn't a social call. Harry, I need your help."

Val climbed into the pilot's seat and watched as a drone fed a pallet of dry goods onto the loading ramp of a waiting freighter. The pressure tent had withdrawn from the *Lucky Rabbit's Foot*, and Val was prepared to take off as soon as possible.

A twinge of guilt stirred inside of him for abandoning Ulysses on a place like this. Val stomped down on that feeling. He couldn't allow himself any doubts now. He and Harry would be a much better pair, anyway. Neither one of them had adjusted well to civilian life. Maybe, together, they could finally help each other move on. It was more likely that they'd both get themselves killed, but Val had to hope for the best.

Charity climbed the ladder to the cockpit. "Still no word from Station Control?"

Val shook his head. "It's been twenty minutes since the last update. It's a miracle anyone is willing to do business here at all."

"Well," Charity moved over to Val's seat and sat across his lap facing him. She put her hands on his shoulders and pushed him back into a reclined position. "Now that we have the ship to ourselves again we can find something to do with this extra time."

"That sounds very—" Motion inside the station caught Val's eye. "What's that?"

Charity sat up and rolled her eyes. "Geez, Val. I know it's been a while, but do I really have to spell it out for you?"

"Not *that*," Val said. He pointed at the viewport. "That." Through the windows into the station itself, Val and Charity watched as the throngs of people parted and a squad of khaki-clad men raced across the promenade.

"Aw, crap," Charity said. She hopped off Val's lap and jogged to her station.

"Now, we don't know that it has anything to do with Ulysses," Val said.

Charity brought up the comm ripper. It was a piece of military hardware that used brute-force decryption to access encrypted comm channels. The Centrality Navy defeated them by shifting the encryption at random intervals based on a highly classified schedule, not to mention the advanced capabilities of their artificial intelligence systems. But police and local militia didn't have those resources, which meant that the comm ripper was perfect for listening in for nearby patrols.

A male voice came over the speaker. "—squad is en route to Heaven's Gate. Requesting backup."

"Copy that, Sergeant." The dispatcher sounded like a woman. "Backup inbound from Ring 2."

"Ulysses," Charity said.

"I'll try to raise him on the comm," Val said. He tried entering the correct frequency. "No response."

"Try again," Charity insisted.

"It's not a problem on our end. We're broadcasting, but he isn't getting our signal. This whole station is a maze of dead zones and interference. He probably doesn't even know we're trying to call."

"We have to help him."

"I'm not so sure," Val said. His hands were frozen above his console.

"What are you saying?"

"The war is over. Ulysses isn't my commander any more. He's his own man. If he wants to get in trouble with the law, why should I risk my life to save him?" His voice softened. "Why should I risk your life?"

"Because you're a good man."

Val gave her a sad smile. "I'm not so sure."

"You need my help?" Harry frowned. "What can I do? I'm not a medic anymore." He held up his hands. They were shaking. "I just can't."

Ulysses shook his head. "I don't need a medic." Hikaru scoffed. "Well, I'm not here for a medic. I'm here because the Centrality sentenced you to five years hard labor breaking asteroids in the Kuiper Belt. From what I heard, you were damned good at it."

"It's the only thing I can do right anymore," Harry said. "It's why I came here. The Solar system had nothing but ghosts for me. Tau Ceti gave me a chance to get away from all the noise and the people. It's just me out there, and I get to play in the densest asteroid belt in known space."

"Exactly," Ulysses said. He pointed to Harry. "You're fearless and have a nose for finding the best rock. Those are the skills I need."

Both Hikaru and Harry shared a doubtful look. "What does the leader of the Martian Volunteers need with a rock-hopper like me? I don't have a ship of my own, and I barely have enough cash to afford my next meal. And if you're looking to crew up with anyone I know, you can forget it. I barely scrape by on scratch jobs put up by freelancers looking for some quick scales."

"But you know how to mine newtonium, right?"

Harry ran a hand through his beard. "Well, yeah. Those jobs pay well, though there's barely enough out there to be worth the trip. Not to mention the fact that what little we know about is so tightly controlled by the Centrality that you can barely even think about it without a permit."

"Suppose that was the job, though," Ulysses said. "Would you be able to do it?"

Harry shrugged. "Sure, I guess."

"What are you planning, Walden?" Hikaru asked.

Ulysses looked around the hallway. Satisfied that no one was close enough to overhear, he said, "The Centrality found something at the edge of the system. They didn't recognize what it was, but that could change at any moment. We need to move quickly before they realize their mistake."

"What did they find?" Harry asked.

A manic gleam shone in Ulysses's eyes. "Something impossible. Something that could change the course of history. And I want to be the one to claim it." He folded his arms across his chest. "Harry, have you ever heard of Newton's Moon?"

CHAPTER SEVENTEEN

SERGEANT Koizumi signaled for his men to move forward. The people who clung to life in this pitiful station were filth, but even filth knew to get out of the way of a *kempei* in pursuit of his duty. The sergeant's khaki-clad squad hustled through the promenade at a brisk pace, and those few who did not stand aside willingly received blows to encourage their loyalty.

Other members of the Eternal Dragon's secret police force expressed displeasure for their assignment to this lawless station. Of course, they did so behind closed doors in what they foolishly believed to be private conversations. But Sergeant Koizumi couldn't agree. The people here were immoral dogs, either unwilling or unfit to find their place in the great society. As such, no tactic was off-limits. No interrogation could go "too far."

Koizumi could allow himself to have a lot of fun here. His men called it a hellhole. He called it a playground.

The disk around Koizumi's ear chirped. "Second squad is in position at the dock."

He tapped the disk. "What's the status on that backup?"

The dispatcher replied in a crisp tone. "Arriving on Ring 3 now."

Koizumi swore under his breath. This was taking too long. Their target was slippery and had already evaded arrest on Ranginui. "Tell them to secure the perimeter. First squad will handle the arrest."

"Don't let your pride overcome you, Sergeant," the dispatcher warned. "Wait for backup to move in with you."

How *dare* that woman tell one of the Eternal Dragon's most feared and loyal servants how to do his job? Rage boiled in Koizumi's blood, and it turned his words to ice. "It is not my pride that will allow the target to escape but your cowardice. Koizumi out."

The neon sign for Heaven's Gate came into view. Koizumi cursed again. If this had been on any other Ring, his men would have been swarming the place by now. As it was, they had to take the long way around to avoid the Empty Quarter. Koizumi was a good citizen of his Eternal Dragon and would never sully his thoughts with religious nonsense. But the catastrophe that struck Angel Station had been the closest thing to divine judgment Koizumi would likely ever witness. What was important now, however, was that the vast section of habitat ring exposed to vacuum meant that his squad was forced to waste precious time avoiding it.

His squad stacked up along the sides of the automatic doors. Koizumi was the first man on the left side, and he avoided standing in the way of the door's sensors until they were ready to move. He felt a tap on his shoulder, meaning that the man behind him was ready to move. It was a gesture that would have been repeated down the line. The team on the opposite side was doing the same thing, and the other breaching team leader gave Koizumi a thumbs-up.

Koizumi held up a hand with three fingers raised. Then two. Then one.

Koizumi pumped his fist, the signal for the team to move. They didn't carry fancy mag rifles like the Imperial Army, instead relying on classic chemical propellant handguns and shotguns. Koizumi lifted his weapon and made a buttonhook turn.

Directly into a closed door.

Koizumi's nose collided with the unresponsive door and he felt something pop. He swore again, loudly, and slammed the butt of his pistol against the door. The impact jarred the door loose and it slid open. Koizumi moved forward, unwilling to look any of his men in the eye after his outburst.

The tactical light attached to his pistol lit up the otherwise dim lobby. It reflected off the thick glass of a man's spectacles. The old man raised his hands. "They're down the hall. C-11."

Koizumi ignored the pain in his nose and waved his men forward with his free hand. They were so close now. He was a predator closing in on his prey. And this time there would be no escape.

"Newton's Moon." Harry's jaw dropped. "You must be joking."

Ulysses smiled. "Nope."

"I always thought it was an old spacer's myth," Harry said. He was speaking to himself as much as anyone. "But if it's true . . ."

"It would change everything," Ulysses agreed. "So how about it? Are you ready for the discovery of a lifetime?" He held out his hand.

Before Harry could reply, armed men burst into the hall. Blinding light poured from the front of their guns, forcing Ulysses to cover his eyes with his forearm. The men wore depressingly familiar khaki uniforms, and the man in the lead had two silver studs on his collar. Ulysses was unfamiliar with the rank insignia of the Eternal Dragon Empire, but he knew that this man was in charge.

Harry began backing away from the men. Hikaru and Ulysses did likewise, though they had the sense to put their hands in the air. Ulysses, walking backwards, stumbled over the edge of hatch C-11, but he recovered quickly.

"Stop right there," the lead agent yelled. "By order of the Eternal Dragon, I am placing you under arrest."

Ulysses lowered his head. Guilt weighed on him. He wasn't sure how the Kempeitai had tracked him here, but he knew that his friends were in trouble and it was all his fault.

The lead agent said, "Harold Lee of Mars. You are under arrest for illegal mining operations, theft of government property, sedition, and terrorism."

Ulysses turned his head to look at his old friend. "What?"

A change came over Harry's features that sent a chill down Ulysses's spine. The bleary daze was gone, replaced with a sharp, hateful gaze. They kept moving down the hall, and the agents kept closing in on them.

When the lead agent's foot reached hatch C-11, Harry gave him a cold smile. "I would not stand there if I were you."

He reached into his robes and pulled out a cylindrical device with a bright red button. He pressed down on the button, then turned and ran down the hallway. Ulysses, still in shock, stood blankly until Hikaru grabbed his sleeve and pulled him along.

Nothing happened.

Sergeant Koizumi smirked. Well, that was anti-climactic. He raised his gun and pointed it at the fleeing men. He didn't know who Lee's companions were, but they could examine the bodies at the morgue.

His finger tightened on the trigger.

Just before the bullet fired, an emergency bulkhead slammed down in front of him. The bullet, designed to pierce flesh without endangering the structural integrity of the station itself, shattered upon impact.

Sergeant Koizumi turned around to see a second bulkhead had separated him from half of his squad. Koizumi frowned. Those were decompression seals, an automatic failsafe to prevent catastrophic decompression from crippling the whole Ring. But no one else had fired, and all his men were equipped with the same frangible rounds that he was.

What was going on?

The hatch beneath him blew open with a shriek of tearing metal. The explosion had been small, but the bomb wasn't intended to kill them. It was simply intended to open the hatch to the room beyond. The room which was now nothing more than a gaping hole in the hull of the station.

The deck plating beneath his feet buckled and Koizumi's eyes widened in horror. With a scream of escaping air, the entire section of flooring was sucked into space.

The last thing that Koizumi saw was Angel Station as he floated into the void. His men were right. It really was a hellhole.

Hikaru and Ulysses followed Harry down the short hallway away from the Kempeitai agents. "What just happened?" Ulysses asked.

Harry glanced over his shoulder. "What do you mean? I always leave breaching charges in my room. Why did you think I was sleeping on the floor? I'm not sleeping in any room that has my name on it." He returned his attention to the rapidly shrinking corridor ahead of him. "Always wondered if it'd work."

"How much damage did you just do?"

Harry shrugged. "This place is built to isolate explosive decompression. It was just the one room. The other rooms will automatically seal until a rescue team arrives. No one got hurt."

"What about those agents?" Hikaru asked.

"No one real," Harry clarified. "No one who will come back to bother me about it."

Hikaru gave Ulysses a wary look. Ulysses ignored him as well as the unsettled feeling in his gut. "Why are they after you?"

"Did some unauthorized work with a hotshot crew a few weeks back. Kempeitai got wind of it and snatched the rest up." There was a hitch in Harry's voice. "Used the captain's daughter. Broadcast her torture on an open comm channel to draw us out."

"I'm sorry," Ulysses said.

"Yeah." Harry looked back for a moment. His eyes were filled with water, but this wasn't from the booze. "I blew up the broadcast repeater with some leftover mining charges, but the damage had been done. The cap'n surrendered with the rest of the crew."

He turned away from Ulysses and his tone took on a hard edge. "None of them survived."

They reached the end of the hallway. It was a simple bulkhead, pieces of aluminum fitted together with rubber seals. "Is there another way out of here?"

Harry examined the bulkhead like he had never seen it before. "Hmm." He snapped his fingers. "I've got some breaching charges in my room. Let me go get them." He spun around on his heel.

"Harry," Ulysses said in a firm voice. His friend looked around as if unsure where the sound had originated. "Harry," Ulysses repeated. That time, the bald miner snapped back into focus and looked into Ulysses's eyes.

"What?"

"You blew the charges in your room. Remember?"

Harry scoffed. "That's ridiculous. If I did that, I'd have the detonator with me." Ulysses pointed to the metallic cylinder still in Harry's hand. Harry held it up for scrutiny. "Would you look at that?" He turned around and considered the bulkhead. "Well, we could pry our way out if we could get through those seals."

Hikaru pulled the katana from his back. "I'm on it." He inserted the blade into the thin black rubber line that separated two segments of bulkhead. Ulysses and Harry followed his progress with their fingertips, trying to get as much leverage as possible to pry a hole in the bulkhead.

It took the better part of five minutes, but the three men managed to create a hole large enough for them to squeeze through one at a time. Ulysses went first. The shoulders of his jacket caught on some of the internal framework of the thin bulkhead, and he had to adjust the angle to avoid getting hopelessly stuck.

Then he was through, emerging from the hole head-first. Of all the things on the other side of the hostel's bulkhead, Ulysses hadn't expected to stumble into a nail salon. Yet here he was, staring into the trembling face of a young woman who was hunched over the calloused feet of a rotund middle-aged man. The man leaned up from his reclined position and adjusted his wire spectacles. He blinked at Ulysses several times as if trying to will him from existence.

The woman simply screamed.

"Great," Ulysses muttered. He held up a hand in greeting. "Don't mind us, folks. Just passing through." He slid behind the young woman. "Excuse me."

Hikaru emerged next, soliciting a renewed set of blank stares and hysteria. By the time Harry squeezed through the bulkhead, the woman had gone out of breath. The fat man in the chair, however, realized that they weren't here to rob him and sat back in the chair to resume his pampering.

Ulysses emerged from the nail salon and onto the open promenade. He looked around the wide curve of Ring 3, trying to get his bearings. "Which way do we go?"

Hikaru was at his shoulder. He pointed to the left. "We arrived from that direction. If we wanted to retrace our steps back to the docking bay, we could go that way."

They took two steps before a collective gasp went up from the crowd. Ulysess watched as a tide of khaki uniforms emerged from among the civilians. Ulysses backed away and said, "On the other hand, there's so much we haven't explored yet. Why take the familiar path?"

"I agree," Harry said, bolting to the right. "This way."

Ulysses ran through the unfamiliar station while pursued by agents of the secret police. Every part of that made him uncomfortable. But Harry seemed to have some idea of where they were going. He took them through what passed for an open-air bazaar on the station, filled with kiosks and carts of every description. The market on Port Tew was a child's purified water stand by comparison to this wide array of fabrics and materials.

Men shouted behind them as they ran. Children who had been playing in the open lanes between shops ducked to the side to avoid the charging strangers. A woman in a face-concealing robe shrieked and recoiled in terror.

In the midst of the chaos, an arm in a khaki sleeve appeared from behind a stall and caught Ulysses by the collar. Ulysses wasted no time, shrinking out of his jacket. Instead of running, however, Ulysses whirled on his ambusher. He hammered the Kempeitai agent with heavy blows to the throat and abdomen. He delivered a final throw that sent the off-balance agent smashing into a mobile cart, little more than a wheelbarrow, filled with produce that had either recently arrived from off-station or had been grown in a local hydroponics farm.

Ulysses moved in and retrieved his jacket. He patted his chest to ensure that his computer tablet was still in place. Then he stripped the pistol from the unconscious agent's belt and checked the magazine by force of habit.

The owner of the shattered cart gawked at his ruined property. "My cabbages!" he screamed.

Ulysses reached into his pocket and tossed the man a gold-colored scale. Unfortunately, he forgot to take the Coriolis force of the spinning station into account and the gold-colored chit went spiraling away. "Sorry." He gave the man an apologetic glance, then took off to catch up to his friends.

It didn't take long. They were maybe six meters ahead of him, but their progress was cut off by a bulkhead that spanned the width of the entire habitat ring. There was a door with a small viewport in the middle of the bulkhead, and the indicator panel beside it told Ulysses it led to an airlock. Ulysses could see jagged wreckage around the corners of the bulkhead and immediately remembered the massive hull breach that he spotted when they arrived. It looked like he had found it.

"Harry, do you have a way out of here?"

Harry was staring at the bulkhead in confusion. "No. Do you?"

Ulysses shook his head. "Val dropped us off."

Harry twisted his head to face Ulysses. "Val Tanner? Heard he was in-system. Is it true he got married?"

Ulysses nodded. A Kempeitai agent emerged from the maze of stalls, but Ulysses pinned him down with a pair of bullets. "Yeah. She seems like a great lady. You'd like her."

Hikaru drew his katana and lowered it into a ready position. None of their pursuers had moved in melee range, but if they made that mistake he was going to ensure they paid a heavy price. "They are probably halfway to Yu-Kiang by now," Hikaru said.

Harry sighed. "Shame. Would have been nice to see another one of the living ones."

The Kempeitai had them trapped, but none of them had opened fire. That was bound to change at any moment, and Ulysses held his gun steady as his eyes swept across the sea of unfriendly faces. "Without a ship, what was your plan?" Ulysses asked.

Harry reached into the pocket of his worn denim pants and pulled out what looked like a plastic brick. It had a tiny circle of metal inserted inside of it. Ulysses recognized the military-grade explosive, having handled it on a regular basis during the war. Harry hefted the bomb and placed his thumb on the metal circle. It turned yellow, as did the detonator that was still in Harry's other hand. "I'm going to take as many of them with us as I can."

"Oh."

A sad smile crossed Harry's face. "Sorry. Plans were always your job. At least we go together, right? Martian Vols to the end."

A Kempeitai agent stepped forward. "Lay down your weapons. This is your final warning."

"Come and take them," Hikaru snarled.

An idea sprang into Ulysses's mind. "Exactly." He let the stolen pistol dangle from his hand and slowly set it on the deck. "Put down your weapons. Let them come and take them."

Hikaru's face expressed a sense of ultimate betrayal. To surrender when one still had the capacity to fight was a mark against one's honor. But Ulysses gave him a subtle wink, a gesture he hoped the Kempeitai wouldn't notice. Hikaru growled in frustration, then flipped his katana back into its sheath. He gingerly set the sword on the deck.

And Harry slid the explosives back into his pocket.

Ulysses had been standing in the way when he pulled it out, obscuring the view of any Kempeitai agent who might have spotted it. This was the last play they had left: lure as many agents as possible in to arrest them, then blow the explosives and take out everyone within ten meters. The civilians had fled the scene, meaning that Harry wouldn't have to worry about any more ghosts plaguing him in the afterlife.

Harry slid the detonator into the long sleeve of his shirt and raised his arms above his head. Hikaru and Ulysses did likewise, getting down on their knees. Ulysses turned his back to the agents and spared a glance at the airlock. If only he had remembered to take his EVA suit from the *Lucky Rabbit's Foot*. Then at least one of them might have had a chance.

A shadow moved across the viewport.

"Move in," the Kempeitai agent in charge of the situation ordered. Five agents separated from the cluster of men who had taken cover behind the abandoned shops of the bazaar and stepped forward to secure the prisoners.

Ulysses kept his head turned away from the Kempeitai agents but tracked their movement by the sound of their footfalls on the metal deck. Just a little bit closer. If they timed it right, they could reopen this bulkhead with the blast. Such a move could effectively condemn Ring 3 to be completely abandoned, but if they were lucky they could take out most, if not all, of the secret police force stationed here.

Ulysses gave Hikaru a look. This wasn't exactly the warrior's death Hikaru would have wanted, but this way they would be able to achieve a greater victory than simply making a noble last stand. His gaze shifted to Harry. His former squad medic had his eyes closed in a gesture of serenity.

The first agent got within arm's reach of Ulysses when the indicator light on the airlock changed. That tiny green light changed everything.

Ulysses snapped out with his legs in a vicious kick that knocked two of the agents onto the deck. He dove for the gun and landed on his back, putting two bullets each into three more of the agents.

Hikaru recognized the change in strategy. He bared his teeth in a predator's grin and snatched the sword from the deck. In one smooth motion, he severed the outstretched hand of the Kempeitai agent who had been reaching for it.

The airlock cycled open and Charity emerged holding a break-action shotgun. She fired as she walked, not aiming for anything but forcing the larger force of Kempeitai to stay behind cover. She fired again, emptying the double-barreled gun into a hand-painted sign for ramen noodles.

Ulysses yelled, "Harry, hand it over!" He reached his arm back and felt the pliable brick of explosives sink into his palm. "Go, go, go!"

Hikaru moved first, withdrawing from the Kempeitai man who was clutching his missing wrist. He slid past Charity who still stood in the airlock door brandishing her shotgun. Harry moved next, and he pulled the detonator out of his sleeve as he ran.

Ulysses locked eyes on the lead Kempeitai agent as he chucked the brick of explosives into the midst of the agents. Rather than a smooth arc, the explosives sailed in a spiral that sent the brick behind the first row of carts. Khaki-clad men ran from the threat in shameless fear.

Ulysses never turned his back as he boarded the *Lucky Rabbit's Foot*. The Kempeitai were scrambling, trying at once to get to the fleeing fugitives and escape their own imminent demise. Once Ulysses was inside the airlock, Charity slammed the button to seal the door.

Ulysses turned around and followed Charity through the short pressure tent into the *Lucky Rabbit's Foot*. Hikaru and Harry stood in the entryway. Harry had the detonator in his hand with his finger on the button.

Ulysses extended his hand. "Give me the detonator."

Harry looked confused, then did what Ulysses asked. Ulysses took the metal cylinder, then twisted a knob at the bottom. The dull indicator light on the detonator went dead.

Now it was Hikaru's turn to be confused. "You're not setting off the bomb?"

Ulysses shook his head. "We've done enough damage to this station for one day. We made it out safely. That's all that matters." The pressure tent withdrew from the airlock and Ulysses felt the rumble as the ship began to hover off the station's deck.

"Go strap in," Ulysses ordered. Hikaru nodded and moved to one of the crash seats in the crew area, but Harry hesitated. He was looking all around with his mouth agape. He ran his hands along the sides of the bulkhead.

"Harry," Ulysses said.

Harry snapped out of his trance and followed Hikaru to the crash seating. Charity and Ulysses moved up the ladder to the cockpit. "Let's get out of here," Charity said as she strapped into her seat.

Ulysses sat in his now-customary chair behind Val. "Val, you don't know how much—"

Val's face was tight with concentration. "Shut up. Thank me when we survive this."

He pulled back on the yoke and the *Lucky Rabbit's Foot* twisted upward. They were inside the ruins of the old promenade, which was still filled with debris. There wasn't a neat entryway carved into the exterior hull. Rather, the huge breach consisted of a winding pathway of twisted metal that opened to a spot just wide enough for the light transport to squeeze through.

Everyone on the cockpit held their breath as the hull grew larger in the viewport. Val had gotten them inside the station, but getting them out would be at least as tricky. Further complicating matters was the fact that Val didn't dare use his engines for such delicate maneuvers, instead relying on his positioning thrusters to put his ship in the precise location.

Val reached the open portion of hull and tilted down. The nose of the *Lucky Rabbit's Foot* slid through the opening. An alarm sounded and Val made a quick adjustment. Even that wasn't quite fast enough to avoid scraping the paint as the starboard wing bumped against the edge of the station's hull.

Charity looked at her board. "Starboard impact. But it looks like superficial damage." She waited another moment and consulted another screen. "You're clear of the station. Punch it."

Val reached over and ignited his engines. "Going for hard burn."

All six engines roared to life as Val hit the throttle. The sudden acceleration forced Ulysses back against his restraints, but he was prepared for it. Within a minute, the gravity drive was active. Thirty seconds after that, the *Lucky Rabbit's Foot* was nothing more than a memory to the inhabitants of Angel Station.

CHAPTER EIGHTEEN

ONCE they were safely away from Angel Station, Val turned the control of the *Lucky Rabbit's Foot* to the ship's computer. He leaned his head back against the headrest and let out a deep breath. Then he unhooked his restraints and rose to his feet.

Val moved behind his seat, then looked down at Ulysses. "That's twice I've saved you now."

Ulysses met his gaze without blinking. "Are you going to hit me again?

"Maybe," Val said. "Depends on if you lie to me again." He gestured to his wife. "We risked our lives for you. Again. I'd say we deserve some answers."

Ulysses nodded. "I agree. In fact, it's time I explained everything." He stood and moved past Val to the pilot's console. He pressed the button for the internal comm and said, "Harry, Hikaru, please assemble in the mess. We need to talk."

Ulysses, Charity, and Val made their way through the ship to the dining area. Ulysses refused to say anything more until they arrived. This was a revelation that everyone needed to hear.

Harry was already seated at the round table when they arrived. Hikaru was standing near a metal cabinet bolted onto the port bulkhead.

Harry stood when Charity entered the room. He extended his hand. "You must be the missus I've heard about," he said. "Pleasure to meet you."

Charity, initially taken aback by the greeting from this wild man, took his hand. "Please, call me Charity. You must be Harry Lee. My husband mentioned you."

"Did he, now?" Harry glanced at Val. "And how is our Mr. Tanner these days?"

"Irritated," Val said. "And hoping for some answers."

"Take a seat," Ulysses said. "I wanted everyone here so I didn't have to give this speech multiple times."

Charity, Val, and Harry sat down around the table. Hikaru remained in place against the bulkhead, but Ulysses had his attention. Once everyone was settled, Ulysses stood on the side of the table opposite Hikaru so he could face the whole crew at once.

"Okay, Yule," Val said. "Talk. Why did you need Harry? What's really going on here?"

Harry raised his hand. "I can answer the first part," he said. "Major Walden needs someone who can mine in microgravity."

"But why?"

"Dunno." Harry scratched his beard. "But it could be because he said he found Newton's Moon."

Val shook his head and climbed out of his seat. "I knew I shouldn't have gone back."

"Val, sit down," Ulysses said.

Val slammed his hands on the table and leaned toward Ulysses. Charity and Harry jumped at the impact, but Ulysses and Hikaru remained still. "The Kempeitai will figure out which ship got you off Angel Station," Val said. "Unless I want to end up in a secret prison strapped to electrodes, I may as well kiss Yu-Kiang goodbye. Savimbi wants us all dead, so Ranginui is also off-limits. You ruined our lives."

He glared at Ulysses. "But I guess all that is worth it because Ulysses Goddamn Walden did it to find something that doesn't exist."

The two men locked eyes across the table. No one spoke for a long moment.

"I'm sorry," Charity said. Her voice broke the tension brewing in the room. "I don't understand. What's Newton's Moon? Is it a settlement?"

"I've never heard of it," Hikaru said.

"That's just a nickname used by pilots and treasure hunters. It's not a real moon," Ulysses said.

"It's not a real *anything*." Val's voice was thick with anger. "It's a myth. A legend. Something bored spacers talk about when they've run out of meaningful things to say."

"The stories go back as far as interstellar travel itself," Harry explained. "Val's right. It isn't so much a location as much as an idea. The motherlode. Rumors floated around about an asteroid, maybe as big as Deimos, made entirely out of newtonium."

Charity frowned. "But that's impossible. Newtonium is never found by itself, least of all in those amounts. And I thought all the astrophysics guys said there wasn't that much newtonium in explored space, much less in one place."

"That's because there isn't," Val said. "Hundreds of spacers have gone looking for it. Some of them came back broke, wasting all their money on a fool's quest. Most of them never came back at all. Suicide by stupidity."

"That's what I thought, too," Ulysses said. "But there was another inmate at Venus. Professor Eugene Oke, one of the 'astrophysics guys.' I helped keep some of the uglier inmates away from him on his first day inside and we became friends. He showed me the math."

Val slid back into his seat, but he kept his eyes on Ulysses. "And we're going to take the word of some crazy prisoner?"

"No offense," Charity said.

Ulysses smiled at that. "Professor Oke had been a scientific advisor to the Martian Congress before the Centrality invaded. He refused to play by the rules of the new administration and got sent to Venus as an example to the rest of the academic community that free speech was no longer tolerated."

"Not that you're biased," Val muttered.

"Professor Oke told me that he looked at the numbers and came to one conclusion: Newton's Moon was real. And it was here in the Tau Ceti system."

"What made him think that?" Harry asked.

"The orbital mechanics in this system are weird," Ulysses said. "Ryujin, the outermost planet is famously unstable, to the point where establishing even orbital cities is too expensive to be worth the investment. Professor Oke said that the problem has only gotten worse within the last decade, and he thinks he knows why."

All eyes were on Ulysses as he spoke. Even Val had allowed his glare to simmer into grudging interest. "Professor Oke's theory was that a sizeable chunk of newtonium had been moving through the system and had begun to tug, however slightly, on Ryujin's orbit."

"But that doesn't make any sense," Charity said. "Newtonium is inert until it's exposed to an electrical current."

"True," Ulysses said. "But Professor Oke said a cloud of ionized plasma could produce similar effects."

"The Tedros Cloud." Charity's eyes were wide.

"The what?" Harry asked.

Charity turned her head to look at him. "It's an anomaly on the edge of the system near Chelsea Station. It's a field of ionized plasma that spans millions of kilometers. And that's just the portion that lies within the boundaries of the system. It's a tiny fraction of a much larger plasma cloud that stretches for lightyears into the void between stars. It's one of the weirder spots in explored space. I use that term loosely since people tend to avoid the Cloud. No one knows why it exhibits such high amounts of ionization despite being so far from the system's star. The prevailing theory is that the Tau Ceti system was on track to become a binary system, but the second star failed to materialize. The Tedros Cloud is simply the remaining stellar material from that failure."

"The professor had some thoughts on that, as well," Ulysses said. "But I couldn't figure out anything he was talking about. What's important to us is that the Tedros Cloud has some latent electrical properties, enough to generate an effect on newtonium. It wasn't enough to produce stable results, but stable results weren't what the professor was seeing."

"This professor doesn't sound too stable, either," Val commented.

Ulysses took a slow breath. "I wasn't convinced either. When I got out of that prison, I wasn't coming here on a treasure hunt. I simply wanted a fresh start. But then I saw the information on that data core and I realized that the professor was right. The navy had sensor records of an uncharted gravitational anomaly within the Tedros Cloud."

"You mean the data core that nearly got us all killed?" Val asked.

"It still might, for all we know," Charity added. "Savimbi's hardly the forgiving type."

"Yes, that data core. Why do you think I wanted to keep it out of his hands? Imagine what would happen if a warlord like Buti Savimbi seized control of the largest reserve of newtonium in explored space."

"There'll be no living with him after that," Val agreed.

"But doesn't this Savimbi still have the core?" Harry asked. "Once he figures it out, won't he be going after it?"

"For that matter," Charity added, "why hasn't the Centrality already sent a fleet in to claim it?"

"During the escape from Ranginui, Walden managed to slag the data core," Hikaru said. "Savimbi won't be an immediate contender, but I would caution against underestimating him."

"And as for the Centrality, it's doubtful that they know what they found. This wasn't a record from a formal astrological survey. It was a brief contact in the middle of the plasma cloud by the destroyer *Antonia Estrada*. An ionized plasma cloud would play havoc with a ship's sensors, and they likely wrote it off as a false contact."

Ulysses leaned on the table. "But here's where the story gets interesting. The *Antonia Estrada* was only in the Tedros Cloud as a shortcut to get to Chelsea Station. But the destroyer never arrived. The last known communication from the ship was that automated sensor update. After that, it's like she jumped into a black hole."

"Well, that's not spooky," Charity said.

"It's a nice story," Val said. "But, like Hikaru said, you slagged the data core. Unless you plan to break into a naval outpost to recover another one, we don't have the sensor data to find this supposed contact." He tilted his head toward his wife. "Like Charity said, the Tedros Cloud is millions of kilometers across. Our grandchildren would die of old age before they'd have a prayer of just stumbling onto it. It's a shame, too. If anyone could pull something like that off, it would have been—"

Ulysses tossed his tablet onto the table. It skittered across the surface, stopping just shy of Val's lap.

Val reached down and picked it up. "You." He studied the tablet for a moment, then looked at Ulysses. "You bastard. You made a copy, didn't you?"

Ulysses grinned. "Not of the whole core. Just the part I needed. I have the coordinates of the sensor contact and the flight path of the *Antonia Estrada*. Between the two pieces of information, we should be able to pin down a reasonable search area."

The smile faded from Ulysses's face. "I've laid it all out for you. But I won't make the decision for you." He swept the room with his gaze, meeting each person's eyes in turn. "If you want out, you have every right. But, if you go with me, we're in this all the way."

Ulysses put his hand palm-down on the table. "Who's with me?"

Harry laid his hand on top of Ulysses's. "I'm in."

Hikaru stepped forward and followed Harry's lead. "I've come this far."

Charity moved her hand forward but held it a few centimeters above the others. She looked to her husband. "Val? I'm not going to do this without you."

Val considered them all, arms crossed in front of him. "You're crazy. You're all crazy." He reached out and took his wife's hand. "Aw, hell. Someone has to keep you idiots alive." He put his hand, still holding Charity's, on the pile. "We're in."

CHAPTER NINETEEN

ULYSSES climbed the ladder into the cockpit as the *Lucky Rabbit's Foot* came out of its grav jump. Val didn't turn around, but he said, "Hey. How'd you sleep?"

Ulysses rubbed his eyes. "All right, I guess. I could hear Harry muttering to himself outside my compartment the whole time. They must have done a real number on him in the Kuiper Belt."

Val draped one arm across the back of his chair. It was just the two of them in the cockpit for the moment. "Yeah. From what I heard, he was considered a 'special combatant' because of his status as medic. Instead of executing him or locking him up on Venus, he was shipped to the edge of the Solar system."

Ulysses nodded. "That much I'd heard. Had him breaking rocks by hand."

Val looked at Ulysses. "That's the thing. He wasn't supposed to be part of the forced labor detachment. He was sentenced to what was effectively extreme community service as a 'volunteer' medic for the prisoners. But the files were corrupted during transmission and the warden assumed he was just another convict. I don't know how long the poor guy was stuck out there before they realized their mistake, but he moved out here to Tau Ceti three years ago."

"And you never bothered to look him up in all that time?" Ulysses asked.

Val shrugged. "Why would I? I was trying to leave that life behind me."

Ulysses barked out a laugh. "And look how well that turned out."

Val smiled at that. "I did my best." His console chirped. He examined his display, and his eyes tightened with concern.

"What is it?" Ulysses asked.

"Radiation spike," Val said. He pointed to the viewports, which were still encased in armor. "We'll be fine as long as we stay inside the ship. But it's driving our sensors crazy."

An alarm sounded. Val gripped the yoke and jerked the ship to the side. Ulysses felt the dull vibration of the auto-cannons firing beneath his feet. "What's happening?"

Val clenched his teeth. "Rock. Big one, too. Just popped up out of nowhere. The sensor feed was nothing but white noise, and by the time it came up on visual it was damned close. Thank God the AKER doesn't seem to be affected, otherwise I'd turn this ship around and never look back. I don't care how much money we're talking about. I'm not diving into a cloud of asteroids and debris without having any way of protecting myself."

Charity clambered up the ladder. "I thought I heard the auto-cannons. Are we in trouble?"

Val shook his head. "Not anymore. Rock nearly clipped us. Can you see if you can clean up the sensor feed?"

Charity slid into her chair. The sensor feed was little more than a field of static. "Wow. That's ugly. If Newton's Moon is out here, it's no wonder no one's found it. We'd almost be better off opening the viewports and just eyeballing it."

Harry's head popped up into the cockpit. "Do you guys hear that?"

Val flipped a pair of switches. "Yes, Harry. It was just the AKER taking out a stray rock."

Harry climbed into the cockpit, then sat so his feet dangled in the ladder well. "Not that. I mean the voices."

Everyone was silent for a long moment. The only sounds came from the ship's computer. "I don't hear anything," Charity said.

"Huh," Harry said. "I could have sworn I heard whispering."

A red light flashed on Val's console. "AKER's out."

"What?" Ulysses asked. "How?"

"I don't know."

Charity examined her screen. "I don't see a fault. It's probably just this radiation messing with the external connections. The AKER is fine, but our indicators are giving us false returns."

Val shook his head. "I'm not risking it." He pulled the yoke hard and the ship began to bank to starboard.

"Val," Ulysses said. "You heard Charity. It's fine. We can't give up now."

"I can do whatever the hell I want," Val countered. "This is *my* ship. I make the calls. You're not in charge now, Ulysses. We tried that a decade ago. And do you remember what happened when we let you lead?"

"Val, don't do this," Charity said.

"Our friends died," Val said. "And for what? For a government that turned its back on us? For a war we couldn't hope to win?"

Ulysses's face darkened. "Our friends died because you weren't there. You could have gone with us to Olympus Mons. We could have escaped to fight another day. To live another day. But we were stuck there because you abandoned us."

Val leapt out of his chair and jabbed his finger in Ulysses's chest. "I warned you that Olympus Mons was a trap, but you were too arrogant to listen. You could have gone with me instead of leading your men into such an obvious set-up."

Harry was still seated on the edge of the ladder well. He let out a sudden shriek. "How can you not hear it?" he screamed. "The voices . . ." He gripped the sides of his head and his face twisted in pain. "Turn around. Turn around. Turn around."

"Look at what you did," Ulysses said.

"What I did?" Val scoffed. "You're the one who dragged Harry into this in the first place. This whole thing is your mess. Just like before, you made a rash decision and then expect everyone else to clean it up."

Charity looked at her console. "Guys."

No one heard her over their own shouting.

"—can't believe that you would blame me for—"

"—dead and you can't handle the responsibility—"

"Turn around. Turn around. Turn around."

"Guys!" Charity yelled, her voice carrying over the din. Everyone stopped and looked at her. "We have something."

Ulysses, Val, and Harry raced toward her console and crowded over it. She pointed to her display. "Gravitational surge at the edge of sensor range."

Val rolled his eyes. "It's just another false contact."

Charity shook her head. "No. It's consistent, but the computer can't figure out what it is. The closest match is a ship with a critically damaged gravity drive."

"Or an asteroid made of newtonium." Harry's eyes were wide, but the crazed emotion was replaced by sharp focus.

"We did it," Val said. He covered his mouth and let out a gasp. "My God, we really did it."

Ulysses held up a hand. "Hold on. Don't spend your fortune just yet. We don't know for sure this is what we're looking for."

"Come on, Yule," Val said. "This was your idea to start with. Can't you get excited like the rest of us?"

"Oh, I'm excited. I'm just trying to figure out the catch." Ulysses smiled. "Still think I'm crazy?"

Val nodded. "Absolutely. But you're not wrong. This matches everything you told us. It's off the reported coordinates, but it makes sense there would be some drift since that destroyer first spotted it. This is it."

"Newton's Moon," Harry said. His voice was touched with awe.

Then the red light on Val's console turned off. The AKER system was back online.

And it started screaming an alert.

"What the hell is that?" Harry asked.

Val jumped back into his seat. "Harry, get back down and strap in. Tell Hikaru to do the same. We're going to be moving around, and I don't want you pulverized if it's too much for the gravity drive to handle."

Harry didn't argue. He gripped the sides of the ladder and swung over, sliding down to the lower deck. Ulysses hooked into his crash webbing. "Another rock?"

Val frowned. "I don't know. AKER just picked up something headed our way and fast." He pushed the yoke forward and the *Lucky Rabbit's Foot* went into a steep dive. "Damn it."

"What?" Charity asked.

"It's following us. Can't get confirmation, but it's acting like a missile."

"How is that possible?" Ulysses asked.

"I don't know, but . . ." Val's voice drifted off. "The contact is gone."

"Another glitch?"

Val sat back in his seat and took a deep breath. "Possibly. But it seems like—"

The alarm screamed again.

"Six contacts," Charity said, reading her own display. "Confirmed missiles."

"Where the hell are they coming from?" Val growled. He punched the button for the internal comm. "Emergency.

Emergency. Prepare vac suits immediately." He reached under his seat and pulled out the distinct orange garment. Ulysses and Charity did the same.

It only took them a few seconds to pull the suits over their clothes and establish a seal. If the ship lost pressure or atmosphere, they would need the suits if they wanted to make it out alive.

Val didn't wait for everyone to get strapped into their seats before he whipped the ship around. The artificial gravity held, so the maneuver was minimally felt inside the ship. The *Lucky Rabbit's Foot* spiraled into a corkscrew away from the incoming threats.

"Thank God you picked up those countermeasures on Ranginui," Val said. His voice was tinny coming out through the mask of the vac suit instead of through the internal comm. "Dump 'em."

Charity nodded and hit a button on her panel. Thin slits at the rear of the ship slid open and spewed a few dozen metallic rods. They spread behind the ship. Val immediately spun away from the collection of devices intended to draw the missiles away from the ship.

The rods were designed to distract a wide variety of the most popular missile guidance systems. Some of the rods were signal emitters for missiles that tracked electronic emissions. Others were visual dazzlers that produced laser pulses to blind missiles that relied on visual scans. A few of the rods disintegrated into minute clouds of reflective dust to disrupt missiles that carried internal lidar tracking. And others were old-fashioned flares that used a magnesium-based chemical compound, combined with an oxidizer that allowed it to burn in vacuum, to fool heat-seeking missiles.

Charity watched the progress of the incoming missiles on her screen. "Splash one," she said. "Wait. Two. They hit the countermeasures."

"And the rest?" Ulysses asked.

Charity bit her lip. "Another missile is just flying straight into the void."

"This plasma cloud can't be any better for their sensors than it has been for ours," Val said. "But that leaves three missiles left within the threat envelope." He kicked the ship around so that the nose was pointed toward the approaching missiles. He put his thumb on the trigger on his yoke. "AKER is online."

Beep beep beep.

"They're closing in fast," Charity said.

"I see them," Val replied.

Beeeeep.

Val pushed the trigger, sending a burst of explosive shells to intercept the oncoming missiles.

"You got one." Charity said.

Beeeeep.

There was a second burst from the auto-cannons.

"You got another one. But that leaves—"

Charity didn't have time to finish before the final missile struck home. The countermeasures and plasma cloud must have had some effect because it wasn't the instant kill shot it should have been. The warhead detonated a little outside the ideal kill radius, but destructive shards spread out in a deadly spray all the same. These weren't random chunks of metal but rather shrapnel designed specifically to puncture the armored hulls of spaceships.

The ship shuddered like a wounded animal. The groan of the engines could be felt as well as heard inside the cockpit. Charity checked her screen. "We've been hit!"

"How bad?" Val asked.

Charity gave him a look. There were tears in her eyes. "She's hurt, Val. Hurt bad. Upper engines are scrapped, and I'm getting decompression alerts from the cargo bay. The dorsal radiator is just . . . gone."

A second groan tore through the ship like a wave, and Val felt a familiar sense of nausea surge in his stomach. Small, unsecured items began to float inside the cockpit. "And the gravity drive is down. Damn it!" he slammed his palms onto his console.

"It could be worse," Ulysses said. His tone was low and calm, the voice of reason to offset rising panic. "We're alive and we still have most of our engines."

"Even if I redline our remaining engines, there's no way we can reach a settled planet before our life support runs out."

"Not to mention the fact that, without a gravity drive, maintaining that level of acceleration for that long will kill us all long before we suffocate," Charity said.

"That's why we need to pull a hard burn for Chelsea Station and put out an emergency broadcast. We're only a couple AU from the main travel lanes. Someone is bound to hear it and check it out."

"What if the Centrality picks it up?" Val asked.

Ulysses shrugged. "So what? We haven't done anything wrong. Certainly nothing they'd know about. We'd just be another wayward ship that took damage after a bad grav jump."

"But what if they were the ones firing at us in the first place?" Val asked.

"Why would they do that?" Ulysses asked.

"If it's not the Centrality, who else could it be?" Charity added.

As if to answer her question, the sensor screen on her console lit up. She bent over the display, then frowned. "Is that what I think it is?"

Val and Ulysses were looking at the same feed she was seeing. There was another contact, much larger than the missiles, which had appeared well within the edges of the sensor envelope. Even ships traveling in from a grav jump were moving much slower than the speed of light and could be detected by lidar at extreme range. But this ship remained cloaked by the sensor-damping properties of the Tedros Cloud.

"I can't tell for sure," Val said. "It's only showing up as an echo on the scope."

"Wait," Ulysses said. "Right there. We had a solid lock, but we lost it again."

"The computer will have processed it, anyway," Charity said. "Let me bring it up." She accessed the ship's simulated intelligence and had it recreate the sensor profile for the brief contact. She snapped her head to look at Ulysses. "What the hell?" she breathed.

Ulysses looked at the information and shivered. "It's the *Antonia Estrada*," he said. "She never left."

"Then this *is* the Centrality," Val said.

"The official report said she was believed to be lost with all hands," Ulysses said. "But it wouldn't be the first time the Centrality used misinformation to their advantage."

The ship reappeared on the scope. It was moving closer. "What do we do?" Charity asked.

"We run," Val said. He looked to Ulysses, expecting an argument.

But Ulysses was in complete agreement. "We run. She stopped launching missiles, so it's possible the captain believes that we were destroyed. Their sensors can't be doing any better than ours are in this plasma cloud. Our only hope is to not be where they expect us to be."

"Right," Val nodded. "Get ready. Even with two engines out, this burn is going to hurt."

Charity nodded. Ulysses said, "Go."

Val activated his vac suit's microphone. "Harry, Hikaru, I pray to God that you're still with us. We are being pursued by a Centrality destroyer and have suffered damage. We are burning toward Chelsea Station, but without the gravity drive this could kill us if we keep it up for too long. Stay secure and prepare for hard burn."

He threw the throttle to maximum and felt his eyeballs try to pull out through the back of his skull. It felt like someone had dropped the entire ship onto his chest. Black spots swam at the corners of his vision.

Fighting the pressure, he turned his head to look at his wife. He watched as she struggled to maintain consciousness under the strain of their rapid acceleration. His bones and muscles were on fire with pain, but he pushed it aside. He still had a job to do.

Charity's console chirped, but she was on the ragged edge of passing out. Val used the keypad on his armrest to pull the data onto his screen. He looked at it, fully expecting the sensor alert to be a new batch of missiles. Instead, a red-tinted sphere appeared at the edge of the scope. It was small, not quite as large as Pluto, but it held a trace atmosphere. Nothing breathable, but in their vac suits they wouldn't need to breathe the planetoid's air.

Val frowned, and even that exertion cost more than he would have expected. During his years in the Tau Ceti system, he had never heard of any sizeable planetoid beyond Ryujin. But it *had* been surveyed, and a single word appeared next to the dwarf planet: Uaigneas.

To his left, his wife's eyes fluttered closed. Val could hear Ulysses behind him as he made weak gasps of pain. He was the only one left fully awake in the cockpit, and he could feel the pressure starting to drive the blood from his brain.

He typed orders into the computer, transferring control to the ship's SI. He gave the ship a simple command: reach Uaigneas at all speed.

Val could feel himself slipping away. The last thing that he saw before losing consciousness was an update on the sensor display. It read "Research Station Uaigneas. Population: Unknown."

Then all was darkness.

CHAPTER TWENTY

ULYSSES opened his eyes. He struggled to remember what had happened to lead him to this point. The memories were fuzzy, as if covered by a layer of gauze. Then impressions began to form. These slowly coalesced into the solid shapes of reality.

Venus. Port Tew. Ranginui. Angel Station.

Val. Charity. Hikaru. Harry.

The *Antonia Estrada.*

Ulysses bolted upright to find himself, to his complete shock, in a genuine bed. The room was cold, but Ulysses was covered by a thick fur blanket. Beneath the blanket, Ulysses had been stripped to his undergarments. His head pounded with a dull ache, and when he put his hand to his forehead he felt the adhesive of a bandage across his temple.

As his eyes adjusted to the darkness, he began to pick out the details of his room. His bed was small but comfortable, and the frame appeared to be hand-carved from wood. The room itself was devoid of any ornamentation save for a crucifix on the wall across from the bed. A squat nightstand against the wall beside the bed held a single lamp and a worn Bible. Beyond that sat a simple chair, and Ulysses could see his clothes folded neatly on top of it.

Ulysses flipped on the lamp and slid out of the bed. He grabbed his clothes from the chair and started to get dressed. Just as he was buttoning his pants, the door to his room opened.

Ulysses, still shirtless, spun around to see a man enter the room. While Ulysses looked younger than his thirty-six years, a side effect of the transformative surgeries that allowed him to assume his new identity, he guessed that the stranger was roughly the same age. His plain attire matched the spartan décor. His brown robes and leather boots looked hand-made, just like the bed. Another wooden crucifix, this one much smaller than the one mounted on the wall, hung from a cord around the man's neck.

"Good," the man said. "You're awake." If he felt awkward about walking in on Ulysses half-dressed, he didn't show it. For his part, Ulysses was accustomed to changing clothes in front of other people. It was an expected part of life aboard a small transport with a dozen other soldiers. "The others will want to see you."

Ulysses frowned. "Others?"

"Your friends," the man said.

An electric shock ran through Ulysses at the news. "They're alive?"

The man nodded. "Yes. How much do you remember?"

"Our ship . . ."

Ulysses stopped himself from going further. He didn't know this man. What if he was working with the *Antonia Estrada*? Furthermore, what if he knew nothing about the destroyer in the plasma cloud but felt forced to report an attack to the government? Ulysses didn't need official attention. Even if the destroyer had gone rogue, he didn't need investigators wandering around the Tedros Cloud. Not when he was so close.

"We came out of grav jump into the plasma cloud," he finished. He wasn't sure what the others had said, so he didn't want to invent a contradicting story that could get them all in trouble. Best to keep this as basic and true as possible. "Our sensors were basically useless, and something hit us. The last thing I remember is making a hard burn for Chelsea Station. Is that where we are?"

"No. You are still quite a distance from Chelsea. You are on a world known as Uaigneas, a dwarf planet at the edge of the Tau Ceti system."

"I've never heard of it."

That drew a smile. "Not many have. Get dressed. Your friends are waiting."

Ulysses tossed on his shirt and jacket. He turned off the lamp, then followed the man through the door. Outside the room, the architecture changed. Whereas the décor of his room had been all earthy browns and dark yellows, the corridor outside was stark white. The roof of the corridor was curved and had support arches every five meters. There were doors on either side of the corridor, and Ulysses could only assume they led to rooms similar to his.

"What is this place?" Ulysses asked.

The man glanced over his shoulder. "This was a research facility built by the early colonists to study the Tedros Cloud."

"You're a scientist?"

The man let out a quiet laugh. "No. The scientific expedition left decades ago. The facility was abandoned, but still viable. It's a basic dome colony, sturdy and functional."

Ulysses ran his hand along the wall. "I thought this looked familiar. It's like the first settlements on Mars."

"You've been to Mars?" the man asked. Ulysses nodded. "What's it like?"

The question gave Ulysses pause. How did he explain it to someone who had never been there? How did he describe the lush greenery of Blackwell Park, one of the largest botanical gardens in mankind's history? How did he convey awe-inspiring sight of Olympus Mons rising into the heavens? How did he translate the center of culture and trade that was Utopia?

How did he explain his home? It was everything he had fought to protect. It was everything he found right in the universe.

And all of it had turned to ash on that fateful day on Olympus Mons. His homeworld had abandoned every ideal it held most dear in the vain hope that the predators that stalked the stars would spare them. Everything he loved there was gone. But the memories remained.

"It's beautiful," he said at last. "I was born there. We made field trips to Kitrell's Landing when I was a kid. I recognize the architecture." Kitrell's Landing was the first permanent colony on the Martian surface. It was named for Courtney Kitrell, the first human to set foot on Mars. It was nothing more than a tourist destination now, but it was a source of pride for all Martians.

They emerged from the corridor into one of the facility's wide domes. The ceiling was eight meters overhead and featured glowing panels that provided illumination as well as some heat for the open space. The dome appeared to be a common room that was currently set up in a hybrid of cafeteria and chapel, with rectangular tables and benches along Ulysses's right and a pulpit and small altar to the left.

Val, Charity, Harry, and Hikaru were gathered around one of the tables with trays of food. More men in brown robes walked around the space, but none of them seemed to be keeping a watchful eye on their guests. If this was a Centrality prison, it was the weirdest one Ulysses had ever seen.

Charity spotted Ulysses and gave him a cheerful wave. She patted an empty spot on the bench next to her. Ulysses took her up on the offer and slid into the seat.

"You're awake," she said. She slid her tray of food to him. It held a half-eaten slice of toast and a bowl of thick chili. "Here. Eat something."

Ulysses held up his hand. "No. Thank you. I'm not going to take your food."

"Of course not," the stranger said. "I will be right back." He walked toward a small swinging door that separated the dining area from the small kitchen.

When he was out of earshot, Ulysses whispered, "What's going on? Where are we?" Val shrugged. Hikaru and Harry both shook their heads. "Okay. Have any of you heard of a dwarf planet called Uaigneas?"

Val's eyes lit up. "That's right. The computer picked up a planetary body on the edge of the Tedros Cloud. We were beginning to black out, so I set the computer to set us down here."

"But what is this place?" Charity asked.

"Feels like I'm back in Catholic school again," Val said.

"Yeah. It's odd," Ulysses said. "Do any of you get the impression these guys knew about the *Antonia Estrada*?"

"No," Harry said. "But we haven't been holding any long conversations with our hosts, either."

"Just be careful," Ulysses said. "Stick to the basics of our story. We're lost travelers and our ship was damaged. If we're lucky, this place has an emitter relay we can use to contact Chelsea Station. We should still have enough money to afford a tow to a shipyard and the repairs we'll need."

"You're not thinking of going back out there, are you?" Val asked.

Ulysses nodded. "Why not?"

"Why not? How about the missile-spewing death machine that—"

Val stopped talking as the robed man returned with a tray of food. He set it down in front of Ulysses along with a spoon for the chili. "My apologies. We consume only what we can grow here, but you are free to eat as much as you'd like."

"You're too generous," Ulysses said. Despite his reluctance to accept Charity's offer, Ulysses was starving. The chili had no meat, which made sense if what the stranger said about self-sufficiency was correct, but the vegetables were fresh and delicious. It was hardly the fresh steak dinner served on Ranginui, but his host had already proven to be infinitely better company.

Between bites, Ulysses said, "So you're not a scientist. But what exactly are you? Why are you here?"

The stranger sat down. "My name is Fernando Garza. Like you, I was a traveler who found himself stranded out here. It was the grace of God that led me here, and the grace of these men that allowed me to make it my home."

"And who are these men?" Charity asked.

"Refugees. Pilgrims. Seekers of God." Garza sighed. "When the current empire rose to power, the so-called 'Eternal Dragon' banned any organized religion that did not conform to the state's demands. These men fled persecution and made their way here. They reclaimed this old scientific outpost and turned it into a monastery where they could worship God in peace."

"And you believe in their God?" Harry asked.

"I should have died out there in the void. But I survived. So, yes, I believe in God. And I believe that He still has a purpose for me." He gestured around the table. "Just as He has a purpose for all of you. In time, I hope you will come to accept that."

Ulysses frowned. "What do you mean, 'in time?' Are you trying to keep us here?"

Garza held up his hands. "You misunderstand. I am not attempting to hold you against your will. But your ship crashed on the bluff just outside the monastery. It is heavily damaged, and I do not know if it will fly again."

Charity gasped and Ulysses saw an expression of pain flicker across Val's face. "We have to try. It's not safe for us here. And I don't want our presence to draw you into our trouble."

"I wish you would reconsider," Garza said. "But everyone must find God in their own way." He paused. "Perhaps there is a way for you to get off-world safely."

"You have a ship?" Ulysses asked.

Garza shook his head. "No. The best we have is a small orbital flyer, but it isn't built for deep space. The ship that carried these pilgrims here was torn apart and used to restore the facility's operations. But there is another ship out there. The freighter *Eiyachu* crashed here much like you did. In another life, I was her junior engineer. Perhaps we could cannibalize the parts you need to restore your ship to working order."

"If you came here on a freighter, what happened to the rest of your crew?" Hikaru asked.

Garza hesitated. "They . . . did not survive."

The table was silent for a long moment. "I'm sorry to hear that," Charity said. "And we would be grateful for any assistance you could provide."

Garza rose to his feet. "I will speak to the abbot and secure the equipment we will need. I am sorry that you must leave so soon, but you will always be welcome here if you choose to return."

He started to walk away, then turned back to face the table. "God brought you here for a reason. Perhaps you should ask yourself what that is."

CHAPTER
TWENTY-ONE

VAL sat in the rear segment of the sealed rover that had been adopted by the monks. With him in the rear compartment were Charity, Harry, and Hikaru. Ulysses sat up front with Garza. He had offered the seat to Charity, but she had elected to stay with her husband.

The impact site was only a short distance from the collection of domes that made up the monastery. The *Lucky Rabbit's Foot* must have detected the facility and attempted to come in for a landing, but the damage had prevented her from achieving a clean touchdown.

When they reached the site, Val opened the hatch and hopped out onto the rocky surface of the dwarf planet. Like the rest of the crew, he wore the standard orange vac suit while outside of the monastery. Gravity was incredibly low, and each move had to be taken with care to avoid careening across the landscape.

The *Lucky Rabbit's Foot* had landed on its belly and carved a short trough on impact. When Val first saw the extent of the damage to his ship, cold rage settled in his gut. The upper engines were still attached, but ugly gouges pierced the outer casing and exposed the power transfer cables. They had been lucky. If the ship's SI hadn't automatically shut down power flow to the upper engines, the weakened cables would have vented thrust through the cracks in the casing. The engines could have exploded, taking half the ship with them and leaving the rest to drift in space forever.

The hull on the bottom of the ship was dented and scratched from the impact, but everything appeared to be structurally sound. The belly armor of Jackrabbit transports, particularly those retrofitted as troop transports, was outstanding for its size and was the only reason the ship hadn't broken up on impact. The front landing skid was bent and the ship's nose dipped into the rocky soil. The armored curtains were still lowered, which meant that the cockpit was still sealed against vacuum.

But the auto-cannons had caught on an outcropping during the descent and were little more than dangling wires. The starboard stabilizing fin, too, had taken damage on impact and was twisted at an odd angle. Until he was sure that the engine mounted within the fin hadn't been ruptured, Val didn't dare put any power through it.

That left the *Lucky Rabbit's Foot* unarmed and with half of its engines unusable. Despite these problems and all the cosmetic damage, the real problem was going to be the gravity drive. Without it, they might as well simply abandon any hope of leaving Uaigneas.

Val turned to see the wreckage of another ship roughly a kilometer away. Unlike the *Lucky Rabbit's Foot*, the gray-green hull that jutted out from the rocks was a tail-lander. Artificial gravity had made belly-landers like the *Lucky Rabbit's Foot* the most popular option for spacers, but tail-landers had the benefit of reducing power requirements for the gravity systems while under power. The freighter was much larger than Val's light transport, and from the angle of the wreck Val knew that a considerable portion of the ship had to have been scattered across the surface of Uaigneas. Val just hoped that enough of the freighter had survived to be useful.

Garza may have adapted to the life of a monk, but he certainly knew his way around starships. Between his knowledge and Charity's expertise, the repairs on the *Lucky*

Rabbit's Foot went rapidly. The rest of the crew helped where they could, hauling equipment and removing ruined pieces to clear space for replacements.

To keep the work flowing, they worked in shifts. Garza oversaw Harry and Ulysses while Val and Hikaru worked with Charity. When one team began running low on oxygen, they would return to the rover to recharge while the second team went out to resume the work. It was a tedious process, but they were making progress.

After five hours, the rover's oxygen reserves were depleted. The erstwhile repair crew had to return to the monastery. When they arrived, they were greeted in the rover bay by a somber looking man with a halo of bushy black hair on his head and prominent laugh lines on his wizened face.

"Welcome back, Brother Garza. I trust everything went well."

Garza shrugged out of his vac suit. "As well as expected, Father Abbot. Their ship suffered a great deal of damage, and there is only so much we can do without a proper shipyard. The ship may be spaceworthy, but we did not have enough time to run the proper tests."

Val kicked out of his vac suit and stepped toward the old priest. "Father, I have to thank you for your hospitality. You saved our lives, and we are forever in your debt."

The abbot shared a look with Garza. "There is no need to thank me, my boy. God delivered you to us, and God demands that we show His grace to all who would receive it." The old man frowned. "But we have a problem."

"What's that?" Garza asked.

"A warship just appeared on the scanner. It's headed directly for us."

"Scanner?" Val asked.

Garza nodded. "Yes. As I told your friend, this used to be a scientific facility. My brothers and I have maintained the equipment and have kept up the research. The Tedros Cloud is God's handiwork. By studying it, we can draw closer to Him."

"Huh," Charity said. "You're not exactly the anti-intellectuals the Imperial Palace makes you out to be, are you?" Garza simply smiled.

"I'm sorry, Father," Val said. "But did you say there was a warship? What kind of warship?"

"Brother Muturi was formally a member of the Imperial Navy, and he says it looks like one of the smaller ships," the abbot said. "No larger than a destroyer."

Val glanced at Ulysses. "Do you have any weapons, Father? Anything you can use to defend yourselves?"

The abbot gave him a flat look. "You realize this is a monastery and not a barracks, right?"

Val put his hand up. "I just thought I'd ask. It's time we came clean. We weren't just hit by a random meteoroid. We were here looking for something and we were attacked by a Centrality destroyer called the *Antonia Estrada*."

"You were looking for Newton's Moon," Garza said.

Ulysses's jaw dropped. "How did you know?"

"Because my crew found it five years ago. And it got them all killed."

"We're not going to let that happen to us," Val said.

Ulysses nodded. "Right. We can't fight and we can't run. But maybe we could shut down any emissions and the destroyer will keep moving. We're still not sure what they want, but launching missiles at a seemingly abandoned facility isn't going to give it to them."

The abbot nodded. "I'll shut down the transmitter array and the active sensors. We'll be blind until the ship is right on top of us, but unless they know exactly where to look they should cruise past us without noticing."

"I'll shut down any exterior lights," Garza said. He followed the abbot out of the rover bay. He grabbed a passing monk and held him by his shoulders. "Gather the brothers and meet in the observation room. Make sure all active emissions are disabled."

The monk nodded and ran off to fulfill his task. Garza started to leave the rover bay, but Val called out after him. "What can we do?"

Garza looked over his shoulder. "Pray."

Everyone gathered in the observation room. Decades ago, this room had been built to study an oddity of interstellar space. The monks had adapted it and resumed that study as a form of meditation. Now twenty souls gathered around the terminals, waiting for any sign of the destroyer's approach.

The room was half the size of the common room and was filled with computer equipment and large displays. It hadn't been intended for a crowd like this, and everyone had to watch out for random elbows as they tried to find space.

All of the active sensors were disabled. To an outside observer, the monastery was a dead facility like it had been when the original scientific team left it decades ago. But the passive sensors were still online, scrubbing through the blinding cloud of plasma to find the threat that loomed above them all.

Garza's suggestion in the rover bay hadn't been a simple turn of phrase. He and his fellow monks were deep in prayer, heads bowed and hands clasped around beaded rosaries. One of the monks shifted nervously and fumbled his words and the abbot in charge snapped his eyes open to glare at the younger man.

Oh yeah, Val thought. *Just like Catholic school.*

His mother had been a deeply religious woman, but his father had always scoffed at the faith. "Mankind has reached the stars," he would say. "We are the gods we were always looking for." Of course, that self-styled "god" abandoned his family for a younger woman on Ganymede when Val had been nine years old.

Val always admired his mother's faith, and her religious phrases were familiar to him. Yet, when it came right down to it, he had become just like his father. Val never put his trust in a higher power. There was nothing but cruel, random chance. The best you could do was to tilt the odds in your favor.

Val never abandoned his sense of self for a larger calling. He had only been tangled up in the war by a quirk of fate. He hadn't signed on to be a hero. He was just paying for flight school on the government's tab. He had seen the true believers die all around him while he survived to fly another day. What had their faith gained them?

He told himself that no one was genuinely that altruistic. Everyone had an angle. Everyone had stakes. But as he looked at the monks deep in earnest, heartfelt prayer, he felt the long-dormant sense that something greater than his own understanding was at work.

Val shifted his gaze from the monks to Ulysses. His former commander was leaning over a console, helping a dark-skinned monk interpret the data that was coming into the passive sensors. Ever since Ulysses had reappeared in his life, Val had felt like someone had reopened an old wound. He told himself that seeing Ulysses dragged up the memories of friends who had only died because they followed him into battle. But that wasn't it. Not entirely. Ulysses represented something else. A belief that, maybe, there was a reason they were here.

Maybe Garza was right. Maybe God did have a purpose for them all.

"We've got something," Ulysses said. "Visual scanner just picked it up heading into orbit."

"Brother Muturi, put it on the screen," Garza said.

The dark-skinned monk nodded and typed in a command. A screen in the center of the far wall lit up. It showed the computer-augmented image of a shadowy shape moving against the haze of the Tedros Cloud. The monk shifted the display through the spectrum until the stark outline of a ship appeared.

For being an instrument of destruction, it had a strange sense of grace to it. Wide curved wings formed the front half of the hull and gradually tapered to a narrow tail section. Two large cylindrical engines attached to pylons at the front of the ship provided primary thrust, and the ship had a smaller cluster of engines at the tail of the ship for additional power.

As the ship drew closer, Val could see energy hotspots on the hull where her weapons were located. The brightest sections were thin rectangular banks along the top and bottom of each wing as well as one on the port and starboard sides of the tail. Val knew that these were the ship's Direct-Energy Threat Elimination and Response system, a much deadlier version of the AKER system. Rather than the classic auto-cannon system, however, the DETER system used directed energy bursts to disable and destroy incoming threats. Combined with a ship's onboard AI, those DETER systems made approaching the destroyer a suicide run for any torpedo, drone, or fighter that attempted it.

It was a fraction of the size of the cruiser they had encountered near Bakuwana. It didn't carry the devastating railguns used by the larger ships in the fleet. These ships were designed for fast attack missions, not the brutal slugging matches of cruiser or battleship combat. Instead of railguns, the tail section contained a large collection of launch tubes for the ship's magazine of missiles and torpedoes. The coilguns, auto-cannons, and directed energy banks were merely there to keep the ship alive until it could deliver its payload.

The ship grew ever larger in the visual scanner. It entered low orbit around the dwarf planet. Even the ship's heraldry was visible when the light amplification was activated. The flag of the Centrality was painted on the dorsal side of the ship. The distinctive emblem featured an eight-pointed starburst containing a black circle. That black circle contained a starfield in the background and three white dots of various sizes in the foreground. Val had heard different stories about the meaning of those white dots. Some said they represented Alpha Centauri A and B along with Proxima Centauri, while others said they represented the three star systems occupied by mankind.

Val heard someone gasp when the bold letters beneath the flag became visible: CNS *Antonia Estrada*. It seemed like they had found their missing ship. Or, more accurately, it had found them.

The prayers drifted away until the whole observation room was quiet. Only the hum of the air scrubber and the whirring of the computer broke the silence.

The destroyer loomed over the dwarf planet. It was inverted so that the dorsal half of the ship was facing toward Uaigneas. The warship blotted out the stars as it moved directly above the monastery.

And stopped.

Everyone in the observation room held their breath. Then a peal of high-pitched static came over the comm. Everyone recoiled at the sound. Brother Muturi checked his console and said, "The ship is putting out a broadcast on all open frequencies."

The abbot nodded. "Let's hear it."

Brother Muturi flipped a switch and a voice came over the comm. It was a man's voice, though it was heavily modulated. Whoever it was, they were in the middle of a speech. "—trespassers must surrender. If they are not turned over to my charge within the next ten minutes, all will suffer the consequences."

The color drained from Garza's face. "No. That's not possible."

"We've been hearing that a lot lately," Val quipped.

The monk turned his head to face Val. "You don't understand. That voice belongs to a dead man."

"What?" Ulysses asked. "How do you know that?"

"His name is Thomas Malak." Garza said. There was a hardness in his eyes that surprised Val. "And I'm the man who killed him."

CHAPTER
TWENTY-TWO

"WHAT are you saying, Garza?" the abbot asked. Val noticed the clear absence of the word *Brother*. "What did you do?"

Garza sighed. "When I served aboard the *Eiyachu* as junior engineer, it was the first time I had ever left Dulcinea. I was so proud, so excited. I thought I was going to be doing something good for once in my life."

His gaze shifted around the room. "But then I found out that Captain Thomas Malak was a real piece of work. He was abusive, physically and verbally, to his crew. Once a pipe burst in the corridor to his quarters. He pulled it down to hit me with it. I hadn't been on the ship for three days. I had nothing to do with it, but he took it out on me anyway. When I went to the ship's medic, I found out things like that happened all the time."

"Why didn't anyone report him?" Charity asked.

"To who?" Garza scoffed. "The Imperial Palace? They don't care what a tyrant captain does to his crew as long as he pays the right taxes. But pay was key. The money was incredible. Far higher than average for merchant spacers. I'd been out of engineering school for two months and was making more than chief engineers with years of experience aboard other ships. We kept our mouths shut and took the abuse. Whatever Malak's secret was, it was worth a few bruises and shouting matches."

He lowered his eyes. "But one day I was following an unusual drain on our ship's fuel reserves and I found what the captain had been hiding from us. Somehow Malak had gotten his hands on a bootleg artificial intelligence. I don't mean a ship's normal SI. I mean a full military-grade thinking computer. That gave him his edge."

"If the Centrality found out about that, they'd kill him on the spot," Ulysses said. "It doesn't matter how much he paid in taxes. They'd never allow anyone else to have that kind of advantage."

"Is that what you mean about killing him?" the abbot asked. There was hope in his voice. "Did you report this to the authorities?"

Garza shook his head. "No. God forgive me, but no. I threatened to report it, but Malak offered to pay me triple if I kept quiet. I agreed on the condition that I'd get off as soon as we delivered our run to Chelsea Station. But we never arrived."

"You came here instead," Val guessed.

"As potent as the AI was, it was essentially in its infancy. It had been patched together, hybridized from other systems, and occasionally it made some glaring mistakes. All routes drawn up by the navigation officer were run through the computer to ensure the most efficient travel plan, but this time an error occurred. Instead of putting us close to Chelsea Station, we wound up in the middle of the Tedros Cloud.

"Captain Malak was furious. He was berating the navigation officer, threatening to toss him out the airlock, when the ship's computer picked up a gravitational anomaly."

"Newton's Moon," Harry said.

"Exactly." Garza turned to his abbot and explained. "It's an asteroid made of newtonium. It should be impossible, but I saw it with my own eyes on the visual scanner. It wasn't a phantom contact. It's real."

Val felt something inside of him surge at the news. Even after seeing his own sensor readings, he hadn't been sure. But Ulysses was right. Newton's Moon was out there.

"Before we did anything, the captain needed to make sure that we could get back to civilization with word of our discovery. Since I was the only one who knew about the AI, I volunteered to check on the connections between the computer and the rest of the ship. Some of those connections were on the exterior of the ship, so once I was off the bridge I pulled on a vac suit in case I needed to go for a walk. That decision saved my life."

Garza swallowed hard. Val could see that recounting the story after all these years was taking its toll on him. "While I was examining the cables inside the computer room, Captain Malak had a realization. With the AI integrated into the ship, he didn't really *need* a human crew to get him home. In fact, we were a liability since we could expose his illegal practices. I don't know where he got the implant to control the damn thing, but he was able to issue orders without the rest of the bridge crew overhearing. He left the bridge to 'assist with repairs' and climbed into one of our EVA suits."

Garza closed his eyes and took a deep breath. "Once he was outside, he ordered the AI to vent the ship. I could hear the screams of my shipmates through the comm in my vac suit. They were begging for help. They were begging for God to save them." He opened his eyes and looked at the abbot. "But He didn't."

Silence reigned. "What did you do?" the abbot asked again. This time the accusation was gone.

"I realized that the ship's computer was responsible. I was up to my elbows in circuitry and didn't have time to figure out a clean shut-down. I just tore pieces out of the computer towers until the lights in the room went dark. Then the emergency systems kicked on and air began to circulate in the ship once more. But it was too late for the rest of the crew. I wandered through the ship, hoping to find other survivors. But I was alone.

"I had to act quickly. Once Captain Malak came back onto the ship, I knew I was dead. His suit was built for mining and salvage and the tools at his disposal would cut through my vac suit like it was nothing. I had some sharp pieces of computer tower in my hands, but no proper weapons. Even without his suit, Malak knew how to fight. He would kill me with his bare hands if he needed to. I only had one option."

"You severed his safety line," Ulysses said. Garza nodded. "That must have taken a lot of work without dedicated tools."

"I had enough motivation to make up for the faulty tools," Garza said. "Malak must have, I don't know, 'felt' the AI shut down. He started ranting at me over the comm, screaming about how he was going to murder me and about how he should have killed me on day one. He had gone completely mad. Then the safety line snapped and he was adrift. I ran to the bridge and fired up the engines. I didn't care where I was going. I just had to get away."

Tears streamed down his face. "I watched as a dwarf planet appeared on the scope. I pointed the *Eiyachu* at it and hoped for a quick death. After what I had done, surrounded by the bodies of my friends, I had nothing to live for."

He swept his arms out to indicate his fellow monks. "But I survived. I was shown grace and mercy. I was given a new home. And I have lived on with the knowledge that God let me live for a reason."

The air was heavy with tension. No one spoke for a long minute. Then Brother Muturi held up a hand. "I am sorry, Brother. But the countdown has reached four minutes. What should we do?"

Garza wiped the tears from his eyes with his sleeve. "Contact the ship. Tell them that I am willing to surrender."

"Brother Garza—" the abbot said.

"You can't!" Charity gasped.

"My life has not been my own since I arrived here," Garza said with a sad smile. "God put me here for a reason. I believe that this is it."

"I'm going with you," Ulysses said.

"For God's sake, Yule, stop playing the martyr," Val said.

"I can't ask you to do that," Garza agreed.

"And what if this Malak guy doesn't buy your story?" Ulysses asked. "You have been in this monastery for years. If he asks you simple questions about current events, he'll know that you weren't the one flying the ship he wanted to destroy. Then he'll kill you and wipe out the rest of us anyway. We can't risk that."

"No," Charity whispered. "You can't." She held out her hand, palm down. "We're in this together."

Ulysses's lips tightened. He shook his head. "Not this time, Charity." He looked at Val. "This time I'm letting my team survive. I'm not dragging you into the obvious trap."

"God *damn* it, Yule." Val's voice was trembling.

"He's right," Hikaru said. "There's no guarantee this Captain Malak will buy Brother Garza's story." Val raised his eyebrows at the use of Garza's religious title, but he said nothing. "Major Walden will have his back. Just as he will watch over Walden's."

"If we're lucky, we can talk Malak down," Ulysses said. "But if not, we should at least be able to divert his anger."

"You're going to need all the luck you can get," Val said. He reached into his vest and pulled out his lucky charm. Val tossed it to Ulysses, and he caught it in mid-air. "I'm going to want that back."

Ulysses choked out a laugh. "You got it."

The abbot looked at Ulysses, then at Garza. "God bless you both."

Garza smiled. "He already has, Father Abbot."

CHAPTER
TWENTY-THREE

WHEN newtonium's gravity-influencing properties were first discovered, the media popularized the idea that flying cars and other anti-gravity vehicles would be just over the horizon. The extreme rarity of the substance and the power requirements for maintaining a stable field meant the vision of flying cars on every world would likely never become a reality. But the low gravity of many settled moons meant that even simple chemical engines could be built to provide efficient levels of thrust.

The orbital flyer operated by the monks used these engines to take advantage of the low gravity of the dwarf planet. The flyer was equipped with only stubby wings, but there wasn't enough air pressure to provide the needed lift anyway. Instead, rotating engine nacelles at the ends of the wings provided vertical lift off and landing capability as well as forward thrust.

The flyer was the closest thing to a flying car Ulysses was likely to ever see. The main body of the craft was actually built around the body of a sleek rover that was sealed against vacuum. It featured a wide viewport to allow for maximum visibility. Even though the flyer itself was pressurized, Ulysses and Garza put on vac suits in the event of a breach.

The flyer emerged from the small launch pad at the edge of the monastery. Ulysses was unfamiliar with the operation of such craft, but Garza had experience and was at the controls. While the flyer soared above the monastery to meet with the destroyer, Ulysses pulled Val's rabbit foot out of a small pouch on his vac suit.

Garza spared a glance from the controls. "What is that thing?" his voice carried over their shared comm channel.

"Rabbit's foot," Ulysses explained. "Val keeps it as a charm. It's supposedly lucky."

Garza chuckled. "Not for the rabbit."

"Yeah. I guess not." Ulysses smiled, but it didn't reach his eyes. He tucked the charm away. "I've been meaning to ask you something."

"I have no secrets left," Garza said. "Feel free to ask."

Ulysses crossed his arms. "This Malak guy. You said he could fight. Was he Centrality Navy?"

Garza frowned. "I don't think so. But I didn't meet him until after the Centrality had already moved into the system and forged their partnership with the Eternal Dragon. It's possible he was part of the original crew to move into the system. Why do you ask?"

"Here's what I don't get," Ulysses said. "Malak goes insane and slaughters his crew. You sever his connection to the ship and take off. He's left floating in space forever, the treasure that he killed to acquire just out of reach. That kind of seems like it should be the end of the story."

"That's what I thought for all these years," Garza agreed.

"Then how did he end up on a Centrality destroyer? I mean, it's possible that they picked up a distress beacon, but you said this happened five years ago, right?"

"Correct."

"But, according the records that brought us here, this destroyer came out here for the first time about a year ago. It made an automated sensor report to Fleet HQ, then vanished from the face of the galaxy. There's no way Malak was just floating around out there for four years plotting his revenge."

"It does sound unlikely."

"And let's say, through some incredible string of luck, Malak survived on sheer will until he was picked up by this passing destroyer. He should be sent off to Chelsea Station for debriefing and a nice long chat with some corporate lawyers who represent his insurance agency. Instead, he's still out here, and now he seems to be calling the shots."

The *Antonia Estrada* grew large in the viewport. "What's your point?"

"I don't know," Ulysses said. "But none of this makes any sense. Keep your eyes open."

Garza smiled. "Your ninja friend said we should watch each other's back. Maybe he was right."

"I think he's supposed to be a samurai," Ulysses said. Garza glanced at him and Ulysses shrugged. "Look, I didn't ask. He's deadly in a fight and helped me out of a tight spot. If he wants to play dress up that's his call."

"How open-minded," Garza teased.

The flyer wasn't complicated enough to warrant a simulated intelligence program, but its basic navigational computer beeped a warning. It was receiving coordinates from an external source that was overriding manual input.

"Looks like Malak saw us coming," Garza said.

"Let's hope so. That was the plan, after all."

The thrusters cut out. But instead of falling back toward the surface, the orbital flyer began drifting toward the *Antonia Estrada*. Ulysses's stomach turned upside-down as they entered the gravity envelope of the destroyer. With the flyer fully captured by the more powerful short-range gravity field of the destroyer, the thrusters swiveled to reorient the flyer to its new "down."

The cargo bay of the large ship split open and a robotic arm emerged. It clamped down on the landing strut of the orbital flyer and secured it, slowly pulling it into the open bay.

Ulysses looked up to see the dwarf planet of Uaigneas one last time before the exterior doors sealed.

They had arrived on the destroyer. The question now was what came next.

The robotic arm, at once pulling the orbital flyer down and supporting some of its weight, guided the craft to the deck. The flyer shuddered as the struts connected with the metal plating. There were no lights in the cargo bay, but a green light by the door indicated that it was safe to leave the flyer. Ulysses opened his door and stepped out of the craft.

And immediately tripped over an outstretched arm.

Ulysses landed on his backside. He stared down at the cadaverous arm that had caught his heel. It was attached to a corpse that had been practically mummified by the dry, nearly airless conditions of the cargo bay. The corpse was dressed in dark grey fatigues with subdued rank patches, and a ragged hole above the sternum stained with long-dried blood attested to the cause of death. The dead man's mouth was pulled back in a macabre mask of pain, and one of his teeth gleamed in the light from the head lamp built into Ulysses's vac suit.

"What the hell?"

Garza came jogging around the front of the orbital flyer. "Are you all right?" he asked. His own headlamp was active, projecting a stark beam of white light into the cavernous space. "What—" He froze as he saw the body sprawled out on the deck. "Oh, dear God."

Ulysses propped himself up with his hands and knees, then stood. "I doubt this was His handiwork." Ulysses studied the body for another moment. "Centrality Marine," he stated. "And his gun is missing."

Garza pointed to a spot on the deck a meter away. "Those look like shell casings."

Ulysses tracked Garza's finger. "And more blood."

He took a few steps forward, then recoiled as another corpse sprang into view. Unlike the first man, who had been strewn across the deck, this body somehow remained locked in place balanced on his knees. The man's throat had been torn open almost to the spine. The deep scarlet of his Centrality Navy uniform matched the dried blood that ran down from the wound. The officer's name patch was obscured by blood, but the two black bars and two gold stars on the shoulder boards indicated that the man had reached the rank of commander. On a ship of this size, that would have made him the highest-ranking officer on board.

Ulysses had a sick feeling that he knew why Malak seemed to be running the ship.

Ulysses knelt to examine the body. A pistol lay abandoned by the corpse's right hand. Ulysses picked it up. Empty. He was willing to bet this was the dead Marine's sidearm. That was one riddle solved, anyway.

"What did this?" Garza asked.

"Nothing good."

There was a soft whir of power as the lights inside the cargo bay activated. Ulysses fully expected to find himself surrounded by either Marines or pirates. He snatched the pistol from the deck and held it up defensively. He knew it was empty, but anyone who threatened him wouldn't necessarily have the same information.

The cargo bay was empty.

A bad feeling crawled up Ulysses's spine. He really wished the dead officer hadn't wasted all of his ammunition. He performed a cursory check of the dead Marine, but it appeared that the man had not thought to bring spare magazines with him. That was unfortunate. Ulysses could have gone looking for the ship's arms locker, but that would have been a bad start to the negotiations.

"What do you think?" Garza asked.

"It's possible Malak was picked up by pirates who were fleeing pursuit and he made them a deal."

"And these pirates took over a powerful navy warship?" Garza asked. "And then, after they did that, they simply returned to the Tedros Cloud instead of using their new toy to become rich by plundering the shipping lanes around Ranginui? I don't buy it."

"One thing is certain," Ulysses replied. "We won't find the truth sitting around in here. Come on."

Thomas Malak sat in his space suit and watched the intruders progress through his ship. They were pitiful, worthless creatures. But the man in the brown robes looked familiar.

Something stirred in Malak's memories. Nebulous shapes of events long past began to crystallize into coherent forms. But they were still frustratingly out of reach.

"Captain, they've made it out of the cargo bay and are headed to the bridge." The voice belonged to Malak's Tactical officer. "Shall we seal the door?"

"No," Malak replied. "I want them here. These animals think they can steal what is rightfully mine. I want to hear their excuses before I end their pathetic lives."

"Yes, sir."

"Captain, our return course to Newton's Moon is laid in," the Navigation officer said. "But the debris field was heavier than we anticipated on our way here. We didn't plan to be here this long. If we wait too much longer, we will have to recalculate the path to avoid the hazards."

"Patience," Malak said. He raised one gloved hand. "This will not take long. But this is a lesson all of humanity must learn. Never come between Thomas Malak and his rightful prize."

Malak leaned back in his chair and considered the scene before him. It seemed like he had spent a lifetime adrift in that forsaken plasma cloud. But he had endured. And he would not let anyone threaten what belonged to him ever again.

The fingers of his suit tapped against the armrest of his command chair as he watched the men move through the corridor. Soon he would be finished here. Soon he could return home. The Navigation officer had been right about one thing. He had been gone too long already. But the risk was worth it if he could snuff out these vermin and make an example for the rest.

He simply had to wait. After all that time adrift in space, Malak had become quite adept at waiting.

There were more bodies in the corridor. But, as Ulysses looked at the young woman crumpled on the deck in front of him, he noticed that something was different. Her uniform was pristine, and there was no evidence of blood or any other injuries. Decomposition had been slowed by the conditions on the ship, but Ulysses didn't have the kind of forensic training needed to determine cause of death.

Garza, however, had far too much experience with this particular matter.

"They asphyxiated," Garza said. His voice was cold and distant. "Malak did it again."

It certainly seemed that way, but Ulysses said, "Let's not jump to conclusions. The only way Malak could have done that is by physically overriding the systems, which seems like a difficult task on a secure naval ship."

"The AI could have done it."

Ulysses scoffed. "A Centrality Navy ARTI system? Sure, if he could overcome the layers of defenses surrounding it. Not to mention its own capacity for self-preservation or the fact that the system has failsafes to prevent the computer from taking human lives without a direct order from the command staff. Malak could try it, but he'd be better off trying to take over Yu-Kiang with a screwdriver. The only way to actually command one of these systems is with a cybernetic implant."

Garza nodded. "In the neck of the commanding officer." He pointed behind them to the cargo bay. "That was him back there, wasn't it? The body whose neck had been torn open. What if he had gone hunting for that implant?"

"To do what with it? Those things are genetically tied to their hosts. They're hard-wired into their nervous system. It wouldn't do him any good."

"Unless he found a way to clone that information onto the implant in his own neck."

Ulysses frowned. He hadn't thought about that possibility. It was a reach, but it was the only scenario either of them had discussed that could explain what they were seeing.

"If he tries the same trick again, our vac suits will protect us," Ulysses observed. "If Malak wants to play dirty, I'm perfectly willing to fight back."

"Agreed."

Ulysses decided that he liked this monk. "Come on. The bridge is this way."

"Right. Let's get some answers and put an end to this once and for all."

CHAPTER TWENTY-FOUR

GARZA and Ulysses stood in front of the door to the bridge. Instead of activating it and entering the room beyond, however, Ulysses gestured for Garza to stay back. Ulysses crept up to the door. It wasn't motion activated, so he could approach without worrying about exposing himself to anyone on the other side. He leaned against the metal door and listened.

"Navigation, keep an eye on that clock." Malak's weird, flat voice could be heard through the metal. Ulysses couldn't hear a response, but from what he knew of Centrality bridge design the Navigation station would have been on the other side of the room and likely out of earshot.

Ulysses backed away from the door. "He's in there. And he's not alone. I'd expect a full suite of officers, Centrality Navy or otherwise."

Garza nodded. "I'm ready."

Ulysses reached for the door controls, but the door slid open before he could touch them. Of course. Malak had been watching them since they climbed on board. It made sense he'd be waiting for them to show up here. He must have been watching as Ulysses eavesdropped.

Ulysses had never been on one of these destroyers. They had only deployed at the end of the war, and the Jovian forces never had a chance to capture one, intact or otherwise. His old commando training kicked in, studying every feature and design choice to find any weakness he could exploit.

His expectation had been correct. Despite being a newer ship by almost fifty years, this *Scorpion*-class destroyer shared the same bridge layout of a *Crusader*-class cruiser. That made sense for a standardized crew experience, but Ulysses was surprised that the design hadn't been updated to center around the ARTI computer which had become the beating heart of naval doctrine.

The bridge was laid out in a semi-circle facing wide display screens built to resemble viewports. They weren't really viewports, of course, because those would have been a structural weakness too easily exploited in combat. The various department officers had their stations here, ranging from port to starboard as Engineering, Sensors, Navigation, Tactical, Communication, and Supply. The ship's Helmsman was not a department officer but held a station between the Navigation and Tactical consoles to enable rapid course adjustments in battle.

The captain's station was on an elevated platform above and behind the rest of his officers. His chair swiveled so he could face any department officer without having to move, and his higher position meant that he could keep an eye on all of his officers at once.

The captain's chair was occupied by a figure in an EVA suit at least a generation older than the one Ulysses picked up on Chelsea Station. Its motorized joints whirred with every motion. The chair swiveled slowly as if examining the officers at their stations.

Ulysses hadn't been expecting to see Malak still wearing his EVA suit on board the destroyer. But that part barely registered with him. The thing that stood out the most, to his horror, were the bodies draped over the command stations at the front of the ship. Every one wore the uniform of a Centrality officer. Every one bore bloody gashes where a blade had cut the life from them.

Malak didn't even seem to notice the corpses. "Sensors," he barked from the captain's chair. "Clean up the feed from Zone 3." He paused. "I don't care about the plasma cloud. Get it done." The voice was the same as the one that they heard on the comm in the monastery. At least Ulysses had learned the source of the weird, tinny vibration in his tone.

"What the hell is going on?" Ulysses breathed.

Garza stepped onto the bridge. "Captain Malak? We are here to discuss your terms."

The captain's chair spun around until the suit was facing the two men in the doorway. "Don't be shy. Come on in." The voice somehow became even more threatening. "I have been waiting for you."

Ulysses followed Garza onto the bridge. The sight was almost unbearable, but the vac suit kept the smell out and he managed to keep his gorge from rising. "We're here to discuss the terms of your peaceful departure from Uaigneas."

The man in the suit ignored him. The suit's helmet tilted quizzically as it considered Garza. "You are familiar. What is your name?"

"Garza, sir"

"Garza," the voice droned. "Fernando. Junior Engineer aboard the freighter *Eiyachu*."

Garza stepped forward. The door to the bridge led directly onto the officer's level, so Garza was forced to look up at Malak. From this angle, Ulysses could only see his own reflection in Malak's visor. "That's right, Thomas. It's me."

"Fernando Garza." He said the words faster this time as if processing their meaning. The suit's helmet straightened. "You killed me."

Ulysses frowned in confusion. Garza had said the same thing in the monastery. It was rare for both sides of a murder to be mistaken about the event.

"I'm sorry for everything that happened," Garza said. "I acknowledge my guilt." He gestured to Ulysses. "But these people are innocent. Take your revenge on me, if you must. But let them live. They have done nothing to you."

The suit was motionless. Not in the way a human is motionless, with slight shifts of balance and the movement of breathing. It was utterly, completely still.

"You killed me," the man in the suit repeated. He rose to his feet. "Did you think you could get away with your crimes?"

Ulysses swallowed. This was getting out of hand. He opened his mouth to intervene, but Garza met his eyes and stopped him with a microscopic shake of his head.

"I didn't want to hurt you, Thomas. But you had gone mad with greed. You—"

"*Mad*?" Malak thundered. "The captain is the ship. The ship is the captain. How dare you question *anything* I decide?"

"You slaughtered your own crew."

"They were parasites. They did nothing but feed on my success. I didn't need them. I don't need you."

Garza took another step forward. "You were killing everyone on the ship. You had to be stopped. I wish there was another way. I truly do." A slight smile broke across Garza's face. "But you survived. It's a miracle. God must have had a plan for you."

"God?" Malak mocked. "Aboard this ship, *I* am god. And I will show you the consequence of disobedience." The suit turned to face the officer stations on the starboard half of the bridge. "Tactical, engage nuclear torpedo. You may fire at will."

"No!" Ulysses screamed. He rushed forward, but it was too late. The center display screen changed to show a thermal image of five domes connected by sturdy tubes half-buried in the rock. It was a live feed of the monastery where their friends all waited for the *Antonia Estrada* to leave orbit. From this angle, neither the *Eiyachu* or *Lucky Rabbit's Foot* were visible, but Ulysses knew they were just behind the rocky bluff southeast of the monastery.

Ulysses could only watch in stunned horror as the flare of a torpedo's engine came racing in from the top of the screen. It impacted on the northern edge of the dome complex. The extreme release of energy blinded the thermal imager, but not before Ulysses saw the domes get ripped apart and scattered for kilometers by the force of the explosion. It was an image that was burned into his mind forever.

His hands clenched into fists. In that instant, he vowed that Thomas Malak would never hurt anyone ever again.

Malak didn't seem to pay any attention to him. The man in the suit was wholly focused on the monk in front of him. Ulysses didn't understand what was happening between the two men, but he knew an opportunity when he saw one.

He withdrew from the bridge slowly to avoid attracting Malak's attention. He knew that Malak still had access to the internal cameras, but he hoped that Garza would be able to distract him long enough for him to accomplish one last mission.

He made his way to the rear of the ship. It was time for one final act of defiance.

Garza watched out of the corner of his eye as Ulysses shrunk away from Malak. At first Garza thought he was crippled by his sense of loss, but then Ulysses kept moving until he was outside of the bridge entirely.

Ulysses had a plan.

But for that plan to work, Garza would have to keep Malak occupied. "You didn't need to do that, Thomas," Garza said. His own rage was nearly blinding, but he forced himself to remain focused. "The people down there did nothing to you. They were innocent."

"They threatened everything," Malak said. "It's mine. All of it. And I won't let any of you steal what belongs to *me*."

Garza's voice hardened. "You haven't changed. You're still insane."

The man in the suit sprang forward and vaulted over the railing separating the captain's section from his officers. The heavy suit smashed into the deck, denting the plating on impact.

Garza stumbled back onto the Navigator's console. He managed to catch himself with his hand before his back collided with the corner of the terminal, but it still hurt. He thanked God for his vac suit. Otherwise the stench of death would have been unbearable. Perhaps that was why Malak was still walking around in his armored EVA suit. It allowed him to avoid the grisly result of his handiwork.

"You *dare* to call me 'insane' after everything you did to me," Malak said. "You tore me to pieces. I could do nothing as you left me to die, shattered and alone."

"What are you talking about?" Garza asked.

"You left me to die! And now it's your turn." The suit looked down at him. "Fernando Garza, as captain of this ship I sentence you to immediate execution."

There were more corpses throughout the ship. Many of them were collected around emergency hatches or escape pods. But the doors remained closed, and the poor souls had been granted just enough time to realize their fate before succumbing.

Ulysses shook his head. There was a chance he had actually fought against some of the older crew members of this ship during the war. In combat, he would have done anything to see them eliminated. But this was different. They weren't threats to his team or mission objectives. They were people who had spent their final moments knowing that they were going to die and that nothing they did would save them. They may have been his enemies in a past life, but they were still human.

Malak was nothing short of a monster.

Ulysses bent down by one of the bodies. The weathered middle-aged man wore the patch of a ship's engineer. Ulysses rummaged through the man's pockets, which was not an easy task in the bulky gloves of the vac suit. He found what he was looking for, however: a pocket knife with a folding blade. He would need this for the next part of his plan.

Ulysses made his way quickly through the destroyer. It had been almost a decade since he had been expected to sneak through an enemy warship like this, but the lack of Centrality Marines made things a lot easier. The ship's layout was also much more straightforward than the convoluted tunnels of a *Champion*-class battleship. The battleships were built with the railgun first and the rest of the internal structure wrapped around it. It was efficient for construction, but less so for finding your way to the toilet once on board.

It only took him a few minutes to reach the launch cells at the tail of the ship. Garza's distraction must have been working. The door to the launch cells was marked with big, bright warning signs, and Ulysses took those as a good indicator that he was on the right track.

When Malak destroyed the monastery, the time from order to launch had been virtually nothing. That meant that at least some of the tubes were loaded with nuclear torpedoes ready to launch at a moment's notice. If Ulysses could find one and sabotage it, the resulting detonation would destroy the *Antonia Estrada* once and for all.

He found a door marked with the universal radiation warning symbol. Ulysses felt a smile cross his face. Despite all the pain, despite the tragedy and loss, Ulysses could go out doing the one thing he was any good at.

He pried the access hatch to the launch tube open and crawled inside the tube. He would need to be right next to the torpedo to work on this. The torpedo itself was as long as Ulysses was tall. The differences between torpedoes and missiles like the ones that took out the engines on the *Lucky Rabbit's Foot* came down to speed, maneuverability, and the strength of the warhead. Missiles were built to take out small, fast threats like fighters or light transports filled with Martian

Volunteer commandos. Torpedoes were true ship-killers which sacrificed the tight turn radius of a missile for devastating warheads.

Ulysses began to pry his way into the casing that surrounded the warhead. The pocket knife was essential, serving as both cutting tool and improvised screwdriver. But it wasn't exactly built to be used this way. It would have been better if he had been able to borrow Charity's tool kit than Val's lucky charm, but Ulysses had made due with less.

He paused, then took out the charm and ran a gloved finger along the fur. A pang of guilt shot through Ulysses at the thought of his friends. His only hope was that they had died suddenly, without any pain. They deserved better than a slow death by radiation poisoning.

They were just the latest casualties in Ulysses's quixotic quest to right the wrongs of a universe that didn't give a damn about what anyone "deserved."

Ulysses had given everything in service to a cause he believed was right. That cause had collapsed, leaving his sacrifices a vain and wasted effort. He told himself that he did the right thing. But did that matter when the right side wasn't the winning side?

It had to matter. Everything he built, everything he lost, had to matter. He wasn't sure if he believed Garza's line about God's purpose, but he knew that the men who had given their lives under his command hadn't sacrificed everything just so he would have the luxury of self-doubt. He was here, in this moment, to do a job.

He returned the rabbit's foot to his pouch. He ground his teeth and got to work. This ship wasn't going to nuke itself. *Wait*, he thought. *Actually, it is.*

Garza's back was bent over the Navigator's console and his eyes widened in terror as the suit loomed over him. But he wasn't afraid of his own death. Rather, he finally got his first look inside the suit, and what he saw made him question his own sanity. Light made its way into the deep well of the suit's helmet for the first time, and Garza felt his knees go out from under him in fear.

There was a body inside of the suit. A shriveled, cadaverous skull wrapped tight in leathery skin. Bits of hair and flesh remained, but they were haphazard and uneven. As the suit leaned toward Garza, the skeletal head inside the helmet lolled forward.

"God save me," Garza mumbled. "What are you?"

"I am what you made me," Malak's modulated voice replied. Whatever it was, it had Garza cornered, the imposing suit moving with glacial inevitability toward the cowering monk. "And you have the nerve to stand here, on my ship, to tell me—"

The suit's helmet snapped around to face one of the officer stations. He paused as if listening to someone, then said, "That's impossible. Run it again." Another pause. "Well, how did you miss that? You useless piece of filth. I should toss you out the airlock with the rest of the garbage."

The suit returned its attention to Garza. "My Sensor officer says there is a ship approaching."

Garza glanced over, his hands still pinned behind his back, at the station to his right. The Sensor officer had patches of his dark hair remaining, but the rest of his head had been bashed into unrecognizable sludge by series of heavy blows. Ulysses had been right. They truly had no idea what was going on here.

"Who are they?" the suit asked. "Are they working for you? Is it the same ship that tried to sneak past me yesterday?" The thing that had stolen Malak's voice raised a gauntleted fist and a wicked blade emerged from the armored vambrace.

"Why won't you just leave me alone?" the suit asked. "Why won't you . . ." The suit sagged, and Garza thought he heard a genuine sigh emerge from the suit. "What now?" The suit turned to face the Tactical station. "Well, how did he get back there? Then jettison the whole cell. Do I have to do everything myself?"

The suit returned its attention to Garza. "Though I admit some things do require a personal touch." The bladed vambrace shone in the light from the display. "Your friends can't save you now."

Garza wasn't sure how a lifeless suit could seem happy, but that was the impression he picked up. Whatever this thing was, wherever it had come from, it had picked up Malak's delight for causing pain.

"Tactical, get a solution for that ship. Hit them with the port coilguns. Don't stop firing until they are atomized."

Despite the fear, despite the rage, and despite the desperation, Garza allowed himself a smile. "Are you sure you have time for that?"

The helmet tilted again in confusion. "I have all the time I need."

"Really?" Garza asked. He moved away from the console for the first time, revealing that he had been inputting a manual override for a grav jump into the Navigation station. A red *Launch* button on the Helmsman's station lit up beside him.

"Navigation, belay that order," the suit bellowed. "What do you mean, you can't cancel a manual override?"

"We're about to go on a long trip," Garza said. "You may want to take your seat."

The suit roared in rage. It drove forward with unnatural strength and sunk its blade into Garza's belly, lifting the monk off his feet with the force of the blow. "Now I can watch you die," the flat, robotic voice said.

Garza coughed and blood sprayed out of his mouth. Fiery lances of pain coursed from the wound in his gut. Darkness crept in on the edges of his vision. Despite his mortal wound, his smile remained, though it was tinged with sadness. "I hope you find peace."

He slammed his palm down on the glowing button.

CHAPTER
TWENTY-FIVE

ULYSSES smirked as an electric spark jumped between two wires. *There*, he thought. *That should do it.* A flashing indicator light inside the warhead let Ulysses know that his work had been successful. The torpedo was live, and the timed activation had been set. If Ulysses did his job correctly, it should be a matter of minutes before it took out the whole ship.

Satisfied with his work, Ulysses shimmied his way around the torpedo to the open access hatch. Once he was outside the launch cell, he'd meet up with Garza. He briefly considered making a run for the cargo bay. They could get to the orbital flyer and try to take off before the ship turned into a fireball.

He shook his head. Even if they made it off the ship and survived the ensuing explosion, the orbital flyer could only take them back down to the surface of Uaigneas. Without the shelter of the monastery, they'd be dead as soon as their vac suits ran out of oxygen. No. Better to go out in a blaze of nuclear fire.

His head and shoulders were through the access hatch when the launch cell behind him made a metallic *screech*. He turned his head to see the whole cell begin to slide "up" and away from the ship.

"No, no, no," Ulysses muttered. He tried to crawl through the access hatch in time, but the edge of the launch cell caught him around the waist. Rather than allow himself to get torn in half trying to fight it, he pushed back from the access hatch into the departing launch cell. He succeeded in part, but the launch cell was still moving away from him just as he was moving away from the shelter of the ship.

Ulysses was exposed, floating through space in orbit around a dwarf planet at the edge of the settled universe. The launch cell must have had a magnetic detachment system, essentially a slow coilgun, because Ulysses couldn't see any thrusters driving the cell away from the ship. But leave the ship it did.

Ulysses's heart sank. The torpedo could still do damage from outside the ship, but Centrality warships were built to withstand punishing fire and keep fighting. Unless the torpedo went off a point-blank range, there was no guarantee the *Antonia Estrada* would be utterly destroyed. If the destroyer could limp away for repairs, then Ulysses's final sacrifice would have been for nothing.

The engines of the destroyer roared to life, though the sound couldn't reach Ulysses through the vacuum of space. "Damn it," Ulysses said. Malak was getting away. After all the destruction and death, Malak would not be forced to answer for his atrocities.

It wasn't fair.

Then the ship surged forward, disappearing from view in an instant. Ulysses frowned. A grav jump? But that didn't make any sense. If he was just trying to get back to Newton's Moon, a grav jump would have been unnecessary. They were only a few hours away from the site under conventional power. Making a grav jump, especially in the conditions of the Tedros Cloud, added the possibility for complications that could have been otherwise avoided.

Then again, Malak hadn't shown himself to be the most stable man Ulysses had ever met. Their brief interaction left Ulysses with far more questions than answers. But, drifting around a dwarf planet within spitting distance of an active nuclear torpedo about to detonate, Ulysses realized those answers wouldn't save him now.

He looked up and gazed upon Uaigneas. The red-brown world had a stark beauty. The dust cloud that had consumed his friends was clearly visible from orbit. It seemed so small from here. Such a little thing in such a big universe. And yet it had taken everything from him.

A ping in his ear told him that his oxygen was nearly depleted. Now it was a race to see if he would die from asphyxiation or nuclear fire. What a grand choice.

Ulysses sighed. He would not let himself be drawn into despair. He returned his attention to Uaigneas above him. If he had to die, he'd rather die admiring the beauty of nature. It could be harsh, it could be unforgiving, and it usually killed you in the end. But even this lifeless rock held a majesty that words could not express.

If only that idiot in the EVA suit would get out of his view. Then it would be perfect.

Ulysses frowned. Wait. That was *his* EVA suit. The one that he left aboard the . . .

His vac suit had no maneuvering thrusters, but he was able to twist his body to get a better view of his surroundings. There, grey-and-white paint shining in the light of the distant star, was a light transport with the words *Lucky Rabbit's Foot* stenciled onto the nose.

Ulysses choked back tears. He didn't understand, but he was too happy to question it. Maybe this was a delusion of his oxygen-deprived brain. Maybe these were visions of dead friends who would spirit him into the afterlife.

Then the EVA suit reached him. A thick gloved hand grasped his ankle. Ulysses couldn't hold back his tears. This was real.

He saw the bald head and bushy beard of Harry Lee through the visor. Harry held fast to Ulysses's ankle with his right hand and used his left to activate the thrusters on his EVA suit. The two men began to fly toward the light transport and away from the torpedo.

Ulysses's eyes widened. The torpedo. They didn't know.

"Harry." There was no response. The EVA suit had to be on a different frequency. Ulysses moved his hand to his belt and fumbled with his suit controls. "Harry." Nothing. "Harry."

"Yeah, Major. I'm here. Save your breath. You're almost out of oxygen."

"I know, but this is important." He gestured to the slim metallic rectangle floating away from them. "That nuke is active. I set it on a timer to blow the *Antonia Estrada* but she got away."

"Huh." Harry did not seem alarmed by the news. "That sounds like something I would have done."

"Is that a compliment or condemnation?"

"Both." Ulysses could hear the smile in Harry's tone. "Charity, did you hear that?"

"I heard. I'm pulling you in. Val's got the grav jump set as soon as you're on board."

It only took two minutes to reach the cargo hold of the *Lucky Rabbit's Foot*, but it felt like hours. Ulysses could feel himself losing consciousness from oxygen deprivation, but he forced himself to stay awake. Either they'd make it in time or they'd all die together.

He didn't even feel it when Harry dragged him into the cargo hold and tossed him onto the deck.

"In. Go."

The gravity drive activated. The *Lucky Rabbit's Foot* lurched awkwardly to safety. And, three seconds later, nuclear fire erupted in the skies above Uaigneas.

CHAPTER TWENTY-SIX

ULYSSES woke up on his back. The last time that had happened, he found himself in a nice, soft bed. This time, he was on the cold steel floor of ship's cargo hold.

No. Not just any ship.

"Out of the way." Ulysses heard Val's voice echoing in the open space of the hold. He opened his eyes to see his friend slide down the ladder from the control platform. Val raced over to Ulysses's side and knelt down. "How is he?"

Harry's voice came from the direction of Ulysses's feet. "His oxygen levels were low. We'll keep an eye on him, but I think we made it just in time."

"Ugh," Ulysses propped himself up on his elbow. "He's right here, you know."

Charity's voice came from the side opposite Val. "You're okay!" She lowered herself to give him a hug.

"Yeah," Ulysses returned the hug as best as he could. "Yeah, I'm okay. Thanks to you. How did you guys—"

"—survive?" Val asked.

"—find you?" Harry asked.

"—get the ship working?" Charity asked.

Ulysses smiled. "Yes. All of those."

Charity spoke first. "Garza did good work. We're not in top shape, but our gravity drive is working again. We took a chance that the repairs had gone well when we fled the monastery."

"It was a close thing," Val said. "If we had waited any longer we would have been vaporized."

"Mr. Lee got us out," Hikaru said. He was leaning against the bulkhead behind Ulysses's head. "As soon as you went up to meet the destroyer, he kept insisting that he was hearing voices telling him to leave."

Ulysses looked at Harry's bearded face. "Really?"

Harry shrugged. "Hey. I know I'm not completely whole. I may be crazy. But I wasn't wrong."

Ulysses laughed. "You and me both. But how did you find me?" His eyes widened and his hand went to the external pouch on his vac suit. "Your lucky charm. It has a beacon, doesn't it?"

"Wouldn't be very useful as a remote caller if it didn't, would it?" Val asked.

"You bastard," Ulysses grinned. "You knew something like this would happen."

"I did what I always do. I made my own luck."

"I believe the term is 'God helps those who help themselves,'" came the familiar voice of the abbot.

Ulysses sat up and looked around the cargo hold. The abbot stood behind Harry and gave Ulysses a satisfied smile. Elsewhere in the cargo hold, thirteen men in brown robes sat on the folding chairs or stood around talking in hushed tones. "The monks," he said. "You got them out."

"Not that they were eager to leave," Val said. "We practically had to drag them on board."

The abbot dipped his head. "Forgive our pride. We owe you our lives. Thank you."

"Just returning the favor, Father," Val said.

"We didn't save everyone," Ulysses said. "Garza's still on that ship. There's no way Malak let him live after that."

"Brother Garza knew that his life was forfeit when he volunteered," the abbot said. "His sacrifice allowed the rest of us to survive. We will treasure his memory forever."

"Then there's only one thing left to say." Ulysses looked down at himself. Besides the open mask, which allowed oxygen to flow, he was still wearing the orange vac suit. "Can someone help get me out of this thing?"

Val leaned back in the pilot's seat. He twirled the end of his thin mustache absently between the fingers of his right hand. The ship was still in the middle of its grav jump, and he wasn't needed at the controls. But this was his home. This was where he belonged. To borrow a phrase from Fernando Garza, this was God's purpose for his life.

His wife sat at her station. He looked at her for a long moment, just admiring the beautiful, talented, gutsy woman who meant everything to him. Her brow was tight with concentration as she studied the display on her screen. Then she saw Val watching her and she turned her head.

"What? What's wrong?"

"Nothing," Val said. "For once, everything's perfect."

Charity snorted. "Let's see how long that lasts."

Val smiled. "How are our levels?"

"Holding," she replied. "Garza really was a damned fine engineer. It's an ugly patch, but we'll make it to Paikea."

Ulysses clambered up the ladder behind Charity. "What's on Paikea?"

Val smirked. "With our luck? An army of Kempeitai, a Centrality battleship, Savimbi's personal hit squad, and a black hole."

Charity shot her husband a look. "We have friends who can put the *Rabbit's Foot* back together and get us armed up. We don't know what else is out there, and Malak could come back at any time. We need to be ready if we're going to make it back to Newton's Moon."

Ulysses shook his head. "We can't go back. I can't put you at risk again. You've saved me three times now. All I've done in return is ruined your ship and dragged you into a mess you had no business in."

"You're family, Walden," Charity said. "That's what families do."

"There's no way we're giving up now," Val agreed.

"I can't ask you to take that risk," Ulysses said.

"You're not asking," Val said. "We're telling you that we're going to take that risk. Together."

"And if everything goes wrong?"

Charity shrugged. "Doesn't it always?"

"If luck doesn't go our way, we'll just make our own," Val said.

"Well, when you put it like that," Ulysses said, "how hard can it be?"

CHAPTER
TWENTY-SEVEN

STEALTH ships had long been a dream of modern navies, but the rapid advance of sensor technology made it expensive to allow a ship to remain functionally undetectable. Few of these ships ever saw production, but someone with sufficient resources could procure one of these rare and valuable ships.

One of these stealth ships emerged from a grav jump well beyond sensor range of Ranginui. The onboard computer determined precise navigational data, then the ship maneuvered toward the moon with a quick burst from its twin fusion engines. It would run cold and quiet until the last possible moment to maximize the element of surprise, but it had a few other tricks up its sleeve.

The black ship was nearly invisible on visual sensors against the backdrop of the cosmos. Special heat sinks allowed it to remain difficult to detect on thermal scans, at least in the short term. The configuration of the angular design combined with light-absorbing tiles helped to baffle lidar and older radar systems alike.

The ship's pilot slid into his seat and hooked into his crash webbing. When he was secure, he flipped a pair of switches to restore manual control. His first order of business was to shut down the gravity drive. With all of the precautions the ship took to stay unseen, it would be foolish to allow his position to be broadcast to any ship or orbital station running a basic gravity sweep.

He flexed his fingers and sighed. He had been on this journey for too long already. It would be nice to get out and stretch his legs. He would need to relish this opportunity. If his employer was correct, his travels were only beginning.

Ranginui, unlike many other moons of its size, was not tidally locked to its parent planet. As such, it maintained a day-night cycle, even if it was a protracted one. ArgoTech City was just edging into the daylight side when the sleek black ship raced into the atmosphere.

The ship's comm board lit up with a contact from ArgoTech City Traffic Control. Despite his ship's stealth characteristics, it was still visible to visual scanners against the dim light of Ranginui's sky. He could have taken a more roundabout route to arrive truly unseen, but the pilot had neither the time nor need to take such measures.

The spaceport's automated system picked him up and sent a hail as standard protocol. The pilot ignored it. He wasn't going to the spaceport. His destination was on a hilltop north of the city.

Even from this distance, his ship's visual scanner showed him a scene of devastation. The pilot studied the images in grim silence. The burned wreckage of vehicles still simmered beyond the stone walls of the compound. There were no bodies visible on the hillside, but the pilot knew that there would have been significant casualties. The clean-up was under way, but there was still a lot of work to be done.

The black ship fired its landing thrusters. The pilot came in over the wall and landed directly in front of the imposing stone pyramid that dominated the complex. Despite all the destruction around it, the pyramid appeared untouched, an immovable object in a sea of chaos. The pilot allowed himself a slight smile. He liked this man's style.

His ship wasn't large, barely fit for two or three passengers. Fortunately, the pilot worked alone. He retrieved his belt with all its attachments and slung it around his leather pants. He tossed a leather coat over his black silk shirt and moved toward the boarding ramp. The ship had a small, cramped airlock, but it was not needed within the confines of the moon's atmosphere.

The pilot descended the boarding ramp and stepped onto the paved courtyard. He was immediately surrounded by eight men with mag rifles pointed at his head. The pilot was unfazed, and his dark eyes made a slow sweep of the men assembled in front of him. "Take me to your master. I have business to discuss with him."

"And what if the boss doesn't want to see you?" one of the guards sneered.

"He will."

One of the men lowered his rifle and put a hand to his ear. "Boss, we've got some company out here. Some guy in black leather just landed in the middle of the courtyard. He's asking for you." The guard examined the pilot. "No, he doesn't look like much. Do you want us to get rid of him?" The man's expression fell. "Are you sure? Okay. Yes, sir, we'll be right there."

The guard looked up. "The commodore wants to talk to you. Follow me."

The guard led the pilot through the heavy blast door into the pyramid. As they walked through the entry hall, the pilot studied his surroundings to get a sense of the man in charge. A pair of marble and bronze statues flanked the short hallway that led into the pyramid. The pilot recognized them. Each one had been created by a famous Tau Ceti sculptor, and both predated the formation of the Eternal Dragon Empire by at least a decade.

The commodore was a man of the past, then. That was fine. But the pilot was a man of the future.

The pilot was led to what could only be described as a throne room. A curved metal chair with thick cushions sat on a raised dais at the center of the room, and a series of workstations surrounded it. It took the pilot a moment to realize that it was built to resemble the bridge aboard a Centrality capital ship. Though, the pilot admitted, the intricate tilework and furs were not precisely standard naval decorations.

The workstations were empty, leaving only six people in the room. Beyond the pilot and his escort, there were two additional armed guards as well as a white-clad technician. They all stood at the feet of the raised dais, looking up at the muscular dark-skinned giant of a man who sat on the throne. The man, for all his projections of power, looked ragged and his hair was a mess.

"The project may never recover," the technician said as the pilot and his escort entered the room. "Tobias tried to warn them, but your trigger-happy goons mistook him for a threat and put him down."

"Unfortunate. One more thing Walden has cost me." The giant leaned forward in his chair. "Very well. How long until the project can move forward?"

"I don't know that it can," the technician said. "Neural processing has already begun to degrade. The system was . . ." His voice trailed off as he saw the stranger enter the room.

The giant saw him, too. He dismissed the technician with a wave. The balding man gave the pilot a terrified glance as he shuffled out of the room. With the technician gone, Buti Savimbi cast his gaze on the intruder.

"I must say, you have picked a poor day to play games with me," Savimbi said.

"Commodore, I am not here for a game." The pilot's voice was clear and strong and echoed in the open room like a bell in a cathedral. "I have come with a request that I am sure you will find mutually beneficial."

"You saw my compound as you came in," Savimbi said. "I'm growing tired of so-called 'business agreements' that leave me with nothing but regret."

The pilot inclined his head. "And rightfully so. In fact, it was your previous deal that interested my client."

Savimbi sat up. "Does your client have a name?"

"He does, indeed. And, given that it is *his* name, it is his responsibility and not mine to share it."

Savimbi frowned. "Well, what does your mysterious client want with me? If he needs protection for his shipping, he can send a request with my office in the city."

"My client is not interested in falling into your extortion racket," the pilot said. Anger flashed in Savimbi's eyes, but the pilot continued. "What he wants is a copy of the data you retrieved from the Centrality Navy."

Anger was replaced with shock, but Savimbi recovered after a moment. "I don't know what you mean." As he spoke, he gave a brief gesture with his head. The guards stepped toward the pilot, but otherwise made no threatening moves.

"Then let me elaborate," the pilot said, unmoved by the encroaching guards. "A ship arrived here two days ago, a *Jackrabbit*-class light transport owned by Val Tanner."

Savimbi looked to the nearest guard and shrugged. "Val Tanner owed me a great deal of money. He came to negotiate."

The pilot smirked. "It appears he got the better end of that negotiation. But Tanner sold you something to wipe away his debt: a series of data cores salvaged from a naval dumping ground. One of those cores still had its sensor data." The smirk disappeared. "My client wants that data."

"Even if I did have these data cores you mentioned," Savimbi said, "they wouldn't be of any use. Not unless your client collects slagged electronics."

The guards took another threatening step. "As I said, my client is interested in the data, not the hardware. I know you made a copy of that data core. I also know that you can't have had time to properly examine it, so you have no idea what it contains. My client simply wants a copy for himself. You keep the cores, as well as your original scan of the data."

"Well, perhaps the next agent your client sends will show more respect." Savimbi snapped his fingers and his guards leapt for the pilot.

The pilot sighed. He tossed the leather jacket back and pulled out a short, straight blade in his left hand. At the same time, he drew a small pistol from its concealed holster with his right. His escort never saw the blow coming. The blade simply drove up through his neck and into his brain.

The pilot released the blade and swiveled to face the oncoming guards. He pulled the trigger twice and each man collapsed with a neat hole through their tinted visors.

Savimbi rose to his full height, but the pilot was fast. He ran forward and slapped Savimbi's hand away from the alarm built into his throne, then slammed the pistol up beneath Savimbi's chin.

The big pirate went rigid. He choked out, "All right. But tell your boss it's going to cost him."

The pilot allowed a wide grin to cross his face.

The hunt was on.

ABOUT THE AUTHOR

Ben Schafer has always had an interest in storytelling. From a young age, he would invent stories and games to entertain his friends and family. After his plans to attend the United States Air Force Academy were cut short by an unforeseen medical event, Ben began to take a closer look at writing as a serious career. An avid student of history and politics, Ben found that world events held infinite possibilities for storytelling. When he's not spending hours at the library or working at his day job, Ben enjoys creating and running tabletop role-playing game campaigns.

To find out more about Ben and keep up with his latest work, visit TheBenSchafer.com and sign up for the mailing list for exclusive content. You can also follow Ben's social media presence on Twitter @TheBenSchafer and on Facebook at TheBenSchafer

SPECIAL THANKS

This book's awesome cover was created by **Oliviaprodesign**. She turned my vague cover concept into a wonderful piece of art.

To **Amy Schafer**, my Social Media Manager and still the best sister I could ask for.

To my **Launch Team** for helping me to turn my dream into reality.

To my father, **William Schafer**, for always letting me bounce crazy ideas off him.

To **Taylor Giblin** for inspiring me and being a constant source of support and encouragement.

To my **friends** and **family** who were patient with me as I disappeared into stacks of science fiction books while creating my own world.

And to **you**, my readers, for taking this journey with me. I look forward to continuing our adventure together.